I0576026

SOMEONE TO HOLD

MICHELLE MAJOR

Copyright © 2025 by Michelle Major

All rights reserved.

No part of this book may be reproduced in any form or by any electronic or mechanical means, including information storage and retrieval systems, without written permission from the author, except for the use of brief quotations in a book review.

Cover Design: Shanoff Designs

Editing: Michelle Fewer

Proofreading: Laura Horah

For the ones who fought hard for their happiness.
Savor every second. You earned it.

Dear Reader-

Welcome (or welcome back!) to Skylark, Colorado. It's my current favorite small town, and I'm honored to have you a part of it.

I've been so excited to share this story because Molly and Chase had my heart from the start. Their journey is tender, complicated, a little angsty, with the emotional swoon I live for when I'm writing (and reading).

I'm guessing a lot of us can relate to Molly. She's the the one who puts everyone else's needs ahead of her own. Watching her learn to make choices for herself was incredibly powerful. And Chase...oh, Chase. There's so much inherently alpha swagger in a bull rider, but I loved peeling those layers back and letting him fall *hard*. He's rough around the edges, but his heart is all in, even when he doesn't think he deserves a second chance.

You'll also find some cameo appearance from other members of the Cool Girls Book Club. We all need a ride-or-die friend group cheering us on (and occasionally pouring the wine).

At its core, *Someone to Hold* is about hope, healing, and the kind of love that makes you believe in the power of choosing your own happiness.

I hope you love reading it as much as I loved writing it.

Big hugs from Colorado-
   Michelle

Playlist

- **"exile"** – Taylor Swift feat. Bon Iver
- **"Burning House"** – Cam
- **"In Case You Didn't Know"** – Brett Young
- **"White Horse"** – Taylor Swift
- **"A Song For You"** – Zach Bryan
- **"Cowboys and Angels"** – Dustin Lynch
- **"Tennessee Whiskey"** – Chris Stapleton
- **"Poison & Wine"** – The Civil Wars
- **"The Bones"** – Maren Morris
- **"Say You Won't Let Go"** – James Arthur
- **"Lady May"** – Tyler Childers
- **"Just The Way You Are"** – Bruno Mars
- **"Slow Burn"** – Kacey Musgraves
- **"You Were Meant for Me"** – Jewel
- **"Better Man"** – Little Big Town
- **" Nothing at All"** – Alison Krauss
- **"Heaven"** – Kane Brown
- **"Come Away With Me"** – Norah Jones
- **"Chasing Cars"** – Snow Patrol
- **"Home"** – Phillip Phillips

1

CHASE

I HEAR SHOUTING AS SOON as I open the truck's door, and my booted foot pauses in midair. Definitely kids' voices—high-pitched and squeaky. It doesn't *sound* like trouble, but something's going down in that house. A smarter man might shut the door and drive away.

I've never been much for kids. Way too much noise, especially with the headaches that still plague me since being trampled by an angry bull six months ago. But I'm here at my childhood best friend's house on the edge of Skylark, Colorado, for one reason.

I made a promise.

Not to Teddy McAllister himself. We hadn't spoken in almost four years before he drowned in a rafting accident two summers ago. Nope, I'm here for his mother.

And if I'm being honest, for me too.

Helping Linda McAllister means giving myself a shot at purpose again, something that's been in damn short supply since that bull wrecked my body and my career.

Linda told me Teddy's widow, Molly, won't be able to put weight on her sprained ankle for at least a month. The right ankle so no driving. But Linda also wasn't about to cancel her five-week European cruise and land tour to play nursemaid.

So she called in a favor, and here I am.

My boots crunch across the gravel as I climb the three front steps. One of them has a loose board, but I'll fix that. I'm a hell of a lot more comfortable being handy than trying to be a manny. But here we are.

I knock and take a step back, bracing myself for round one with Molly McAllister.

I've seen her around town since my accident. She's polite— barely—but we both know she can't stand me. Not that I blame her.

I was there the weekend she married Teddy six years ago. The twins are seven now. You can do the math. Let's just say it was a shotgun wedding without the shotgun but also very little romance that I could see.

Teddy acted like he should get a gold star for marrying the woman he knocked up after a one-week fling. Although I probably shouldn't say "knocked up" and definitely won't say it to her.

Regrettably, I said a lot worse that weekend.

To be fair, I didn't realize she was standing in the hallway when I told Teddy to call off the wedding and send his bride-to-be packing. I thought I was being loyal and looking out for him, even after he told me to fuck off.

But when I stepped out of the room, Molly's wide green eyes landed on me with all the force of that goddamn bull. My heart had leapt into my throat, but she'd spun on her heel and retreated down the stairs before I could explain. As if there were words to make her hate me less than she had a right to.

Even though I'd issued the warning as much for her benefit as his.

Teddy McAllister was handsome and charming and had a magnetic energy that drew people—women especially—toward him. He also had a troubled soul and could just as quickly repel those same people, leaving a trail of pain and heartache in his wake. More than anything, Teddy hated feeling like he was tied down.

I knew in my heart that at best he'd make a terrible husband and mediocre father. And although I didn't know Molly, I could tell she needed more than Teddy would be able to give her. Deserved more. She'd been so beautiful and bright, like walking sunshine.

Was I jealous? No. Without a doubt, I knew I didn't deserve someone as sweet and kind as Molly seemed to be. But neither did Teddy.

He went through with the wedding, and she avoided me the rest of the weekend. A few weeks later, I won my first pro rodeo championship. My life got busy, and somewhere between prize buckles and late-night drives to the next town, Teddy and I let our friendship slip away like a mountain creek at the end of summer. Too shallow and rocky to carry anything of value downstream.

I heard from my sister that he and Molly had twins, but I didn't hear another word from him. I didn't reach out either. Maybe I didn't want to hear how wrong I'd been. Or maybe I didn't want to be right.

But I never forgot her eyes that night.

So yeah, I'm surprised as hell she's willing to accept my help now. I'm the guy who called her a mistake, and she's letting me into her home.

I guess in some cases, desperate times call for assholes.

The door flies open before I can knock again, and a tow-headed boy with a smattering of freckles across the bridge of his nose glares up at me. He's wearing cargo shorts, no shirt, and there's a jam smudge on his cheek.

He takes one look at me and backs into the house again. "Stranger danger!" he yells. "Mommy! There's a stranger at the door! He's driving a white van!"

Well, shit.

I glance at my white *pickup* and offer it a silent apology for being mistaken for a van. It's an F-150, extended cab, new tires. Don't get me started on the kidnapping insinuation.

I whip off my Stetson and run a hand through my hair. It could use a trim, but we're not talking "creepy van guy" long.

The kid bolts inside, still shouting, and the door swings wide.

I figure that's my invitation.

I step inside, and the chaos hits full throttle.

"Mommy, my hair's a mess!"

"It's white van!"

"It's a truck," I call out, already regretting what I'm about to step into here. "With an extended cab."

The front door of Linda McAllister's farmhouse opens into the living room, which looks the same as I remember from childhood, even though it's been nearly fifteen years since Teddy and I spent hours playing *Call of Duty* draped across that plaid sofa.

One of the owners before Linda renovated the small rooms into a modified open concept to give the space a larger feel. The kitchen is off to the left and looks like a pancake bomb recently detonated in the center of it. Liquid drips from the linoleum counter, and the cabinet doors under the sink are open, like somebody had been looking for a way to turn off the water.

"Who is this stranger, Luke?" Molly demands as she comes around the corner of the hallway that leads to the laundry room, hopping on one foot as she holds the injured one aloft behind her.

She stops cold, and it takes a moment for her eyes to narrow with recognition.

"What the hell are you doing in my house?" She's brandishing the plunger like a weapon.

I lift a brow. "Can you point that thing somewhere else?"

"Why are you driving a white van?"

"It's a *truck*, Molly."

"It looked like a van." At least the boy's stopped shouting.

"Mommy, what about my hair?" the girl trailing behind Molly asks.

That's when I notice

Oh, fuck me.

I was so distracted by the plunger and her glare that I didn't register Molly's T-shirt is wet. Also see-through.

Her bra is pink.

And she's cold. Either that, or she's smuggling raisins.

I can't seem to look away.

Even worse? She sees me not being able to look away.

She lets out a little yelp, drops the plunger, and hops down the hall again.

I'm left with two smallish humans and about seventeen kinds of awkward.

The boy bolts after his mother. But the girl tilts her head, bright blond hair and skeptical brown eyes reminding me of her dad.

"Hey there," I say with a nod. "I'm Chase. I was friends with your dad."

"Are you the friend that wrestles bulls?"

"I ride them. Or used to."

"Daddy talked about you. He said you were a troublemaker."

Takes one to know one, but I don't want to speak ill of the dead. Not to the dead guy's daughter, anyway.

I smile despite myself. "He wasn't wrong. Your dad and I had a lot of adventures. Maybe you, your brother, and I will as well."

She studies me. "Mommy doesn't like adventures."

"She doesn't have to come along then."

"Come along where?" Molly's back and still glaring.

She's using crutches now, though she doesn't look much more stable than she did with the hopping. But she's swapped out the wet T-shirt for a red flannel buttoned up all wrong.

She's a mess but still manages to look like sweetness and sin wrapped up in a soft plaid shirt.

"Seriously, why are you here?"

"I'm here to get the kids to the bus on time."

Her mouth opens, then closes again. She's unknowingly flashing glimpses of creamy skin between the gaps in the front of that flannel, but I keep my eyes at eye level. Barely.

I could fix those buttons for her. I'd like to. Maybe brush my knuckles across her collarbone. I bet she'd be the softest thing I've ever touched. It's also the dumbest thought I've ever had, and there have been some real winners.

Sure, I noticed Molly that first weekend, even though she was marrying my best friend. It's hard to ignore a woman like her. But now she's both more appealing and also more off limits.

"Are you the nanny?" the girl blurts.

"He's not the nanny," Molly says through gritted teeth.

"I prefer *manny*," I say with a wink.

The girl giggles. Molly doesn't.

The boy looks horrified. "Grandma said she hired a *girl*."

"I'm not a girl," I say.

"Yeah, we get that." Molly puts a hand on the boy's head. "It's okay, Lukey. I'll figure this out before you get home from school. Grab your jacket from the kitchen."

"You need a shirt," I tell him.

"It's in the dryer," he says, voice trembling.

"You've only got one shirt?" I tap the watch encircling my wrist. "Because we gotta go, buddy."

"It's his Thursday shirt," the girl explains which makes zero sense to me.

"So wear your Friday shirt."

His chin starts to quiver.

Shit.

"It's okay, sweetie," Molly says gently. "Check the dryer. Your Thursday shirt should be good to go. Laurel, get the backpacks and grab your lunches, please."

She flicks a dismissive gaze in my direction. "Chase, you've done plenty. I'll walk them to the bus stop and—"

"You know your driveway's a quarter mile, right?"

"I can walk on crutches."

"I never said you couldn't."

If looks could kill, they'd be digging my grave right now. I know she has every reason to believe I'm a complete dick.

But I'm not. Not anymore.

"I'll walk with you." I try to make my tone placating. "We have stuff to talk about."

For the record, I don't typically do placating.

She doesn't look impressed. In fact she looks irritated as fuck. "We don't."

"Hey, Luke," I say as the boy returns fully clothed from the laundry room.

He stumbles back a little. "Ye-e-ss," he stutters like I'm some child-eating clown who drags his victims to the sewer.

"Your mom told you to grab a jacket."

"Don't yell at me."

I run a hand through my hat hair. "I wasn't yelling."

"It sounds like you're yelling," the girl says, her chin tipped up like she's daring me to say more.

I glance over at Molly, who raises a brow. A brow that clearly says, *Don't yell at my kid, you stupid fucker.* Message received.

"A jacket," I repeat in a softer tone.

Luke's eyes widen, but he moves to the kitchen and grabs a hoodie from a chair.

The girl grins at me. "Now you're whisper-yelling."

"I'll work on it."

"You won't be here long enough to work on it," Molly snaps.

She turns, the kids in tow, and limps toward the front door like a woman on a mission.

She might not be yelling, but her soft as steel voice gets the message across loud and clear. And damn if it doesn't make me want to follow her anyway.

2

CHASE

As we walk in tense silence down the driveway, I rack my brain to figure out how things went so sideways so fast. I don't know who Molly expected to show up at the house this morning, but it sure as hell wasn't me.

Linda told me her daughter-in-law knew I'd been recruited to take care of the kids and property, which clearly isn't the case. And while we were both misled, I've got to find a way to convince a woman who hates my guts to let me help her in a role with which I have no experience, business, or desire to do.

But I want this property. I need it if I'm going to rebuild my life in Skylark, Colorado.

The price my former best friend's mother agreed on for the sale is more than fair. It will allow me to buy the land. It's the last piece of the puzzle I need and will even leave me with enough money to actually purchase the cattle to start my business.

A lot of retired bull riders get hired on at big cattle operations, but I never liked working for other people. I want something to call my own. One of the old-timers on the circuit used to say there's nothing at the end of the road if you don't own your own land. I took that to heart.

The kids skip ahead, smart enough to want to put distance between themselves and the anger radiating off their mother. This fiercely independent side is one I didn't expect from a woman who initially struck me as the type to apologize for taking up space.

Silence doesn't bother me, but it's hard to tell whether she's planning to stay quiet until after Luke and Laurel are on their way or because the exertion is catching up with her. She seems to be slowing with every step. I've done a couple of stints on crutches over the years. It sucks. No judgment here.

"Mommy, I hear the bus," Laurel shouts over her shoulder. "We need to hurry, or we're gonna miss it."

"I'm coming," Molly answers, sounding winded. And despite the cool morning breeze, I can see a sheen of sweat across her brow. "You guys go ahead. I'll be there."

"Mommy, faster." Luke turns back with an anxious look that says he needs his whole family moving together to feel safe.

Molly lets out a little whimper of protest, and the sound hits me straight in the damn feels. I've never been one to play the white knight, but this woman has been through more than her share of shit. I don't know where the irresistible urge to take care of her comes from but can't deny it.

"Race you to the end of the driveway," I tell the kids as I take off at a sprint.

After a moment's hesitation, they start running along with me. I expect Laurel to keep up, but I'm pretty damn shocked when Luke outpaces us both. Granted, I'm running in cowboy boots and not exactly in my cardio era. My leg, which was broken in three places thanks to Black Tornado crushing it, still protests, but I ignore it.

"Well done, Speed Racer," I tell the boy as the bus pulls to a stop in front of the mailbox.

He shoots me a glare that's about as friendly as how his mom looks at me. "You won't be here when we get home from school, right?"

I let my shoulders lift and lower, trying to catch my breath. "I guess we'll have to see."

"Can you fix the sink before you go?" Laurel asks quietly, glancing around me. Her feathery brows draw together with the worry of a kid who's seen her mother struggle with too many broken things and not enough help.

"Yeah," I promise. I don't know that Molly will let me stick around long enough for that, but I'm going to give it my best shot.

I lift a hand in greeting to the bus driver, who, judging by his age, could have been assigned to this route back when kids still rode to school in horse-drawn carriages.

Both kids wave from their seats as the bus pulls away, but they're not looking at me. I wait until it's almost out of sight before I turn, expecting to see Molly right there.

Only she's on her way back to the house, struggling more obviously now, the crutches catching every few steps on the uneven ground.

I jog past her and then pivot to block her way. "We need to talk."

She licks her lips, and the sight of that pink tongue—well, it does things to my insides. Things I have no business thinking about given who I am, and more importantly, who she is.

"I need to get back to the house," she says, adjusting the crutch under her right arm. It looks like she's working hard not to wince.

"Give me those," I say, holding out a hand.

"I don't want your help."

"I get it. You don't want anything from me. But I can't just watch you struggle and sweat when it doesn't need to be that way."

She lifts one of the crutches and points it in my direction. "Do you have a problem with sweaty women?"

I blink. How the fuck am I supposed to answer that question? Honestly, I guess, because before I can stop my mouth from saying it, my brain spits out, "I've had some of the best times of my life with sweaty women."

And that level of truthfulness knocks Molly McAllister on her ass—literally.

It could also be the fact that she drops the first crutch, bobbles the second, and before I can grab her, she lands with a yelp on the gravel. A cloud of dust swirls around her, and she starts blinking hard, like she's trying not to cry.

We've established that I'm not a prince among men, but I do my level best not to make women cry. I grab both crutches, then hold out a hand. She shies away from it the way my horse would if there was a rattlesnake on the path in front of us.

"Come on, Molly. I understand you have zero reasons to like me."

"More like I've got several reasons not to," she clarifies, still staring at my outstretched hand.

"Not debating that, but give me a tiny break here. I hate to think that Teddy's watching from the great beyond and seeing me let his wife—the mother of his children—wallow in the dirt. He'd want me to help you."

"As if I have time for wallowing," she mutters. It's soft, but there's an edge to it. "Despite your opinion of me back in the day, Teddy would know I can take care of myself. He certainly left me alone often enough to get good at it. So I'd appreciate it if you lay those crutches on the ground and head back to your truck."

"I'm not leaving." I shake my head. "I've got nowhere else to be."

Her eyebrows furrow over those deep green eyes. She considers that statement, which reveals far more than I intended, but eventually places her hand in mine.

To my surprise, the calluses I feel on her palm nearly match those on mine. I shouldn't be surprised since I know she uses the field next to the barn for her flower farming business. Farming of any type is hard work.

I lift her to her feet—well, her one foot—but before she can reach for the crutches, I scoop her into my arms, tucking the crutches under the arm cradling her back.

"You can't carry me to the house," she says.

"Don't squirm, or I'm going to drop the crutches, and we'll have to start this balancing act all over again."

"Chase, you're going to drop me." She's so stiff it feels like I'm carrying one of those department store mannequins.

"I won't, Molly. I've got you." There's no explanation for how rough my voice sounds, but I can feel the heat coming off her. There's the scent of sweat and earth, and the faint smell of sugar cookies, which I figure comes from her lotion. I bite back the urge to lean in and run my lips along the graceful column of her throat. To taste the salt on her skin.

Yeah. I like sweaty women just fine.

But this one is off-limits, I remind myself. I'm here to do a job, and I have to convince her to let me.

The wisps of her hair brush my cheek, sending my blood and brain cells rushing south. A physical reaction, nothing more. I like women—all shapes and sizes. Molly McAllister isn't special to me. There's nothing to see here, folks.

She stops protesting but doesn't relax into me. I'm quickly coming to appreciate that she's got more sense than I gave her credit for the summer she and Teddy married. Back then, I figured she was just young and starry-eyed, but there's a steel in her spine I completely missed.

Back at the house, I leave the crutches resting against the front porch rail while I carry her inside and lower her to the old sofa.

"You want a glass of water?"

"Yes, please." She winces as she lifts her foot onto the coffee table. She fixed the buttons at some point, but this movement causes the flannel to bunch above the waistband of her black leggings, revealing a sliver of skin as creamy as moonlight. I like those leggings, or maybe they're called yoga pants. Who the hell knows. But I thank whoever invented them because they show off every curve of a woman's body.

Note to self: stop noticing Molly's body.

I retrieve the crutches, then place them against the edge of the couch where she can reach them. We need to talk, but I don't want her to feel like she can't get away if she wants to. And that hopping business from earlier will only cause more trouble.

"I need to call a plumber," she announces as I walk toward the kitchen. "The sink in the laundry room works."

Her voice is even, but I hear the frustration in it.

"I bet I can fix the sink." I grab two glasses and head down the short hall to fill them. When I return, she's still eyeing me warily, but takes the glass with a trembling hand.

"Have you eaten today?" I down my water and then turn back for the kitchen, not liking how seeing her so fragile makes my heart twist with something dangerously close to tenderness. "I'll make eggs."

I hear her snort. "No, thank you."

Ignoring her, I open the fridge and peer at the contents. "You've got some veggies and ham. I could—"

"I do not want eggs and ham. Not in a box." Her tone is indignant as she continues, "Not with a fox."

I chuckle and then marvel that she can make me smile in the midst of what is turning out to be a giant shit show of a morning. "Got it, Molly-I-Am. No eggs and ham."

She rolls her eyes, but one side of her mouth curves. It feels like a victory from where I'm standing.

"I don't know what Linda was thinking asking you to help," she says as much to herself as to me. "I don't want to bother her on her trip, but this makes no sense."

She takes another long sip of water, and a few drops dribble down her chin before she wipes them away with her shirt sleeve. Maybe I'm the one who needs help, because why do I find that adorable?

I grab a granola bar from a basket on the counter and bring it to her. She narrows her eyes like it's some kind of a trick. "I'm here to help you and the kids."

She snatches the granola bar and rips open the wrapper. "Why you? Is it your years of experience with children? Your love of the domestic arts?"

My lips twitch. I can't remember the last time a woman gave me this much shit, and I kind of love it. "Because I have a debt to pay to your mother-in-law."

It's the truth, just not all of it.

She inclines her head. "What kind of debt?"

"The kind she's called in," I say. "You're going to have to trust me."

"Hard pass," she answers as she chews. "I don't trust you. Why would Linda have set this up without asking me first?"

"Because she knew you wouldn't agree to it," I say, like *duh*.

"I'm not agreeing to it," she confirms, like *double duh*.

"I owe Teddy and Linda a lot," I say quietly. "Helping you will repay that debt."

That should be a mic drop moment.

She draws in a sharp breath but doesn't exactly look impressed. "What does that mean?"

"Your late husband and his mom saved me. They gave back my future when my asshole of a father took it from me. Hard to tell what would have happened if—"

"I've never been a big fan of puzzles, Chase." She holds up a hand. "Stop talking in riddles or get the hell out of my house."

Her full mouth thins. Like I needed another reason to notice her sweet pink lips.

"I spent a lot of time in this house as a kid." I run a hand over the back of the sofa, tracing the worn spot where we used to vault over the back instead of walking around like civilized humans. "Linda wasn't the greatest mom in the world, but she loved Teddy to distraction."

She closes her eyes briefly, exhaustion written in every line of her face. "He could do no wrong in her eyes." Those quiet words tell me everything I need to know about how the years since Teddy's death have been for her living with his mother. Not that I'm surprised.

"But what does that have to do with him saving you?" she asks before my thoughts wander too far.

"Part of the reason I was here so often is because I didn't want to be at my own house. My dad is...well, things were rough."

She goes brows-up again, and I wonder if she's aware of her ability to have an entire conversation with just her eyebrows. "How rough?"

"Very."

She studies my face for a long moment, and I can see her weighing whether to dig deeper for the details I'm unwilling to share. Whatever she finds there must convince her to leave it alone, because she sighs and looks away.

"I won't pretend to understand what that means, but I'm glad Teddy helped you." Her voice lacks the edge it's carried since I arrived. "And I'll think about letting you help me."

It's not a yes, but it's not the flat rejection she gave earlier.

"That's all I'm asking."

"I'm going to take a shower," she says, struggling to her feet with the crutches. "You need to be gone by the time I get out."

"Understood," I answer, telling myself not to think about this woman in the shower. I head for the door, but pause with my hand on the knob. "I'm willing to do whatever it takes, Molly."

"Don't make promises you can't keep," she says with a tired laugh, and then starts up the stairs.

The urge to beg her to let me follow leaves me wondering what exactly I've gotten myself into.

3

MOLLY

I TEXTED the book club chat an hour ago and asked for an emergency meeting. Within minutes, Sadie Barlowe offered to drive and Avah suggested meeting spots. We're so different as individuals, but I know without question they'd drop everything for me if I asked. Just like they did today. We're having lunch at the diner where Iris's brother runs the kitchen because she convinced him to save the big table in back for us.

I shrug and focus on my half-eaten turkey sandwich. "I told him he needed to be gone by the time I got out of the shower. And he was."

Sloane sits back in her chair and studies me. "You didn't specify whether or not you made it clear he shouldn't come back."

I press my lips together, but don't answer.

Avah lets out a long-suffering sigh. "Molly, come on. This is the guy who tried to convince Teddy not to marry you." She leans forward like I need to focus on her words. "On the eve of your wedding."

"I was there, Avah. I remember. But Linda hired him. She told me she'd pay for a nanny while she's on her trip, and I need the help. If Chase is her choice, how can I say no?"

"Sweetie, we can find a better candidate." Iris Dixon, Skylark's former mayor, reaches across the table and takes my hand. "If your mother-in-law refuses to pay for *your* choice of nannies, we'll pitch in. You have options."

"What options?" I swallow back the emotion threatening to choke me. "This morning proved I can barely get the kids off to school on time, let alone handle my flower business and the farmhouse. It'll be weeks until I'm off crutches, and longer until I'm cleared to drive. Even if I could handle the farm, I can't make deliveries or set up the booth at the local markets like this."

"We'll take turns driving you," Sadie offers without hesitation. "I have lots of flexibility in my training schedule. We'll put together a calendar."

"It'll be like a meal train, only a ride train," Iris adds. "At least until we find somebody else you can hire."

This is exactly what I love about my friends. Sloane—who owns the local bookstore, Cover to Cover—brought us together under the guise of a book club, but somewhere along the way we became each other's ride or dies. I don't bother repeating that my inability to pay someone for the kind of help I need is part of the problem. Sure, I make okay money once the spring and summer seasons kick into high gear and I'm selling flowers to florists, co-ops, and setting up my booth at the weekly farmers market and local art and craft festivals. But still, money is tight.

Teddy lit up every room he walked into, the kind of person who made everything feel like an adventure.

Basically, the polar opposite of me. At least this current version of me.

I was in bad shape after he died. The suffocating guilt over what had pushed him to take those early-season risks on the river —namely the state of our marriage—made it feel like I was the one drowning. Plus, our five-year-old twins missed their daddy and didn't understand that he was never coming back home.

This business I run is one I love and created through my own hard work. It gives me purpose. No one had any reason to believe I could make flower farming a success, even me. But it's going better than I hoped, and I don't want to give it up. Growing flowers means something to me, and finally being independent means everything.

"It's time to stop letting Linda control your life." The words sound so simple when Avah says them. She's gorgeous and confident and has a hot investment banker fiancé. I'm supposed to be providing the flowers for her elopement at the end of the summer, but it's doubtful I'll even be here then.

"What does it matter when we're moving to Albuquerque with her?" I ask, more to myself than my friends.

Silence greets the statement, like no one knows how to pep-talk me out of my sad, small existence. Not that I expect them to. It's a prison of my own making.

"You don't have to live the life everyone expects."

All of us turn at the words spoken by Piper, Sadie's younger sister. She became part of the book club a couple of months ago after she moved back to Skylark at the end of last summer when she broke off her engagement. We all wanted her to join, but it took Sloane to convince her to agree to it.

Sloane doesn't seem to realize that she touches her fingers to the ends of her hair every couple of minutes. It's growing back after months of chemo. First, the brutal rounds last summer and fall, then more treatments leading up to her stem-cell transplant at the Vanderbilt-Ingram Cancer Center in Nashville right before Christmas.

She came home to Colorado in February, and the soft dark fuzz has been filling in ever since. Now it's a bit longer than a buzz cut, making her delicate features even more beautiful. Her doctors say she's doing well, that her counts look good, but I catch the way she still touches her hair like she's making sure it's real, that it's staying this time.

Piper flashes a half-hearted smile. "I mean, do as I say, not as I do. I'm not exactly a role model for making living-your-best-life decisions."

"You made the decision not to marry an asshole." Sadie gently nudges her sister. "That's something."

"I'm not living anywhere close to my best life," I agree, almost reflexively.

"You're a great mom," Iris tells me, and I know I should just accept the compliment. I love my kids more than life, but I'm twenty-seven and have spent almost my entire life letting fear have power over me. Fear of being left behind or a burden to people. Of not being worthy of love unless I'm contorting myself into knots to make other people happy.

I shrug and take a sip of water to ease the sudden burn in my throat. "What kind of example am I setting for my kids? That it's okay to let someone else dictate your life? That you should just accept whatever scraps of affection people throw your way? I'm teaching them that love means being treated like an also-ran, and that terrifies me."

"Then maybe it's time to step up to the bucket list challenge," Iris suggests. "There's nothing like checking something off a to-do list to make you feel good."

"Not all of us are Type A plus," I counter, attempting a smile.

"A plus plus is more like it." Iris pushes a leftover sweet potato fry around her plate, and the din of the crowded diner fills the brief pause in conversation as servers weave between tables balancing plates of Nick Dixon's delicious comfort food. "There's no shame in my tightly wound game. But we all know what it's like to let fear dictate our lives."

Sloane's gaze meets mine. "We do need someone to step up next for the challenge."

"It won't be me," Piper announces. "I'm going to play the new cool girls book club member card."

"I'm going to play the 'I like my life just the way it is' card," Avah declares.

Must be nice, I think, not without a hint of longing. I can't remember the last time I felt content with my life. I don't know what it's like to be satisfied and at peace with the present moment instead of always looking ahead to when things might get better.

My friends wait for my answer, the expectation in their gazes making my cheeks heat and my skin prickle like there are ants crawling across it.

"The plan had been to take the kids on an adventure before we moved, but..." I pat my right thigh. My foot is elevated on another chair because the injured ankle swells if I'm on my feet—or foot, as the case may be—for too long. "I was thinking of a theme park, but we might have to take a rain check on that."

"Riding 'It's A Small World' isn't a bucket list item," Avah says matter-of-factly.

"That's rude," I mutter. Avah is my best friend in this group, and we're definitely an opposites-attract kind of vibe.

Taylor's smile is softer. "The bucket list challenge is about you, not the twins."

I breathe out a laugh. "I'm a single mother of two high-energy first graders. There is no me."

My best friend squeezes my fingers. "Not until you find her," Avah tells me.

Tears sting the back of my eyes. I love these women. I don't know how I would have made it through the past couple of years without their support and friendship. But they don't understand.

"I think she's been gone for too long," I whisper then clear my throat to dislodge the rest of it—my origin story. "I was only five when I went to live with my grandparents after Mom died. From the day I carried a trash bag filled with all my worldly possessions over their doorstep, Nana and Pops made it clear they weren't taking me in because of love. As much of a train wreck as my mom made of her life, they wouldn't let strangers raise her kid."

"Her actions and the consequences from them weren't your fault or responsibility," Iris says. She's speaking from personal experience. Her mom was a magnet for scandal, and my friend paid a price for that.

"My grandparents loved me," I say like it needs explaining, "but they always worried I was going to turn out like my mom. I worried that they'd give up on me if I did anything out of line, so I became who they wanted me to be. Then they died in that car wreck, and I went on my first adventure to Colorado." I throw up my hands. "We all know how that turned out."

"It led to you being part of our lives," Sloane reminds me.

I nod. "Don't get me wrong. I wouldn't trade my vacation fling with Teddy or everything that came after, because I love my kids and you guys and living in Skylark. But I can't let Luke and Laurel feel like a burden the way..." I trail off and use the corner of my napkin to wipe an invisible spot on the smooth tabletop. "I just don't know how to have an identity outside of being their mom. It's the only thing I've been good at in my life. How uber pathetic is that?"

Sloane wraps an arm around my shoulder and squeezes me into a tight hug. "It's not. But you're more than your ability to take care of those sweet kids."

I choke out a laugh. "Not sure my ability is something to brag about when we've been living with my mother-in-law since Teddy's death. I'm hardly the poster child for independent single moms."

"Because you've been busy paying off his debt." Avah's tone is angry on my behalf. "We all know you took a loss when you sold his vans and rafts. All that fancy equipment for a business that never turned a profit."

"Yes, but—"

"Credit cards maxed out," she continues. "Loans in your name...all of it dumped on you after he passed. And with no life insurance. He put you in a bad spot, Mols."

I draw in a deep breath. "I made my last payment to the credit

card company this month. I'm free and clear, at least from that."
It's a small win, but it's mine.

"Why are you moving to Albuquerque with your mother-in-law when you love it here?" Piper asks.

Sadie elbows her, and a silence falls over our group.

"Is that a bad question?" Piper whispers.

"It's not," I answer before anyone else can. "I'm moving because that's where Linda is retiring to, and she wants her grandkids close. It's nice that she wants us with her." Did that sound convincing? Doubtful.

Avah's eyes narrow. "No one in the history of the world has ever described Linda McAllister as nice. She's for sure not nice to you. She treats you like a servant, Molly."

"She took me in after Teddy died," I argue weakly. "I had nothing. No money, no life insurance, no way to pay the bills. Nothing but debt and two kids who had just lost their father. I owe her. If it wasn't for me—"

"No." Iris holds up a hand. "We're not doing that again. The part where you blame yourself because Teddy put a raft in that river when the water was running way too high and fast to be safe, even for somebody with his experience."

"But he—"

"No." Avah leans forward and points a French-manicured finger at my face. "You are *not* responsible for his death, and Linda needs to stop trying to make you feel that way."

"Or you need to stop letting her," Sadie adds in a gentler tone.

"Exactly," Avah agrees. "Was Teddy's death a horrible accident? Yes. Do we feel for you and the kids? One hundred percent. Does it mean you don't deserve to be happy? Fuck no, Molly. You're a good person and a good mother. But you only have one life."

"One wild and precious life," Taylor echoes, and I recognize the line from my favorite Mary Oliver poem. "What are you going to do with it?"

A million excuses fill my brain.

"What do you *want* to do with it?" Sloane asks softly.

"It's not moving to Albuquerque," Piper murmurs, earning another elbow from her sister. The book club's newest member is going to give Avah a run for her money on having exactly zero fucks to give when it comes to calling us out on the ways we play small. The ways *I* play small and let fear rule my world.

"I want my kids to see me live big and take risks..." I shake my head and pat my thigh again. "Even if those risks mean I end up slightly bruised and battered. Piper's right, you know?"

"She is?" Sadie asks, sounding incredulous.

"I am?" Piper echoes, then nods. "Of course, I am. About what?"

"I hate the idea of moving to Albuquerque." I sigh. "And I've been making excuses for a long time. Playing small to please other people." I rest my head on Sloane's shoulder. "I don't want to do that anymore. I want to choose me for once."

"Yaass, Queen," Avah says with a wink.

"I don't know that I've earned queen status, but I want to stay in Skylark more than any place else I've ever lived. It feels like home here."

"This town has that effect on people," Iris confirms with a grin.

"You're staying in Skylark." Avah raises her fist in the air. "Let's f-ing go!"

The table erupts in cheers and applause. Patrons at the neighboring tables glance over at our celebratory outburst, but none of us care. The warmth of my friends' support wraps around me like a blanket.

"I also want to keep the farm."

My friends go silent.

"Are you sure about that?" Taylor asks, her smile dimming slightly. "A property that size is a lot of work."

Avah studies me. "You want to live in Shrine-to-Teddy Manor?"

I roll my eyes. "It's more than Teddy's childhood home. My kids love it there, and so do I. I've put a lot of money and energy into the property—redoing the greenhouse and amending the soil for my flowers. The house has good bones. It just needs a little love."

For the first time, I'm not waiting for someone else to decide my future. I'm actually making the choice myself. "The farm isn't just a place to live, it's where I want to build something lasting and beautiful."

"Honey, you could make an outhouse beautiful," Iris tells me. "But will Linda let you stay there? I thought she was intent on selling."

"I'll buy it from her. I have a little savings, even after paying off Teddy's debt. If this year's flower season goes as well as I hope, I should have enough money for a down payment. A small business loan could be an option. I just have to show Linda I'm capable of making it on my own. Maybe her being gone on this trip is the time I need to pull up my big girl panties and find a way."

Sloane squeezes my arm. "Heck, yeah."

I smile at my friends and realize I haven't felt this hopeful in... well, forever.

"It's settled then," I tell the group. "I'm up next for the bucket list challenge, and I'm going to figure out how to do life on my terms. Like Kristen Quinn said, I'm going to lose my fear."

"What about the hot cowboy Linda saddled you with?" Avah asks.

I think about that long and hard, then shake my head.

"I'm keeping the cowboy. If he wants to pay off the debt he thinks he owes by watching my kids and helping me until my ankle is better..." I shrug. "Who am I to turn away free labor?"

"What about how he treated you the weekend of your

wedding?" Taylor leans across the table. "The opinion he seemed so willing to share."

"Let him have it. I know who I am. You all know who I am. What the heck does Chase Calhoun's opinion matter?"

Sloane sets down her glass of iced tea with a deliberate clink and fixes me with that steely I'm-kicking-cancer's-ass stare. "Look who finally found her backbone. About damn time, Molly."

Maybe she's right. I can stand up for myself, make my own choices, and stop caring what other people think. Maybe I'm finally ready to become the person I want to be, and no one—not my mother-in-law or a hot, broody cowboy—is going to stop me.

4

MOLLY

I'M in the greenhouse an hour later when I hear Chase's truck rumble down the gravel driveway. All the courage I gathered during lunch with my friends vanishes like a plume of smoke. I glance over at the photo of Luke and Laurel I have pinned to the corkboard next to the greenhouse's door.

Remember your why, Kristen Quinn advised in her book. Those kids are it for me. I want to be the mom they deserve as much as I want to be someone I can be proud of.

I smooth a hand over my hair, then realize I've probably left dirt crumbs in it. I don't wear gloves nearly as often as I should because I like the warm feel of the earth on my bare skin.

Avah told me about a podcast she listened to that recommended standing bare feet in grass to ground yourself. It's a shame that people have to be reminded of that. Maybe it's because I grew up on my grandparents' farm, but dirt has always done it for me.

An especially helpful thing these days because it's not as if I'm running my hands through anything else. Like Chase's thick locks, or over the muscles his denim shirt clung to this morning.

I press the tips of my short fingernails into the center of my palm, hoping the bite of pain will ground me in a different way. It might not be the smartest idea in the world to hire a nanny who makes my ovaries stand up and do a little dance.

He thinks I'm weak. And possibly a gold digger, which is ironic since Teddy never had money. But I need to remember the devastation his callous words caused to younger me as I watch him stride across the yard.

I hate him for both his judgment and the fact that I overheard it. Even worse, my husband-to-be agreed with Chase's asshole opinion so I went into my marriage knowing Teddy thought the worst of me.

And rather than leaning into that understanding and fighting to prove I was something different, I let it define me.

I'm not doing that anymore.

Chase opens the greenhouse door, and even with everything between us, my traitorous body notices the way his broad shoulders fill the doorframe. How his work shirt stretches across the hard planes of his chest. His stormy gray eyes find mine, and I mentally curse the flutter in my stomach.

"Okay if I come in?" His voice is gruff and scrapes across my skin like sandpaper, which is an oddly appealing sensation. "Or are you busy?"

"Busy," I tell him, forcing my tone to stay chilly. "But just with transplanting seeds. I can talk and work."

"Should you be standing and working?" He gestures toward my injured leg.

I study him as he studies my ankle. Years of bull riding have honed his frame to perfection—lean hips, powerful thighs, and maddeningly distracting forearms that are strong and tanned in a way that makes a woman curious about the rest of him. His hair is longer than it used to be, but it only emphasizes the sharp angles of his face and a chiseled jaw that could cut glass. It's annoying how devastatingly handsome he is, especially when I'm trying to stay unaffected by his presence. My pulse quickens despite my best efforts, and I hate that he still affects me this way.

Something about him in this space—my sanctuary—puts me on edge. Oddly, not in a bad way. More like my senses are heightened. I can hear the birds outside and feel the tiny breeze that blows in from the windows that are slightly cracked.

"Things aren't going to get done unless I do them." I dust my hands off and grab the handle of the scooter I keep in the greenhouse. "Besides, it's a sprained ankle, not life-threatening."

Chase's eyebrows draw together. "How did you hurt yourself anyway? Linda didn't give specifics."

"I twisted it while sledding with the twins during that big snowstorm a couple of weeks ago."

"Based on your coordination this morning," he says with an amused smirk. "That tracks."

I flip him the bird, and he chuckles. "Did you do all this?" he asks, inclining his head toward the rows of seed pods. "By yourself?"

"Luke and Laurel help sometimes. But it's mostly me."

"Linda said you garden. She made it sound like..." He runs a hand through that sandy blond hair.

"A hobby?"

He nods, and the smile I give him is as brittle as old newspaper. "Of course she did. It's a job. *My* job." I bite my lower lip, and he winces slightly, like the movement causes him pain.

I don't owe him an explanation, but can't stop myself from continuing, "Planting and harvesting are a calling for me. My grandparents were farmers and their parents before them. I think growing things is in my blood." I straighten my shoulders. "But flower farming is also a business. Thanks to my success last summer, I retired from cleaning office buildings every night after I put the kids to bed."

His brows draw together. "After?"

"Normally I'd start around nine or so and finish around

midnight." At his shocked expression, I roll my eyes. "Did you think Linda was bankrolling our lives? Not that I'd expect or even want her to. I know what you think of me, Chase, but—"

He holds up a hand, regret darkening his eyes. "I need you to understand how things were before your wedding." He looks down at the dirt floor like he can't quite bring himself to meet my gaze. "My childhood best friend, who claimed he'd never settle down called and told me to get my ass to Colorado. For his wedding to a vacation fling who got herself pregnant. So, yeah, I was skeptical at best."

"I didn't *get myself* anything, Chase." I breathe out a sharp laugh. "Trust me, Teddy was actively involved in the process."

Chase closes his eyes for a few seconds. "That isn't how he talked about it, and when I met you..."

I feel my eyes narrow. "What happened when you met me?"

"You seemed delicate...fragile. Teddy was always a sucker for wounded birds."

Anger rises inside me, but it's as much directed at myself as Chase. I'm very familiar with the version of me that first caught Teddy's eye.

I came with friends to Colorado only weeks after my grandparents died. I *was* a wounded bird at that point. And Teddy liked it. He enjoyed drawing the smile out of me and playing white knight for the young woman who cried herself to sleep in her tent every night. For better or worse, we both lost interest in me playing that role very quickly.

"Shell shocked," I clarify. "I was overwhelmed and shell-shocked at how my life was changing."

He's silent for a moment before nodding. "You got over it. Linda told me you're a good mom." Is this his way of convincing me he no longer thinks I trapped his friend into marriage? I remind myself that I don't care what Chase Calhoun thinks of me.

"I've gotten over a lot of things," I tell him with a shrug. "Can we be done skipping down memory lane? Like I said in my text, I'd like to take you up on your offer of help, or Linda's offer for you to help me. However you want to phrase it."

"I'm glad you changed your mind." His voice is neutral as he stands there with one hand hooked in his belt loop, the other holding his hat. And looking every inch the rugged bull rider who could probably fix anything that needs fixing and handle whatever problem comes his way.

"I know she talked to you about taking care of the twins, but that will primarily involve driving them when they need to get to town for activities. Otherwise, the three of us can manage around here even with my ankle. I know how to manage."

He's watching me intently, and if he knew Teddy as well as I think he did, he understands what I mean. I was married for four years before my husband's accident, and Teddy loved his kids. But while he could light up a room like nobody's business, I don't think he ever changed a diaper or cleaned up puke when they got sick. And believe me, if one got sick, the other did as well. Teddy wasn't into domesticity.

He liked to float in with his bag of tricks, party magician style. But once he grew tired of being the fun parent or something better caught his attention, my late husband was gone again. Teddy brought home the sugar, but I was the keeper of the recipe box of our lives.

Chase clears his throat, and I realize I've let my thoughts wander to memories better left in the past.

"I'll need your help keeping the flower farm going." It's my turn to study him. "Did Linda happen to mention my business?"

"She did not," he answers before his gaze flicks around the greenhouse's interior once more.

"Right." Because, according to my mother-in-law, flower farming is a hobby. Maybe it started that way, but it's so much more now. It's also how I'm going to make my dream of staying in Skylark come true.

"The work is year-round, but things start to pick up this

month." I move forward on the scooter. "Currently, I use about three acres for the flowers. The bulbs will be coming up soon in the nearest field. I could use another set of hands harvesting and then planting new crops. And someone to drive me into town for deliveries and help with my booth at local markets."

Listing everything out loud makes my chest tighten painfully. There's so much to do. So many moving pieces have to work together if I'm going to make enough money to buy this place. The weight of it presses down on me like a boulder, and I have to force myself to take a steady breath.

"I'll do whatever you need." It's similar to what he told me earlier, and the statement makes goosebumps erupt along my arms. It feels as if he's promising something more than his arrangement with my mother-in-law. Like he's doing this for me. Because of me.

It's probably just my overly-sentimental heart. I tend to latch onto whatever crumbs of kindness people scatter in my direction.

"If you tell me what Linda is paying you, I can try to add—"

"It's worked out, Molly." He shakes his head. "You don't owe me anything. My debt to the McAllisters has been hanging over my head for nearly a decade. I'm grateful for a chance to pay it off."

"The work is physical," I tell him as if that's not obvious. What I really want to do is ask exactly why he owes Teddy and my mother-in-law. But that's not my business. This man is not my friend or my ally. Although he might not be the enemy I thought he was, I need to remember I'm also not the wounded bird he believed me to be. I can take care of myself.

I press my lips together and swallow. "If you have any limitations from your accident, we can—"

"I don't," he snaps, rolling his shoulders like he's shrugging off some invisible weight.

"But you're not going back to bull riding?"

"I already planned on retiring," he says quickly. "Having the shit stomped out of me confirmed that decision."

Chase Calhoun is a lot of things. He's hotter than sin, a little

32

bit mysterious, all confidence and swagger, and about as sexy as any man I've ever laid eyes on.

But he is *not* a good liar.

I don't call him out on it. Not when he's agreed to provide the help I desperately need.

"There's a lot to be done in the next few weeks. The timing of my injury couldn't be worse." My gaze drops to the denim plastered against his powerful thighs. He might look strong as an ox, but I noticed a slight hitch in his step yesterday after jogging to the end of the driveway. People around town talked after his accident at the rodeo last fall. The bull's weight shattered his femur, and the rumor was he'd never walk without a limp, let alone get back on a horse again.

"Linda told me you and the kids are moving with her to Albuquerque."

My stomach ties itself into a knot, and I smooth a hand over the leaves of a nearby plant, hoping the familiar gesture will work its usual magic and calm me. "That's Linda's plan. I have a different one."

He raises an eyebrow. "Care to share?"

Cue the nerves dancing across my belly. It was one thing to commit to a new future with my friends surrounding me. It's quite another to say the words out loud to a man who likely still doubts I'm capable of managing my own shit. But I made a promise to myself, and more importantly, to my children.

"I'm going to buy the farm." My voice only shakes a little as I say the words.

Chase steps back like my statement reached out and slapped him across the face. My grandfather used the term "gobsmacked" when he was particularly shocked about something, and that sums up Chase's expression perfectly.

"Are you sure? Do you have the money for it?"

No and no, I think in my head, but I nod and smile. "Yes, I'm sure, and no, I don't have the money yet. But I will and...well, I will."

He draws in a slow breath and focuses on the rows of raised planters as if it's too hard to meet my gaze. "That's going to come as a shock to Linda," he says after a few moments.

"Yep." My heart hammers against my ribs at the thought of my mother-in-law when she finds out. Her disappointment, anger, and maybe a sense of betrayal that I'm not following through on our arrangement. But I have to do this for my kids. And even more, for me.

"If you talk to her again, I'd appreciate if you don't mention it. Albuquerque's not that far, and we'll visit or she can stay with us. This was their father's home, and it's ours now." I clear my throat, then whisper, "I love it here."

His mouth opens like he's got something to say to that, but he snaps it shut again, then turns to gaze out the greenhouse's west-facing windows. The farm butts up against the National Forest on that edge, the thick trees forming a natural border to the fields.

"It's okay if you don't believe in me," I say, even though I'm a little hurt by his reaction. Not that I have any right to be. Heck, I'm still working on believing in myself, mostly borrowing my friends' confidence in the meantime. "But if I'm going to do this, I need help. At least until I can dr—"

"Once more, I'm here for whatever you need." He's clearly frustrated that I didn't take him at his word the first or second time. "Help with the kids and the flowers, plus acting as your damn chauffeur or—"

"Don't sound too thrilled about it," I mutter, surprised when his shoulders lower like my sarcasm amuses him.

"I've been staying with my sister, which is a bit of a drive." He's finally looking at me again, and the emotion swirling in those pale gray eyes makes my breath catch. "It would be easier if I were closer."

The thought of him sleeping under the same roof sends a

powerful zing through my chest that I absolutely cannot afford to feel. Not with him.

"I'm a single mom with two young kids." As if he doesn't know that already. "I don't feel comfortable with you staying at the house."

He nods. "Totally agree, but if you're okay with me parking my trailer next to the barn...it's where I live when I'm on the circuit. I don't like hotels."

"Oh." A trailer. Not with me. My pulse settles a smidge. "That should be fine."

"I'd also like to stable my horse in the barn."

"Your horse?" I don't mean to shudder but can't quite stop it.

"Fancy." He tilts his head. "Are you allergic or something?"

"Not exactly. I'm just not a fan of animals with giant teeth."

There's a beat of silence, then he chokes out a laugh. "She's not a tiger, Molly."

"I got bitten as a kid."

"Did you provoke the horse?"

My fingers tighten on the scooter's handlebars. "Do I look like the type of person who goes around provoking animals?" His grin widens in a way that feels almost wolfish. Talk about wild animals.

"For your information, I was minding my own business in my grandparents' barn. The horse reached over the edge of the stall and tried to take a chunk out of my shoulder." I rub my shoulder like it was yesterday.

"Fancy isn't going to bite you."

"Damn straight, because I'm not getting close enough for her to reach me."

He laughs again. "You're funny."

"Being bitten by an animal isn't funny."

"The way you describe it is kind of funny."

"You're a dick," I counter.

"*Kind* of a dick," he agrees.

For some reason, that makes my lips twitch. I don't want to be amused by this tall, handsome cowboy. I don't want to be anything by him.

"Fine on keeping your horse here. Fair warning, the barn hasn't been used for anything but storing tools and equipment in years."

"I can take care of any repairs."

"Like you took care of the sink," I say, then force myself to add, "Thank you for that."

"It was as much for my benefit as yours." He gives me a slow wink that does funny things to my insides. "It's been a few years since I attended a wet T-shirt contest. Best part of my morning, but I'm guessing that show is a one-and-done."

My cheeks instantly color in response to his words. "You shouldn't notice that, let alone talk about it."

"I'm only human," he offers like some sort of explanation.

The slow smile he gives me is like a match to a flame, and it's my lady parts catching fire. Allowing Chase Calhoun into my life is a bad idea. The worst.

I shake my head to clear those thoughts. I need help if I'm going to buy the farm, and he's my best option. "I need to get back to work."

"What do you need from me?"

Everything, my body chants like a refrain. "Nothing right now," I say. And do you hear how calm and unaffected I sound? Well done, Molly.

Another nod. "Then I'll grab my stuff from my sister's and move the trailer and Fancy here."

I nod. "The school bus drops off around three-thirty. If you could come back after that, I'd like to talk to the twins about the arrangement before you get here."

Laurel won't mind, but Luke isn't going to like it.

"Yep," he agrees, and I have a feeling he knows exactly why I'm making that request. "I'll be back later." With a final nod, he turns and walks out of the greenhouse.

Alone again, I draw in a deep breath. The earthy, familiar smell of the greenhouse calms my nerves, but underneath it, there's something new. The lingering scent of the man I just agreed to depend on for the next few weeks.

A man who makes me feel like I'm more than just a single mom juggling too many responsibilities. Who looks at me like I'm a woman worth the kind of attention that has nothing to do with school pickups or grocery lists. Chase Calhoun makes me want to upgrade my underwear situation, even though I'd bet my life he's never going to see them.

5

CHASE

"YOU'RE DOING WHAT NOW?" My sister glares at me from the doorway of the spare room in her duplex. I've been holed up in this tiny space since being released from the hospital after my accident. The longest five months of my life.

I continue to pull my clothes out of the dresser in the corner of the postage-stamp-sized bedroom, tossing them in the duffel bag on the bed. "How many different ways can I explain it, Ada?"

"You can't shack up with your best friend's wife," she tells me in no uncertain terms.

I mutter a curse as the drawer I slam shut clips my finger. "For fuck's sake, we're not shacking up. I'm helping with the twins and her flower business while Linda's out of the country." I turn and face her. "I figured you'd be happy to get rid of me."

"First, watch your language," she says with a tilt of her chin. "Second, as a matter of fact, you *are* cramping my style. I met a guy the other night and—"

I clamp my hands over my ears. "La la la la la la."

"Dude. I'm an adult."

"You're my baby sister. I don't want to hear about your sex life."

"Why are you doing this?" Her voice becomes more serious as she tugs on the end of her honey-colored braid. Her eyes are the same pale gray as mine, but infinitely gentler. My sister can light up a room with a smile that comes as naturally to her as breathing, which is probably why she's such a popular elementary school teacher. "You don't like kids."

"I like them better than chicken pox."

"They compare favorably to a communicable disease. A rousing endorsement."

"You know I have a debt to repay. I don't like that hanging over my head."

"You're sure this is the right way to go about it?"

"It's the only way."

"Molly McAllister's a sweetheart, Chase. She volunteers for every class party and school fundraiser. She's good at all of it—from the decorating cupcakes to her flower arrangements. You'd think Martha Stewart was her grandmother."

I blink. "What the hell does that mean?"

"She makes things beautiful."

"What does that have to do with me? She sprained her ankle, not her fingers. If she wants to decorate cupcakes, more power to her. I'm there to drive her kids around and help her take care of the flower farm. Cupcakes aren't in the job description." I could certainly think of some creative uses for icing where Molly is concerned.

"You don't like her."

I zip up the duffel and turn to face my little sister. Thank god she isn't a mind reader because that last thought definitely wouldn't fall under the heading of Ada approved. "First you accuse me of shacking up, which I'm not. I'll be staying in the trailer and coming back here or over to Ray's to shower, shave, and—"

"Use the Poo-Pourri spray," she reminds me.

"I've been using the Poo-Pourri, Ada. Your crapper smells like a damn field of lavender. The point is, I'm not playing house with Molly, *and* I never said I didn't like her."

"You made it clear without words."

I hope Ada takes my low growl as a hint. I'm sure as hell not admitting to my far-too-nosey sister that my opinion of Molly has done a complete one-eighty in the span of a day.

It's better if everyone, Molly included, keeps believing I don't think much of the sweet widow with a soft smile and sad eyes. Unlike Teddy, damsels in distress never did it for me. But Molly has made it clear she's not a woman who needs saving. I not only believe her, I like her more because of it.

"This isn't right," my sister insists, tapping her booted foot against the hardwood floor. "You haven't been right since the accident, Chase. Watching that bull—"

"I know what happened." I sigh and hang my head. "Hell, half of Skylark saw Black Tornado trample me."

"Half the town wasn't at the hospital. It was me who spent hours outside the ICU. They weren't sure if you were going to make it. And later, no one could guarantee you would walk again."

"Yet, here I am." I hold out my arms. "The picture of health."

I know I'm not fooling either of us but ignore the bead of sweat trailing between my shoulder blades. The reminder of that night, and the hell that was my months-long recovery, always triggers some kind of physical reaction. Never a good one.

"Are you sure you can handle this?"

"I'm wiping the slate clean with the McAllisters." I don't mention Linda's promise to sell me her property when she gets back to town or how Molly's admission that she wants to buy it made me second guess every plan I have for the future. "I can manage a few weeks of nannying."

"Well, I like anything that makes you stay longer," she says softly. "It's good having you here."

We both know she's not just talking about geography. Ever since Mom got sick, Ada's been carrying the heavy load.

It's been over five years since our mother accidentally burned down our childhood home, but the memory hasn't miraculously become less painful.

Ada had just moved back to town for a job at Skylark Elementary, and I was checking in by phone a couple of times a week from the road. We hadn't realized that Mom's tendency to forget details and misplace her keys had progressed into full-blown dementia. She left a pot of boiling noodles on the stove while she drove into town because, as she told us later, she'd forgotten to buy tomato sauce. By the time Linda, Mom's nearest neighbor, saw the plume of smoke in the sky and called the fire department, the house was engulfed. Thirty years of memories—not all of them good—literally up in flames. We were able to salvage a few photo albums, but everything else was gone.

It wasn't the worst thing that happened in that house by a long shot, but it did make me aware that my sister needed more help than I was giving her. I pulled out of the events I was scheduled to ride in over the next month and returned to Skylark to get Mom settled in the memory-care unit of a nearby assisted living facility.

Fresh out of jail, Dad had shown up the day we had the charred remains of the house bulldozed. He'd been drunk and belligerent, ranting about how this was what Mom deserved for leaving him. Ada hated it when Dad popped off, but I was immune to his temper, which didn't mean I wanted anything to do with the fucker.

That didn't stop me from coming back to Colorado more often to see my mom and offer Ada what help I could give. I tried to coordinate my visits with events so that I'd have an excuse to get in and out. Too much family bonding wasn't good for any of us given our level of dysfunction. That's why I was home for the event that matched me with Black Tornado, a bull with a reputation for being a mean son of a bitch both in and out of the ring. The kind of animal that didn't just want to throw you—he wanted to make sure you never got back up.

Dad came to see me once in the hospital after the accident, but the minute he started going on about how I wasn't all my reputation was cracked up to be, I pulled the cord for the nurse and had him kicked out.

I felt nothing, my go-to emotional state, as I watched him leave. Which is why it's annoying as fuck that my body, particularly the empty cavity that once held my heart, seems so attuned to every emotion Molly displays—particularly the ones she tried to hide.

"Thank you for caring, Ada." I pull her into a hug. "You're a better person than anyone in this family deserves."

"I know," she agrees and pats me on the back. "Not a chance I'm going to let you forget it."

I don't bother grabbing my toiletries from the bathroom. Like I told my sister, I'll be coming here or going to Ray and Janice's for running water.

It's a short drive over to the Grimshaw ranch where I've got my Airstream parked and Fancy stabled. Unlike most guys who retire from the rodeo circuit, Ray didn't start running cattle or training horses. He and his wife, Janice, bought land, but Ray went back to school for a teaching degree. I lucked out to have him for American History sophomore year. He became my mentor and friend, and we stayed in touch over the years.

He's also the one who drove me to physical therapy appointments before I was cleared to drive. Unlike my sister, he didn't ask questions about whether my recovery was physical or mental. When I told him I was retiring, he nodded and said I had a good run and should be proud of myself.

Proud is another emotion I don't do, so I'm taking his word on that. It sure beats having my dad's voice in my head.

"So you're going to be looking after a couple of first graders," he says as he watches me load Fancy into the trailer after I dropped off the Airstream. "Are you sure that's a good idea?"

"You sound like Ada. Why does everybody think I have something against kids?"

"It's the way your lip curls every time an ankle biter approaches at an event to ask for your autograph," Janice suggests from where she's standing next to her husband.

Ray chuckles. "Yeah, that's why."

"Kids love a sneer. It's part of my lore." That's a term I overheard my sister using, and I like it.

"It's part of your DNA."

My gut clenches in an automatic denial.

"I don't mean it like that," Ray says, reading my reaction. "You aren't like your father. It's just that some people are kid folks and some are horse folks."

I shut the trailer behind Fancy, and then turn to face my friend. "I'm driving the twins to activities and helping with Molly's flower business." I take off my hat and run a hand through my hair. "Shit, you guys. It's not like I hate kids."

"You better watch that potty mouth." Janice points a finger at me. "Little pitchers have big ears."

"I never understood that saying," I mutter.

"Cut the cursing," Ray clarifies.

"I can do that."

They offer matching snorts.

The habit of swearing like a sailor won't disappear overnight, but I've got to start somewhere. "I can try."

"Of course you can." Janice steps forward to hug me. "It's a good thing, what you're doing for Teddy's widow and those kids."

"Paying off one debit, but I still owe the two of you. I appreciate everything you've done for me," I tell her.

She pulls away and narrows her eyes. "You're family, Chase. Even if we're not related by blood. And don't act like you're saying goodbye forever. This is the first step to you putting down roots in Skylark, where you belong."

I swallow against the unfamiliar tightness in my throat. "Thank you for saying that."

Ray claps me on the shoulder with a firm grip. "You bring those kids over to meet the goats when you get a chance. Kids love goats, and ours need the attention."

Ray and Janice's place is on the opposite end of town from Linda's house, and it's half past five when I pull in with the horse trailer. Curtains flutter in the house's front window as I'm unloading, but no one comes out to greet me, so I decide it's best to get Fancy settled in the barn before I knock on the door again.

I've had my horse since she was a yearling and can tell she's looking down her nose at moving from Ray's well-appointed barn to the stall at the McAllisters', which needs quite a bit of TLC. But Fancy trusts me implicitly, a sentiment that goes both ways. Our relationship is the most committed I've ever had with a female, and has seen me through a lot of life's ups and downs.

"It's going to be fine," I assure her as she checks out her new digs. She offers a doubtful whinny in response, but seems happy enough once I give her fresh oats and hay.

"What's his name?" a voice says from behind me.

I turn to see Laurel staring at Fancy, and once again, I'm struck by how much she looks like her father.

"*Her* name is Fancy."

"She looks fancy," she says as she moves closer, obviously fascinated by the animal, who's chestnut coat gleams.

"Exactly."

Her gaze flicks to me. "Can I ride her?"

"Sure," I answer immediately, then shake my head. "I mean, if your mom says it's okay."

She scrunches up her nose. "Mom's scared of horses."

"She mentioned that."

"Does Fancy bite?"

"She's as gentle as a lamb." I reach into my coat pocket and take out the carrot I grabbed from Ada's refrigerator on my way out the door. "You want to feed her a snack?"

The excitement on the girl's face makes me feel like I offered her a pet unicorn. She takes the carrot from my hand and steps forward without an ounce of trepidation. "She likes it when you talk sweet."

Laurel shoots me a dubious glance, also pure Teddy, before focusing on the horse. She looks at the carrot in her hand then up again as she reaches her arm out. "Hey, Fancy. You're a good girl, aren't you?"

The horse takes the carrot gently because she is, indeed, a good girl. Then she snuffles against Laurel's palm, earning a bright giggle as the girl strokes her velvet head.

"I think she likes me," she says.

"She definitely likes you. She also likes being scratched between her eyes."

"I'm *so* going to convince Mom to let me ride her."

"Good luck with that. Speaking of, does your mom know you're out here?"

"Yeah, she told me to tell you she's making dinner."

Shit. "I should be helping with that."

"Probably," Laurel agrees but continues to pet the horse.

"Maybe we should both be helping." I glance down at my dusty clothes and decide fresh ones will have to wait. "What's for supper?"

"Spaghetti," Laurel says. "With Mom's homemade sauce."

"Your mother made homemade sauce?"

"A while ago. She got it from the freezer."

"Is your mom a good cook?"

Laurel lets out her own sort of snuffle. "Duh, she's the best."

"I can't cook for sh..." The kid's eyes cut to me when I stop mid-curse word. But, hell, I stopped. "I'm a terrible cook, but I'm a pro at dishes."

She's quiet momentarily and then says, "Mom doesn't like to admit she needs help, but she does."

"That's what I'm here for," I assure her, thinking this isn't going to be quite as hard as I thought. I don't know what my sister and Ray and Janice were talking about. Laurel and I are getting along like peas and carrots, which is a great start. There's a decent chance the whole thing will be easy-peasy.

6

CHASE

Easy-peasy. Famous last words.

Thirty minutes with Molly's kids, and I'm convinced that willingly climbing onto the back of an angry bull isn't the hardest thing I've ever done. Wrangling seven-year-old twins and not pissing off their gorgeous mother is proving to be a challenge way beyond my limited capabilities.

Turns out, Luke and Laurel could give a rat's ass about my sneer or anything else I do to bring order to their particular brand of upheaval. The girl seemed sweet when we were together in the barn, but once we got back to the house, it became even clearer that she takes after Teddy in looks *and* personality. One moment, she's charming and fun-loving. The next, she's screaming at her brother like a feral cat with its tail caught in a door.

Luke's emotional state is perpetually tuned to the high anxiety station. I stopped counting after the fourth time he burst into tears, prompted by a pointed word or look from his sister. Laurel also inherited the ability to push buttons from her father. For all his winsome charm, Teddy could cut a person off at the knees with his casual criticism.

"You're doing it wrong!" Laurel's voice pierces the air as the two of them sit at the coffee table drawing something for a school assignment. "That's not how farm animals are supposed to look."

Luke's bottom lip trembles. "I like them this way."

"It's stupid," she declares, and just like that, the waterworks start again.

Molly keeps insisting she has things under control if I need to continue getting settled.

"You really don't have to stay," she says for the third time, her voice tight with obvious exhaustion. "You probably have better things to do."

I don't know why she's under the impression I need to spend hours feathering my nest. Or maybe she simply doesn't want an audience as she struggles to handle the chaos swirling around her like a tornado. I can also relate to her determination to get by with the most minuscule amount of help possible.

The farmhouse kitchen isn't big to start with, and Molly seems to have the turning radius of a semi on those crutches. There are about six different times I think she's going to land on her ass. And that's before she grabs the saucepan handle without a potholder and ends up spilling half of it down the front of the stove and herself.

Tomato sauce splatters across the white tile countertop like abstract art, and I watch her shoulders sag. The wet T-shirt business might have been unintentionally hot, but another ruined shirt just makes me feel sorry for her. It's obvious she's on the brink of a total meltdown when she doesn't argue after I suggest she go to her room to change.

I find a jar of sauce in the cabinet to mix with what's left in the pan, then manage to get the pasta, bread, and a bagged salad onto plates at the table before she returns. I'm damn proud of myself, until Luke starts blubbering again because the red sauce slides into his lettuce.

"It's all going to the same place," I tell him. "They're just getting to know one another before they hit your stomach."

"He doesn't like his food touching," Laurel explains with the patience of someone who's had to translate her brother's quirks a thousand times before.

"Do you cry like this at school?" I ask.

He blinks up at me with his mother's big green eyes. "Sometimes," he mutters.

"That's a rough road to hoe, kiddo."

Molly makes her way slowly down the stairs wearing a pale gray sweatshirt that makes her eyes look even more striking. I lean across the table toward Luke, pitching my voice low enough so that only the twins can hear me. "Can you deal with your food making friends on the plate this once? I'm sure your mom feels bad about spilling her homemade sauce, and it might help her mood if you could suck it up."

"Mom says sucks is a bad word," Laurel tells me as Luke frowns.

"I'll remember that for next time, but how about helping your mom out?"

Who knows if it's my brand of tough love works, or if the kid is simply motivated by the thought of taking care of his mother, but he eats everything off his plate without complaint. He even picks up a piece of sauce-drenched lettuce and chews it deliberately, his small face scrunched in concentration.

Molly seems shocked—in a pleasant-ish sort of way—that I managed to keep the dinner train rolling. I shouldn't feel so gratified by her approval, but I do.

I insist on clearing the table and loading the dishwasher while she helps the kids finish their homework, but she tries to get rid of me again as she follows the kids up the stairs for bath and bedtime.

"You've done enough," she insists, her hand resting on the banister. "I can handle the rest."

"No place else to be." Besides, she might need backup and another change of clothes if those two are as rowdy in the bath as they were before dinner.

To my surprise, things quiet down. Every few minutes, laughter echoes down the steps. The sound of Molly's voice drifts down, too, warm and patient as she reads them a story. "And then the knight rode his horse up the mountain." Her voice has a musical quality that makes something in my chest tighten.

I've just finished drying the final hand-washed pot when there's a rustling sound behind me. I turn to find the kids standing side by side at the edge of the kitchen. The girl wears a nightgown with flowers all over it, and the boy is in striped PJs with a space theme. Their hair is still damp from their baths, cheeks rosy, and they smell like lavender soap and something I can only guess is innocence.

"Thanks for your help today," Laurel says, then elbows her brother.

"Thank you." Luke's fingers twist in the hem of his pajama shirt.

"Yeah, sure." I rub a hand along the back of my neck. This obviously forced bit of gratitude touches me, both deeply and rather unexpectedly. They're cute when they aren't being terrors.

"Race upstairs!" Luke says, turning to make a run for it, but Laurel grabs him and tries to muscle her way into the lead. The boy evades her grasp and vaults himself over the back of the worn sofa in some kind of kangaroo hop.

"Settle down." Molly's voice calls from somewhere upstairs, but her tone holds more amusement than admonishment.

Hell, maybe Luke takes after his father in some ways, too. Teddy had the best coordination of anyone I've ever met. As a boy, he could climb like nobody's business—trees or rock faces, and more often than was smart for either of us, the roof of the house.

A smile curves my lips as I watch the kids scamper up the stairs, their footsteps thundering across the floor above. I hang the dish towel I've been using to dry the things that wouldn't fit in the dishwasher.

The house is back in order, so there's no reason for me to stick

50

around, but I do. After all the noise of the evening, I know my trailer will feel especially quiet. Usually, I crave that kind of silence after the lights and sounds of a crowd at an event. Since my accident, I've had too much silence, and now I find myself craving something different—companionship.

The clock on the wall behind me ticks steadily, marking time in the peaceful house. Through the ceiling overhead, I hear the gentle murmur of Molly's voice as she tucks the kids into bed.

As she makes her awkward way down the stairs on her bottom, her orthopedic boot making a soft thump against each wooden step, the need for companionship shifts into outright desire. And when she offers me a tentative smile, her cheeks flushed and her strawberry blonde hair falling in soft waves around her shoulders, it isn't just my heart that rises to attention.

"They're finally down," she says, settling at the bottom of the stairs and looking up at me with those impossibly green eyes. "I can't thank you enough for staying. I don't know what I would have done without you tonight."

The vulnerability in her voice and the way she looks at me—like I'm some kind of hero instead of a washed-up cowboy with more scars than sense—does something to me. It makes me want to be the man she thinks I am.

But wanting and being capable of it are two different things. Let's face it, Molly McAllister deserves a hell of a lot more than what I have left to give.

7

CHASE

The sound of voices wakes me in the morning, and I blink open my eyes to see sunlight peeking through the edges of the trailer's blackout curtains.

Shit.

I jackknife upright after glancing at the clock. It's seven forty-five, which means those voices belong to Luke and Laurel, who are walking past the trailer on their way to catch the bus at the end of the driveway. Which also means I missed helping with breakfast, getting them ready for school, and generally doing the job I'm supposed to do.

Double shit.

I throw on a sweatshirt and jeans, shove my feet into boots, and race out of the trailer like the place is on fire.

"Good morning," I call to the trio moving down the gravel driveway, slowly because of Molly's crutches.

The kids wave and keep walking, but she stops and looks over her shoulder at me. Her eyes widen slightly as she takes in what I imagine is some legit bed head. I'm also still buttoning up my fly.

Her brows furrow. "Long night?"

"Something like that," I say. How do I explain that the hours

52

of sleep I lost were her fault? Or at least dream Molly's fault. I tossed and turned, hard as a rock, even after taking myself in hand once. No, make that twice.

I've had no desire to get back on a bull since the accident, but even less desire to hook up with a woman. Now I can't stop thinking about the one woman I can't let myself want. My type has always been easy on the eyes, hard and fast in the bedroom, with zero strings attached. Molly is none of those things, so there's no accounting for my reaction to her.

"Mom, I hear the bus," Luke calls.

"It's here early," Laurel adds.

Molly's fingers tighten on the crutches.

"I'm sorry I missed breakfast," I say as I finish buttoning my jeans. Maybe it's wishful thinking, but I'm pretty sure the reason her cheeks are suddenly flushed has less to do with exertion and more with the flash of abs I just gave her.

"Chase will walk you the rest of the way," she tells the twins. "Love you both. I'll see you later today at the party."

"Bye, Mom. Love you."

"Love you, Mommy."

"I really am sorry," I say as I move past her. Like she has any reason to believe me.

"I need to leave here at nine to make some deliveries. After they get on the bus, I could use help loading the tubs of flowers into the back of the truck." She gives me a funny look. "And I'm guessing you need a shower."

So maybe she wasn't looking at my stomach. The thought is annoyingly disappointing.

I jog around the curve of the driveway where the kids have disappeared.

"Can I ride Fancy after school?" Laurel asks by way of greeting.

"Good morning to you, too," I answer. "Did you ask your mom?"

"Mommy said no," Luke tells his sister, not meeting my eyes.

"She doesn't want you riding some cowboy horse. It could bite you."

"Do you want to try feeding Fancy a carrot?" I ask Luke.

"I want to feed her another carrot *and* ride," Laurel answers first.

"Mommy said no," Luke repeats, then looks up at me. "You missed breakfast, and Mommy makes the best blueberry muffins, and horses bite."

Before I can explain again that my horse isn't going to bite anyone, the bus pulls up and the door swings open.

Laurel gets on first, and through the window, I see her sit with another girl. The two of them immediately start giggling. Luke is slower to board. He hands the driver a brown paper bag, and the old man offers a stained-tooth grin.

"Thanks, buddy. I appreciate you and your mom thinking of me." He pulls a muffin out of the bag and takes a bite before raising it in my direction. "Molly's the best."

I nod as the door closes, and the bus trundles off down the road. Luke has taken a seat by himself and glares at me as I wave when the bus rolls past.

Teddy and I always sat together in the back. Does Luke have a friend getting on at a later stop? I'm not convinced. And despite knowing better, I vow right here and now that I'm going to help that boy make a friend. For Teddy.

I expect to see Molly still making her way back to the house, but the driveway is empty. There's a flash of movement near the greenhouse as I climb the porch steps, and her apparent industriousness makes me feel like an even bigger loser. More so when the scent of freshly brewed coffee and homemade muffins greets me as I enter the house. I don't deserve to pour myself a cup, but all I've got in the trailer is instant, which isn't going to cut it this morning.

In addition to the muffins, I notice two dozen cupcakes cooling on a wire rack on the counter. It seems like I wasn't the only one not sleeping last night, but she was far more productive during her overnight hours.

I down a giant mug of coffee in a couple of swigs, then wash out the pot and leave it drying in the rack next to the sink. As chaotic as yesterday was, Molly appears to have this morning buttoned up.

I rip through feeding Fancy and mucking her stall before heading toward the greenhouse. Molly's filling five-gallon buckets with tulips and daffodils, their yellow and purple blooms a bright welcome sign to the change of seasons. I may not know much about flowers, but I'm impressed by her operation, especially knowing she's done it all herself.

"What can I do?"

She backs up a few inches on her scooter, her wariness making me want to straighten my shoulders and puff out my chest like I'm back in middle school trying to impress the prettiest girl in class.

Only the stakes feel higher because we're not kids, and the intensity of her gaze has me fighting the urge to check if I've got something stuck in my teeth.

I blink and wait for her to speak, but when she continues to stare, I can't take it any longer and ask, "Is there a problem?"

She shakes her head. "I know you've been through a lot with the accident, and I appreciate your willingness to help while Linda's away. But I can't have somebody who's out of control near my children. Not..." She swallows hard, then adds, "...again."

Her eyes glow like chips of jade, beautiful but sharp enough to cut glass. "I'm sure you know Teddy was typically the life of any party." Her voice is flat. "That partying came with a price. I stayed because...well, I loved him, but he didn't always make it easy. I'm not having that energy around my children again."

"I don't do drugs." I hate that she's assumed the worst even though she has no reason not to. "Unless you count an occasional ibuprofen. And I'm not a fan of hangovers. I might have a beer or two when I'm out with friends, but—"

"Last night—" she begins.

"I'm sorry," I repeat, realizing that I've offered more apologies to this woman in the past twenty-four hours than I have to anyone in years. The need for her to believe in me, to see me as someone worth trusting, burns in my chest like a brand. "I have trouble sleeping sometimes. Because of my no numbing agents rule, it was nearly three before I managed to fall asleep last night, and I overslept. It won't happen again. You can trust me, Molly." At least on that.

Her name is like honey on my tongue, sweet and addictive. I don't realize I'm holding my breath waiting for her answer until she gives a slight nod, and something in me releases. Her tentative acceptance lifts an invisible weight from my shoulders.

I admire the hell out of her already. She's running a business, raising kids, and still managing to look like every version of temptation I've ever encountered.

"The truck I use for deliveries is in the garage," she says, and I'm happy as a pig in shit to be done with that conversation. "Keys are in the console. Could you back it up in front of the greenhouse so we can load the buckets?"

"Of course." I turn and jog in the direction of the garage, grateful to be able to help in some meaningful way.

The truck is a beater with a bench seat that's been re-covered in a thick cotton fabric in a floral pattern. It smells like Molly—a contrasting yet beguiling mix of lavender and sunshine. There are large vinyl stickers on both the driver and passenger doors with a simple but pretty logo for Meadow Blooms, which I assume is the official name of her business.

She's filling the last bucket with water when I reenter the greenhouse. "If you want to stay at the house and rest your ankle, I can make the deliveries."

"I'm fine," she says, but I already hear a tinge of weariness in her voice.

"Are you sure you aren't doing too much?" I ask. "I'm guessing those muffins and cupcakes didn't bake themselves?"

For a moment, it looks as though she's going to give me another one-finger salute, but she settles for an exaggerated eye roll. "A small army of magical woodland creatures helped me."

The corner of her mouth lifts, and that hint of a smile hits me like a sucker punch to the chest.

To be fair, if woodland creatures were going to pick somebody to help, it would be this woman, who seems to be as pure of heart as any damn fairy tale princess I can imagine.

"Good to know," I tell her, not bothering to hide my smile. "I figured it was talking teacups and candlesticks."

"What do you know about talking teacups?" She gives me a sidelong glance, and heat pools low in my belly. Yeah, she's beautiful, but it's more than that. I don't know what the hell we're doing here, but I want more of it.

"My sister was major-league into princesses as a kid," I admit, rubbing a hand across my jaw. "Belle was her favorite."

"I'm partial to Ariel," Molly says quietly.

"Because you both have red hair, right?" I grab two buckets and secure them in the back of the truck.

"That was part of it, but I think it has more to do with wanting to belong and..." She shakes her head. "Forget it. No time for deep thoughts with *The Little Mermaid*."

I don't argue, even though I want to. This glimpse into her thoughts feels significant, and so different from the surface-level conversations I'm used to on the circuit. Talking about ride times, beer brands, and which buckle bunny is causing drama.

Besides my sister, I don't know women who think about the deeper meanings of princesses. I already know Molly is more than I thought, but I want to learn even more. I want to understand the thoughts and emotions that flicker behind those green eyes.

"I've met your sister at the elementary school. She's a popular teacher."

I nod. "Ada's always been great with kids. She loves teaching."

I hold up a hand when Molly starts to move forward on the scooter like she's going to help load buckets. "She's also mentioned your cupcake prowess, but isn't a sprained ankle an excuse to lighten your load?"

She breathes out a soft laugh. "I offered to bring cupcakes before the accident. Luke and Laurel are in the same class this year, which doesn't usually happen with twins. Their teacher's going on maternity leave next week, so the other class mom and I are throwing her a baby shower this afternoon. I didn't want to put more work on the other parents."

"So even with an injury, you're still taking care of everyone?" I lift another bucket into the truck bed.

She ignores my question and gestures to the crutches leaning against one of the benches. "Could you fit those in the back of the truck? They're easier than dragging the scooter to town. I'll need to come back after the deliveries to decorate the cupcakes and then head to the school this afternoon. I can text one of the other moms to pick me up so you don't—"

"I'll drive you back and forth as many times as you need, Molly. That's why I'm here. I can't help decorate cupcakes, but I can carry them without a problem. Let's not have a repeat of the pasta sauce from last night."

I shut the truck bed and expect to find her glaring at me again for hinting that she couldn't handle the cupcakes on her own, but to my surprise, she's smiling outright. And damn if it doesn't hit me straight in the feels.

"Thank you."

Her gratitude throws me off balance worse than any pissed-off bull ever did. I know how to handle anger and push back against resistance. Both are familiar territory. But I'm entirely out of my depth with this woman saying thank you like giving her a ride is the equivalent of hanging the moon. And a part of me I don't recognize wants to do that, too.

"Let's get this show going then." I clear my throat when the words come out more growly than I intend. "You need help getting in the truck?"

The passenger door is open, but she's staring up at the high seat like she's at the trailhead of a fourteener. Even with the running board, it might be a challenge to hoist herself up there with only one working leg.

"I can manage—"

"Let me help." Without waiting for an answer, I lift her into the truck, my hands spanning her waist as I guide her onto the seat. For a moment, she's close enough that I can smell her shampoo, the scent one part floral, one part sweet and totally Molly. I force myself to step back before I do something stupid like bury my face in her hair.

"Thank you." She sounds as breathless as I feel.

"You don't have to keep thanking me. Helping you is why I'm here."

"Right. Your debt to the McAllisters." She gives me a funny look. "Are you going to tell me about that at some point?"

"Not planning on it," I say as I shut the door.

"I guess everybody has secrets," she murmurs through the open window.

Our eyes meet as I walk around the front of the truck, and for a heartbeat, neither of us looks away. There's something vulnerable in her expression. Like she's as surprised by this unexpected connection as I am.

I climb into the truck and head toward town, trying not to think about how much I want to know every one of Molly's secrets.

8

MOLLY

"THAT CUPCAKE IS the ugliest thing I've ever seen."

Chase gasps like I've deeply offended him. "It's a work of art."

"Her shower theme is baby farm animals, not *Silence of the Lambs*."

We're back at the house after making our rounds in town—the florist, two restaurants, the coffee shop, and a local boutique that uses my flowers for their displays. To my surprise, Chase did wonders for my self-esteem with how genuinely impressed he seemed by my popularity around town. The popularity of my flowers, anyway. His reaction was so encouraging, for a moment I completely forgot I was supposed to hate him and found myself inviting him in for a sandwich and to help prep my contribution to the baby shower.

I should have taken him at his word that he can't decorate because he's a terrible cupcake artist.

"You grew up on a farm." He points a finger at me. "My version is more realistic than the *Charlotte's Web* fairy tale."

A laugh bursts out of me. "What do you know about *Charlotte's Web*?"

"That's some pig," he answers, holding up the cupcake frosted in pink icing that looks more like a mutilated animal than a storybook creature.

I feel my smile widen. "Luke loves Charlotte."

"Me, too." Chase places the cupcake on a plate and wipes his hands on a nearby kitchen towel. "He might hate me, but we have the same taste in children's literature, at least with Wilbur and the gang."

"I'm going to give you an A for effort," I say. "But you're forbidden from putting that thing in the carrier with my cupcakes. I've got a rep to protect."

"I heard," he agrees. "My sister told me all about Molly McAllister's domestic diva talents. Wouldn't want to tarnish your reputation."

"I appreciate that." Ugh. Why do I sound so prim and proper? Not that I should want to sound any other way with Chase. Definitely not flirty.

It's hard to remember that when he's so ridiculously appealing. But it's more than his rockin' body and movie-star smile that have had me on the verge of melting all day. Okay, I'll admit I spent far too much time watching his forearm muscles flex as he did everything from shifting the manual truck into gear to toting my flower buckets like they weighed about as much as a feather.

I actually thought about asking him to roll down his sleeves when it felt like I was having a premature hot flash—centered right between my thighs. However, my body's reaction is nothing compared to the cartwheels my heart has been doing. Because I'm a sucker for anything sweet, his inherent kindness—and the fact that he doesn't even seem to be aware of it--gets under my skin most of all. I understand he's helping me out of an obligation to my late husband and his mother, but Chase has more than made up for the missed breakfast this morning.

Half the time, he seems to know what I need before I've said a word. Considering how much we had to do, he made what could have been a difficult few hours feel effortless. And while several people recognized him in town—hometown hero and all that—he deferred questions about himself and kept the attention on me and my flowers.

During my marriage, I tried so hard to carve out my own place in our small mountain community, desperate to be seen outside of Teddy's shadow. It wasn't like I picked up the mantle of tradwife because I thought creating pretty or nice things made me special. It came naturally, just like growing flowers. But no matter what I tried or how much of an effort I made with his friends or coworkers, it was always the Teddy show.

My life became impossibly small, and I stood by and watched as every piece of myself was whittled away until only scraps were left. When the twins started preschool, I tried bringing in some extra money by catering local events. But every time I booked a job, Teddy would either get sick or be called out of town for some far-flung guiding gig. I couldn't even make it to the book club I was invited to join with some local moms because my husband couldn't commit to watching his children for a couple hours a month.

Both he and his mother made it clear that I chose to have the babies—our babies—and he'd done as much as I could expect of him by agreeing to marry me.

I channeled my creative energy into school volunteering, a habit I've continued since moving to Skylark. Sure, decorating cupcakes for a class party is small potatoes, but it was the first thing that gave me some reason to feel capable of creating something beautiful that also matters to someone else.

"If my disfigured piggy can't be part of your perfect barnyard..." Chase starts to unwrap the cupcake, a smirk curving the edge of his full lips.

"Did you do a bad job on purpose so that you could get an early taste?"

His eyes take on a mischievous glint. "Sweetheart, do I look like a man who has to resort to unscrupulous means to get a taste?" His affronted tone is ruined when he gives me a slow wink.

I shake my head even as sparks skitter along my skin. He lifts the fully unwrapped cupcake toward me. "First bite is yours."

It feels strangely intimate to allow him to feed me.

"You go ahead," I say, pulling back slightly. "I know what my cupcakes taste like."

A smile tugs at the corner of his mouth. "That sounds like baking innuendo. I'd be a real goner if you used a British accent."

I breathe out a small laugh. "What do you know about British baking?"

"There's a lot of downtime on the circuit." He studies the grotesquely decorated cupcake. "I've watched my share of baking shows. Obviously none of their expertise rubbed off on me, and I absorbed nothing about technique, but I appreciate watching other people make things pretty."

"You're seriously a fan of baking competitions?"

He shrugs. "They calm me down. Have a bite, Molly. It wouldn't feel right if you don't enjoy this monstrosity along with me."

The way my mouth is watering suddenly has nothing to do with the cupcake. Still, I lean forward and take a small bite, then dab a bit of icing off my upper lip with the pad of one finger.

I watch his chest rise and fall and try not to reveal my own physical reaction, but damn, that's a good cupcake.

"It needs a smidge more salt," I say, because self-critical is my go-to.

Chase frowns and pops the rest of the cupcake into his mouth. His eyes drift closed, and he lets out a small moan. "Fucking perfection," he whispers and licks his lips.

I swallow back a moan and come close to swallowing my tongue.

Perfection. This moment is perfect, all right. Perfect and dangerous.

"I'm glad you approve." I try to sound all business when my body is thinking about anything and everything but business. I distract myself by adjusting the cupcakes in their holders and put the lids on the two plastic carriers. "We should go so we're not late to the party."

"We'll take my truck."

"Sure." I sound like I've just run a sprint, and he gives me a sidelong glance as he stacks the carriers one on top of the other.

"Perfection," he repeats. "I wouldn't change a thing." Something in his tone makes me think he's talking about more than just cupcakes.

He leaves the door open after he exits, so it's easier for me to get out. The porch steps remain challenging, but I manage to get down before he returns to help. I hate being dependent on him, even if he's working off a debt by helping me.

We're mostly silent on the drive into town, and I wonder if I imagined that moment in the kitchen.

"Everything okay?" he asks when I take my phone from my purse as we near the school.

"I'm going to call the secretary and ask her to help me carry the cupcakes inside."

He shakes his head. "I'm going in with you."

"To a teacher's baby shower?" He must be joking.

"You might need help, and that's my job." The words sound too casual.

"Come on. What's the real reason? Are you interested in or already dating one of the teachers?" I have no right to feel jealous, but the emotion spikes in my chest just the same.

"Hell, no," he says with a laugh. "We've already covered that my sister works at the school. Do you know what she'd do to me if I tried to date one of her coworkers?"

"I take it she wouldn't approve?"

"You're familiar with castration, right?"

My eyes widen, and I can't help but smile. "I think I could be friends with your sister."

"A terrifying thought," he murmurs as we enter the school parking lot. "I'll drop you off and then park and bring in the cupcakes."

"You don't have to, Chase. You've gone above and beyond this morning, so—"

"Does Luke have friends?" he asks, the words spoken so gently, I almost miss them.

"Of course he has friends. He's a great kid."

One thick brow arches in my direction as he pulls to a stop in front of the school's main door. "Besides Laurel?"

"Well, his sister is his best friend. That's how it is with twins. They have a bond." He continues to stare, and my chest tightens with the familiar defensiveness that comes from being judged and coming up lacking. "Why are you asking that?"

"I'm trying to get a sense of the situation. Hard to believe, but I was also a seven-year-old boy at one point."

My heart pounds against my ribs as I force myself to sit perfectly still. I refuse to let Chase see how his casual observation has rattled me. I'm a good mother. It's the only thing I'm certain of. With one question, Chase has made me doubt even that.

"Leave the cupcakes at the front office," I say as I climb out of the truck and struggle to pull the crutches from the back seat.

He starts to unbuckle his seatbelt. "I can help with—"

"I don't need help right now," I say through clenched teeth, trying—and mostly failing—to pretend his words haven't cut deep. He thinks my son is a situation. That can't be true. Can it?

The kids cheer as I enter the classroom. I have a reputation as the cupcake mom. Laurel waves to me from her seat at one of the low tables, surrounded by friends. Luke sits on the brightly patterned rug at the front of the room, but there's a noticeable gap between him and the cluster of other kids listening to story time. My stomach drops to my toes. My son *has* friends.

The classroom is already decorated with streamers and balloons in a rainbow of pastel colors. Aimee Bradshaw, the twins' teacher, hasn't found out whether she's having a boy or a girl, so we've kept the theme gender neutral.

The door opens again, and I swallow back a groan as Chase follows the school's principal, Amanda Sinton, into the room.

Sure, Chase is famous in Skylark. The rodeo is a big deal here, especially for long-time residents, but I'm surprised at the reaction he receives, as if he's a movie star who just walked into his big premiere instead of a cowboy walking into a first-grade class party.

I don't think it's the kids who have Chase eyeing the door as if he wants to ensure he has a clear escape path. The expressions on the faces of the female teachers and mothers gathered in the room range from mildly curious to downright voracious. They're looking at him like he's the last chocolate chip cookie at a church potluck.

"Happy baby shower," he says to Aimee with a genuine smile, then clears his throat. "I'm honored to celebrate with you."

I hobble forward, cursing my injured ankle for the millionth time. "I told you to leave them at the office," I remind him in a hushed tone.

His gaze holds mine with an intensity that makes my breath catch. "I tried, but the principal insisted I deliver them myself."

"How do you know Chase Calhoun?" one of the mothers asks the teacher, not even bothering to pitch her voice low.

"I don't." Aimee presses a hand to her basketball-sized belly. "But based on the way he or she is kicking, I think my baby is a rodeo fan."

Chase smiles at the mom who asked the question. "I'm here because I'm helping Molly."

"He's the twins' nanny," Amanda clarifies, sounding astounded at the idea of it. I'm not a fan of our principal. She gives off total mean-girl vibes. But hearing her announce that information like breaking news, and watching Chase give a matter-of-fact nod, still makes my chest skip a beat.

My daughter giggles with her friends while Luke's gaze stays firmly planted on the carpet between his crisscross applesauce legs.

"Do you know Chase Calhoun?" One of the other boys scoots closer and elbows Luke. "Is he teaching you to ride?"

Luke blinks and glances up, clearly shocked to have earned the attention of several of his classmates. He looks toward me and then at Chase.

"Anytime Luke wants a lesson, I'm here for it," Chase tells the boys with a wink.

My son's cheeks flame bright pink, but he doesn't contradict the cowboy. Not when his peers are so obviously impressed.

"How about those games?" I say to the other class mom, sensing Luke needs a little break.

"Sure. Let's get started." She claps her hands, and the students quiet as they wait for her instructions. "Split up into teams of four. Our first game is the Dirty Diaper Challenge."

I smile and nod, even as my skin tingles. Chase is staring at me, so I turn my head slightly, like that will make the intensity of his focus less noticeable.

What I focus on instead is my son standing between two groups of boys. Boys who are arguing over who gets to claim sweet Luke as part of their team. He looks like a deer caught in headlights, and I'd bet money he's never experienced being wanted this way. My mind races as I think of all those playground moments I've pushed aside. Watching Luke build stick forts alone while Laurel commanded armies of giggling girls. My son reading quietly at recess while other kids played tag. Always walking a step behind his sister and her friends.

Oh, no. Chase is right. My son doesn't have friends.

Emotion bubbles up inside me as my heart hurls itself against my ribcage. I've sacrificed so much of myself because I wanted my kids to have the unconditional love I never did from my troubled mom or my grandparents, who became reluctant and resentful guardians after her death.

I thought I could love the twins enough to ensure they'd never feel like outsiders looking in. Or wonder if they truly belonged somewhere, the way I spent most of my life worrying.

It may have worked with my daughter, although more likely, she takes after her naturally self-assured dad. How have I been so blind to the fact that Luke might be struggling socially? And why did it have to be Chase who pointed it out to me?

The man's ability to home in on every single way I'm lacking is annoying as hell. It's like he's a heat-seeking weakness missile, and I'm sending flares into the night sky.

9

MOLLY

IF IT WEREN'T for the crutches, I'd find an excuse to duck out of the room during the games. How many bathroom stalls have I hidden in over the years, counting to ten and willing myself to stop feeling so awkward? What's one more? But I'd probably make a spectacle of myself, and I see Chase moving closer, Amanda stuck like glue to his side.

The kids laugh and groan at the game of guessing the type of melted chocolate smeared across the inside of a diaper.

One of the other mothers leans closer to me. "You've got a hot bull rider for your *nanny*?" she asks with a knowing chuckle.

"He's my late husband's best friend," I say, like that's the equivalent of man cooties. My body immediately calls me out on the lie, but I ignore it.

"Tell me he's living in that house with you."

"He's *not* living with me."

"But maybe he's helping with more than just the kids?" another mom suggests. "Don't tell my husband, but I wouldn't mind hiring a manly nanny."

"Please, stop," I beg. "It isn't like that." My face is on fire because I can't imagine Chase doesn't hear the teasing. They're not exactly whispering.

"Come on now, ladies." His deep voice is pitched low but carries a hint of amusement. A casual smile curves his lips, like he's genuinely entertained by their speculation. "You can't seriously believe there's anything between Molly and me other than helping with the kids and driving her where she needs to."

He shrugs again, and now my face is burning even hotter but for a different reason. Yeah, it was rude and inappropriate for the moms to insinuate anything, especially with my kids sitting a few feet away, but I kind of hate that he practically shuddered with revulsion at the suggestion that there could be more to the two of us. It's not like there is or that I want there to be. But he makes getting involved with me sound about as appealing as eating a wad of chewing gum he found stuck to the bottom of a bleacher at the rodeo fairgrounds.

There are murmurs of acceptance at his explanation, and Amanda gives me a look like I'm the most pitiful creature she's ever stumbled across. But Chase isn't finished. Oh, no.

"I loved Teddy McAllister like a brother, and his mother asked me to do poor Molly here a favor."

Poor Molly.

I feel my eyes narrow.

"The McAllisters were good to me." His smile turns almost nostalgic. "I owe them."

"With Linda away on her trip," Amanda says sweetly to Chase, "Molly doesn't have anybody else. It's so nice of you to take time out of your busy schedule to—"

"I have people," I interrupt. "Friends."

My God, why am I defending myself?

The winners of the Dirty Diaper Challenge are announced and I clap along with the other moms, grateful for the diversion. Luke and his teammates are each given a handful of Bradshaw Bucks, which they can cash in for prizes at the end of the semester. Bradshaw Bucks are worth more than a stack of Benjamins in first grade.

Amanda grips my arm like she's testing my composure with her clammy fingers. "Your book club besties," she says with a smile that doesn't come anywhere near reaching her eyes. "Those ladies are dropping like flies as they couple up, right? Sadie, Iris, Taylor..." I hate her touching me like we're friends but can't force myself to pull away. "Avah Harris is engaged. And Sloane...well, I'm sure she's got her own challenges to deal with thanks to the big C."

"She's beating it." My voice sounds like it's coming from a faraway place.

"I feel for you, Molly." Amanda gives my arm another squeeze and this time I do pull away. "A single mother of twins living off the generosity of her mother-in-law."

"I'm not living off her," I whisper.

"Of course." She makes a face. "But that's a lot of baggage for a man to consider lifting."

What a bitch.

"I hope it doesn't take too much time away from your life, Chase." She turns to him with the practiced smile of someone used to getting what she wants. The other moms have gone suspiciously quiet. "I know we're all rooting for you to get back on the circuit."

The baby shower games continue, and I force a smile as I watch the teams try to guess baby food flavors while blindfolded. Chase looks at me with a funny expression, like I'm not the one who's just been completely humiliated.

"I appreciate that," he says to the group in general, then rubs a hand over the back of his neck.

He does that when he's uncomfortable, which he deserves after what he's done to me. But his eyes have taken on a hollow appearance, one that makes my chest tighten with unexpected sympathy. Because it's a look I recognize staring back at me in the mirror.

"Who wants cupcakes?" I call out suddenly. The other class mom gapes at me, her shock justifiable given that she's just explained the instructions for the next game. She has to be wondering why I've skipped ahead to snack time so abruptly.

"Cupcakes," the kids scream.

Aimee Bradshaw uses her well-honed teacher skills to bring order to the masses and instructs the students to make a single-file line in front of the snack table.

I turn to Chase. "Would you help me pass them out?" I'm still not sure why I'm being the least bit kind after what he did..

"We'd love to have you come back for career day, Chase," Amanda says, again with the fake sweetness. "If you give me your number—"

"I'll coordinate with him," I tell her. "We need to get to the cupcakes."

The look of relief on his face is priceless, and he's surprisingly good with the kids. He keeps them entertained without letting things devolve into mayhem, a fine line to walk.

"You should take a seat," he tells me when the kids are back at their desks, happily munching on cupcakes and shouting out baby name suggestions to their teacher.

I roll my eyes. "I'm fine standing."

"It's obvious you're tired. Your arms are trembling."

"If it's obvious, then you didn't need to point it out," I snap. "But thanks. Both for the reminder and for making it clear you'd have absolutely zero interest in a woman like me." I plop down on the chair he's moved behind the snack table.

My armpits ache more than my arms. The scooter is way more comfortable, even if it's bulkier to maneuver. I'm so lost in my self-pitying thoughts that it takes me a minute to realize Chase is staring at me, slack-jawed.

"What?" I demand, crossing my arms over my chest.

"I never said I wouldn't be interested in a woman like you."

His voice is gruff, and with everyone else involved in baby shower activities, it feels like we're in our own little bubble. But I'm not going down this road when I know where it leads.

"I don't want to talk anymore. You've made your opinion clear on more than one occasion. You were Teddy's friend and owe a debt to the McAllisters. We *all* get it."

He opens his mouth like he wants to argue, then shuts it again and shakes his head. "I didn't say those words."

Laurel skips up to the table with her two best friends. "Can Kate and Melody come over later to meet Fancy?" She offers Chase her most charming smile, which looks just like her father's.

"No," I say before he can answer. "I need your help in the greenhouse this afternoon. Maybe next week."

"Mommy, please." Even Laurel's whine is adorable. "Luke can help you. He doesn't have anything else to do."

Right, because my son doesn't have friends, just like Chase told me.

"Your mother makes the rules," Chase tells her, seemingly unaffected by her cute pout. "When she says the time is right, your friends can meet Fancy. Not before."

My daughter's wispy brows pull together. Laurel isn't used to hearing the word "no" from anyone. I'm not sure how clear her memories of her father are after two years, but Teddy rarely denied her anything. Even when it went against the rules I set.

I'm surprised Chase isn't doing the same thing, and I don't want to admit how much I appreciate it. I remind myself that it doesn't matter if he isn't interested in a woman like me because that's not why he's here. Having Chase around the next few weeks will get me closer to buying the farm and claiming the future I want for myself and my kids.

So what if it means more time with a man who thinks I'm not

worthy of him? I spent enough years married to one of those. It won't kill me.

I'm tougher than people think and more than what Chase Calhoun believes me to be.

I'm more than what *I* believe myself to be. By the end of this flower season, everyone is going to know it.

10

MOLLY

THE NEXT FEW days go by in a flash as Chase, the kids, and I settle into a rhythm. Things between us still feel awkward, but that's mostly a me problem.

Even with my best effort to hate him, it's hard to ignore the fact that this man is quickly becoming someone I both like and rely on. He doesn't treat me as if I'm lame or worthless or a woman he'd never be interested in. Quite the opposite, actually.

I wish he weren't so Johnny-on-the-spot helpful and kind. That he didn't have those intense eyes that bore a hole right through me. Or that almost reluctant smile. Or those muscles that make my mouth go dry every time they tense and flex.

Even Luke is starting to warm up to him—something I didn't see coming.

Chase doesn't act like working in the greenhouse, or helping me with planting and harvesting, is a burden. Or like he'd rather be somewhere else. I spent most of my marriage with a man who—I think—loved me in his own way, but often acted like he wanted to be somewhere else. The only time Chase shows even a flicker of annoyance is when I make one too many self-deprecating remarks or try to downplay my skill with growing flowers.

My mother-in-law likes to joke about me "playing in the dirt." Somehow, I've internalized her opinion like it's my own. I'm trying to change my mindset around that. If I'm going to make this business a success, I need to start treating it—and myself—like something worthy of people's respect.

I don't take compliments well and tend to brush off the praise I get from both vendors and customers. Growing flowers is work, but it comes naturally to me. So while I appreciate the positive feedback, it doesn't feel like I'm doing anything mind-blowing or special. It's not like I'm climbing onto the back of an angry, two-ton animal intent on throwing me to the ground

"Do you need anything else before I head out?"

His voice startles me. I whirl around, nearly jumping out of my skin, and instinctively launch the small hand rake I'd been gripping in his direction. It clatters to the ground at his feet.

Chase arches a brow and bends to pick it up, a slow smile curving his mouth. "I take it that's a no?"

"I need you to not sneak up on me." I press a hand to my chest where my heart is still hammering.

He chuckles. "Not sure walking over here from the barn counts as sneaking."

"Yeah, well." I shrug, trying to shake off the embarrassment. "Part of what I love about this work is that I can get lost in it. I didn't hear you. Sorry I freaked out. As usual, I'm the problem."

Chase tilts his head and studies me in that quiet, unnerving way he has. The one that makes me feel like he sees too much.

"Who hurt you?" he asks softly. And he means it. Not like he's handing me a line, but like he's a man who genuinely wants to know. It undoes me in ways I can't begin to explain.

"No one," I whisper. "Why would you—"

"Who made you doubt everything good about yourself?" His voice is steady but laced with heat. "Was it Teddy or—"

"I'm not hurt," I say quickly. "I'm just...me."

He nods slowly, taking in more than just my words. "It's time to see yourself differently."

My lips roll together as my entire body goes taut with awareness. Oh, no. Helpful Chase is one thing. Perceptive Chase? I cannot deal with that right now. Or maybe ever.

"I'm fine," I say quickly, looking down at my watch when it becomes too much to keep meeting his gaze. "A friend is picking me up in a few minutes. She's getting married, and we're going wedding dress shopping."

He draws in a slow breath. I know he has more to say, but my self-doubt is the last thing I want to discuss with Chase.

"Who's getting married?" he asks.

"Avah Harris. You probably remember her. Blonde, gorgeous, and beyond confident." The opposite of me, I don't add.

Chase shakes his head. "Sort of." He pauses. "I don't remember her being especially cordial to anyone outside her inner circle, if you know what I mean."

"She's the best friend I've ever had, so I *reckon* she's plenty *cordial*." I roll my eyes. "I haven't heard anyone use that term since my granddad died."

Okay, now I'm being snippy for no reason. Avah is a flat-out bitch and proud of it. She'd tell you the same thing. She's like a queen in a castle. Only a few people make it to the drawbridge, even fewer across the moat and into the courtyard. And as far as the throne room, she guards access to that like her life depends on it.

I love her like the sister I never had, so I'm not going to let a guy who doesn't know anything about her or her past talk shit about her. Come to think of it, I don't know a lot about her past other than she's an only child and, by her own account, grew up spoiled rotten.

"Cordial is an old-timey word," Chase says, ignoring my sarcasm. "Got it. I'm sure your friend is great. I wasn't trying to offend you. I'm glad you have a bestie and a squad, or whatever they call it."

My mood does a quick one-eighty thanks to his fumbling attempt at girl-speak. I press my lips together to hold back a grin. "A squad?"

I see the tips of his ears turn pink, which is adorable even as it causes certain parts of my body to tingle. Oh, lord. I'm in big trouble if a blush has that effect on me.

He takes a step back and tips his ball cap toward me. "I should be back in about an hour. If there's anything you need—"

"Where do you go every day at this time?"

Chase blinks like he doesn't quite understand the question.

I roll my shoulders and command my mouth to remain shut, but the words burst from my lips like a tidal wave. "Are you showering at your girlfriend's house after...the sex?

He huffs out a laugh, and I clasp my hands over my eyes.

"I didn't just say that."

"You absolutely did," he says, and I hear the smile in his voice.

"I'm begging you to forget that I mentioned *the sex* and pretend I didn't just ask about your private life, because it's none of my business." I keep my hand over my eyes, refusing to look at him because I might die of embarrassment.

"Molly, I'm not having *the sex* with anyone."

Wait a sec. Does his voice sound deeper than normal? Almost husky.

"I shower at a friend's house," he continues after clearing his throat. "Every day. Trust me, it's a good idea."

I widen my fingers to peek through. "Isn't there a bathroom in your trailer? You said you live there most of the time."

"I have a bathroom, but you have no hookup. It's easier if I—"

"Why don't you use the bathroom in the house?"

His eyes widen slightly. "I didn't want to ask. I know you don't want me here. The less I mess up your routine, the better."

"But you're helping me."

"You're helping me, too, with—"

"I know. The mysterious debt you owe Linda."

"I'm here for *you*," he says, like his motivation or feelings about who I am don't matter in the grand scheme of things. I try to remind myself that's true. Chase Calhoun is a means to an end for me.

So what if it's Chase's eyes and his muscular arms I think of when I unlock the box in my nightstand drawer where I keep my toys? I doubt I'm the first woman who's gotten herself off imagining Chase's hands on her.

"Are you okay?" he asks, snapping me back to the present.

Seriously, someone save me from where and how often my thoughts drift around this man. No wonder he thinks what he does of me.

"You look like my mom does when she's having one of her power surges."

"You think I'm having a hot flash?" I grind out the words. "I'm twenty-seven, not forty-seven."

He makes a face. "I don't know how it works."

"I'm *not* in menopause."

"Okay, I just—" He holds up his hands like he can't win for losing. "I just want to make things easier."

Right now, I feel the opposite of easy, my skin prickling with awareness.

"So try using your muscles more and your mouth less."

Uh, did *that* just come out of *my* mouth?

The air crackles between us. Chase steps close enough that I catch a whiff of sweat, sunshine, and whatever soap he uses. He might need a shower, but he smells delicious.

"You have no idea how good I am with my mouth."

Cowboy mic drop.

"I'm sure plenty of rodeo queens could fill me in." I try to sound disinterested instead of insanely jealous. "I'll take a hard pass on those details."

MICHELLE MAJOR

He flashes a smile, and as irritated as I am, I find myself smiling, too. Not that I'd admit it to him, but the truth is, I like who I am around Chase. A little bolder. Less my usual mouse-in-the-corner vibe.

"You're welcome to use the shower in the house, but you're going to have to navigate around a whole mess of bath toys," I tell him. "I'm guessing you're not as uncoordinated as me."

"Accidents happen," he says with a shrug. "Trust me, I've learned the lesson many times in my career, especially with my last appearance in the ring."

I also know about bad timing and worse luck, and for some unknown reason I feel the need to connect with Chase in this moment. "I lost my mom to an accidental overdose," I tell him. "My grandparents died in a car crash. And then Teddy..."

"I'm sorry, Molly." His voice softens, the teasing gone.

"I don't know why I just shared that." I tuck a strand of hair behind my ear. "Those aren't the same kind of accidents that—"

"You don't have to explain. I'll be quick with the shower and stay out of your way."

"Take your time. I'll be gone for a couple of hours. Just plan on doing whatever you need to during school hours, and we'll figure out a schedule for the weekends."

"Thanks." He starts to turn away.

"Hey, Chase?"

He glances back, hand on the doorknob.

"Do you brush your teeth in the RV?" The words tumble out before I can stop them. "For the record, it's the mom in me asking."

He blinks. "Are you serious?"

"If you don't have running water...I mean, oral hygiene is important."

"It sure is." That lazy smile curves his lips again. "I brush my teeth. Want to smell my breath?"

Yes, my traitorous body practically shouts.

"That won't be necessary."

"Twice a day, for the record."

"I'm sure your dentist is impressed."

"She gave me her phone number along with a new toothbrush last time I was in."

Of course she did.

"I'll see you later." I need to end this conversation before I do something dumb. Like close the distance between us and plaster myself to his hard body.

He tips his cap again and walks away. I don't think I imagine the faint scent of trouble left in his wake.

11

MOLLY

A MINUTE LATER, my phone pings with an incoming message.

> Avah: About to turn down your driveway.

I wash the dirt off my hands in the greenhouse sink, smooth some water over my flyaway hair, and hang the apron I always wear when planting on the hook by the door before hobbling out into the late morning sunlight.

"Can't I just order something online?" she asks in a fake whine as she helps me place my crutches in the back of her compact BMW SUV.

"Nope. Drinking champagne and trying on expensive dresses is part of the bride-to-be gauntlet." I open the passenger door. "But are we cheating on the rest of the book club with just the two of us?"

She flips up her sunglasses and stares at me over the roof of the car. "I don't like to be the center of attention."

I choke out a laugh as I awkwardly climb in after stowing the crutches. "Since when?"

"Not for this kind of girly stuff," she says as she fastens her seatbelt. "What's the point? Jon and I have been dating forever, and we're eloping. None of this is necessary."

"Speaking of that, why aren't you having a big wedding? I know your mom doesn't live in Skylark anymore, but you have friends here. What about the rest of your family, or..." I shake my head. "I don't know anything about your dad?"

Avah shoots me some major side-eye. "What's up with twenty questions?"

"I was just telling Chase how you're my best friend. And somehow I know so little about you when I'm a book that's open so far my spine is cracked. I mean, you know that it's been over two years since I had sex. That's a lot of detail, Avs."

"Jon and I had sex last night. Reverse cowgirl. We're even. Feel better?"

"Yikes," I whisper. "Not the kind of detail I meant. I don't even think I know what reverse cowgirl means."

"Google it," she says as she merges onto the highway, heading west toward the Flatirons and the town of Boulder. Her appointment is at a bridal boutique in the college town. "And then tell me about the hot cowboy. If the Airstream's a rockin', don't come—"

"Hard pass on both."

"You need a dick appointment," she says, like she's talking about the weather. "Chase Calhoun is a viable option."

"He's my late husband's best friend."

"Did they see each other once during your marriage?"

"They lived different lives, especially after Teddy and I got married." I shake my head. "It doesn't matter. I'm not interested."

She laughs softly. "You're lying. *Everyone* is interested in Chase."

I shift in my seat and look out the window at the passing scenery. Spring comes late to the foothills, and while a few of the cottonwoods have green buds coloring their branches, most of the trees are still bare. I'm like one of those naked trees—no one can see the changes taking place in me yet, but when my season comes, I'll bloom in a way that surprises everyone. Myself included.

"I know what you're doing," I tell my bestie. "You're trying to distract me from talking about you by talking about me. You know you can tell me anything, right?"

I see her grip tighten on the leather steering wheel. "I know," she says quietly, "but I don't like talking about myself or my family. My dad's in jail. Has been for years."

The words hit me like a splash of cold water, and my chest tightens. "Avah, I'm so sorry. Are you—"

She waves away my concern. "Suffice to say, he won't make it to the elopement."

"Do you want to tell me why?" I ask slowly.

She glances at me as she pulls off the highway and heads toward the historic Pearl Street Mall. "I know you love a true crime documentary. He's not a serial killer, if you're wondering."

I swallow. "Is he *any* kind of killer?"

"No," she answers with a breathy laugh. "He ran an insurance scam on elderly people. Bilked hundreds of cotton-headed grandmothers out of their savings. It's embarrassing. I grew up as daddy's little princess. The gifts he gave me...the big house and fancy car...extravagant vacations—all of it was a lie."

"You were a kid, Avs. You have no reason to be embarrassed." I pause then force myself to ask, "Did your mother know?"

I see my friend's chest rise and fall with a slow breath. "She denied any knowledge, but I think she understood there was something shady going on. She divorced my dad after the scandal broke. Reinvented herself. Both of us. Harris is my mom's maiden name. She changed our names before moving to Skylark."

"Does anyone in town know?"

Avah shakes her head. "It was like she orchestrated her own version of witness protection. Mom closed her eyes and put her finger on the map. That's how we ended up here. She broke ties with everyone she knew in Connecticut and kept any mention of our past vague. There's a lot you can get away with not saying when you're a bitch to people. I think that's why I got so good at the mean-girl routine. It kept everyone at arm's length so they never got close enough to ask the right questions."

"I like you just the way you are."

"Because you're the nicest person on the planet."

"Because you're a good friend." I reach out and squeeze her arm. "A good person."

She rolls her eyes. "Hardly. I don't know why I came back here after college. Mom packed up for Florida the day after my high school graduation like she was on the run. But there was something about Skylark that stuck with me."

"It's the mountains," I tell her as Belle Époque Bridal comes into view. The shop is adorable. With cream-colored brick and forest-green trim, it's tucked between a pottery studio and a vintage bookshop just off the Pearl Street Mall. "Knowing they're standing strong behind us, reminding us we can survive whatever comes our way, just like they have."

"That's fucking woo-woo," she says, her voice catching. "But maybe you're right."

"You should tell the rest of the book club. We've all been through our own messy family stuff. Trust me, nobody's going to judge you for the mistakes your parents made."

"You're the only one who knows, Molly, and it's staying that way." She pulls into a diagonal parking space and hits the brake so hard I lurch forward as the seatbelt snaps tight against my chest.

"What about Jon?"

"Only you," she insists.

I can't hide my shock that her soon-to-be husband doesn't know. "You're marrying him."

"He's marrying now-me and future-me."

"Is this why you're eloping?"

"For your information, eloping is a trend in Colorado. We can marry ourselves. I've hired an expensive photographer to document the whole thing, and you'll create my bouquet. It's going to be beautiful."

"But is it what you want?" I can't wrap my head around outspoken, attention-loving Avah choosing to get married with just a photographer for company.

"Sadie and Ian had a private ceremony," she says instead of answering my question.

"Piper, Felix, and Riva were there," I counter. "They also had a big party to celebrate a few weeks later."

"I'm going to celebrate on a honeymoon in Tahiti. I don't want anything else. Not with my family's baggage hanging over me, and Jon's high-profile position at the firm. The last thing either of us needs is questions about why my parents aren't there, or worse, having to explain if someone decides to dig into my past."

"Okay," I agree, as we get out of the vehicle, hearing the desperation in her voice. The vulnerability is so at odds with Avah's typical confidence, it makes my chest ache. "I'm sorry I never asked about your family. I assumed your life was perfect."

She begins feeding quarters into the parking meter. "No one's life is perfect, but some of us have perfected the art of smoke and mirrors." She looks up and offers me a genuine smile. "One of the many things I love about you is how you wave your baggage around like a calling card."

"Wait a minute." I lift a crutch and point it in her direction. "Am I your embarrassing-past beard? No one will question where you came from when you're standing next to train wreck Molly."

Ignoring the crutches, she pulls me in for a tight hug and grips my cheeks between her slender hands.

"You aren't a train wreck. You are a badass bitch. A B.A.B. The babbiest of B.A.Bs."

"That's not a thing," I say with a laugh.

"It is if we make it one."

We're almost to the door of the bridal boutique, but Avah stops and grips my arm.

"I don't want to do this." Her voice is serious again.

"The dress shopping or are you having second thoughts about Jon?"

She gives me a funny look. "I don't mean getting married. But you know how the salespeople are at these places. They're going to ask me the same kinds of questions you did. Am I having a big wedding? Are my parents so excited? Do I like my in-laws?"

"*Do* you like your in-laws?"

"Oh God, no." Avah mock shudders. "They're insufferable. But I don't want to play at being rude so that the well-meaning salesperson stops asking questions."

She leans back against the brick wall of the boutique. Her shoulders sag like she's carrying an invisible weight. "I want to order a dress online, get married with just Jon and the photographer, have lots of honeymoon sex, and keep looking toward the future."

If anybody understands the desire to leave the past behind, it's me. "Then let's go home," I tell her. "We'll find you the perfect dress online, and you'll look absolutely stunning. You don't owe anyone explanations or small talk."

"Am I a total wimp?" She scrunches her perfectly pert nose. "Did you go dress shopping before your wedding?"

"Hardly." I cough out a laugh. "I'd just packed up my grandparents' house so I wore one of my grandma's church dresses. Teddy's river rat friends felt even more sorry for him when I showed up looking like one of the *Golden Girls*. But we aren't talking about the awkward affair that was my wedding. This trip is about you. If it's not what you want, then it's not what I want either."

She chews on her lower lip as she studies the mannequins in the storefront window. "I want to go home. Are you mad?"

"Of course not." I manage to hug her without losing a crutch or my balance.

"Do you want to grab coffee or something?"

"To be honest, I'd rather head back and log a couple more hours of work before the kids get home from school. I'm so slow getting things done these days."

She hugs me more tightly. "Please tell me that by *work,* you mean drooling after Chase."

"I don't drool," I tell her. Although I might lust a little.

"Come on, Molly," she says as we climb back in the car. "It's the perfect setup."

"Even if I wanted an appointment, Chase has no interest in a meetup with my lady parts."

She bestows that patented Avah brow arch on me again. "How do you know?"

"He overheard one of the moms make a comment about the two of us at school the other day." I force a smile, ignoring the weird ache in my chest. "Chase made it clear that he's in my life because of his debt to the McAllisters."

"Then he doesn't deserve to be the broom who sweeps away your coochie cobwebs," Avah says primly.

I bust out laughing. "No, he doesn't."

"We'll find somebody, especially now that you're staying in Skylark. It's a shame all the guys Jon works with are uptight finance tools."

In my humble opinion, the same could be said about Jon, but I don't mention that. "I'm fine, Avah. Really. Thank you for sharing more about you."

She gives me a funny look. "You're my best friend. All you had to do was ask."

She's right. I've been complacent in so many areas of my life. I don't just accept whatever people choose to share—I actively avoid digging deeper so as not to make anyone uncomfortable.

Being a single mother to twins demands a lot, but it's also

become my convenient shield against taking any real risks. I let my grandparents dictate every area of my life after my mom died because I knew I should be grateful they were willing to raise me. Then Teddy agreed to marry me when I got pregnant, but he went through the motions of being a husband without ever truly wanting the role. Linda took us in after he died, and once again I became the grateful recipient of someone else's reluctant charity, terrified to ask for more than the bare minimum.

I'm so used to being a doormat, I might as well lie down on the interstate and beg people to run over me.

On the drive home, we switch to lighter subjects, both of us needing a bit of levity. By the time we pull into my driveway, we're laughing about Avah's horror at the idea of sharing one bathroom with seven-year-old twins *and* a dusty cowboy.

I worry I haven't given Chase enough time for his shower—I did tell him I'd be gone a couple of hours—but when we pull down the driveway, his car is gone.

"Have you been in the Airstream?" Avah asks, her voice almost a whisper.

"He's not going to overhear you inside the car," I tell her.

"So have you?" she shouts, causing me to jump.

"Very funny. No, I haven't."

"Aren't you curious how he lives?"

"Not one bit."

She laughs, nearly a cackle. "Then you must have upgraded the toys in your nightstand drawer, because, damn girl, *I'm* curious. You can tell a lot about a man by the way he keeps his house, even if that house is on wheels."

"What does your house say about Jon?" I ask, genuinely curious. Jon Clark is my best friend's fiancé, and they've lived together for the two years I've been in Skylark, but I barely know him.

She frowns as if she isn't quite sure how to answer. "It was my house to start with, but he did add several mirrors when he moved in, and some fancy scale that tracks his body stats. He also has ten pairs of identical sneakers."

"Um, why?" I have to admit, I've never noticed Jon's choice in footwear because he refuses to hang out with us. Sadie, Iris, and Taylor are with guys who make an effort. Maybe it's because Jon and Avah were dating before the book club was formed.

Avah doesn't seem to notice his aversion to her friends. "One pair is for the gym, one is for running, one is for just hanging out on the weekends." She gives a tight smile. "He prefers that one type of shoe."

"I guess that means he's loyal," I tell her, trying to salvage the awkwardness of this exchange.

"I always thought loyalty was a good thing in dogs, but you're right. I want a loyal husband."

"Yay, Jon," I say weakly.

"Do you need help in?" she asks as she pulls to a stop in front of the house.

"I've got it."

"Is that a ramp coming off your front porch?" She lifts her sunglasses to the top of her head.

"Yeah." For some reason, I feel my cheeks heat. "I kind of suck on steps with these crutches, so Chase built it for me. Makes getting up and down a lot easier."

"Okay, that's sweet," Avah says. "And kind of hot."

"It's not," I insist, even though my pulse went haywire yesterday morning watching him through the front porch window, sleeves rolled up, muscles flexing as he measured and hammered, making something just for me.

"He doesn't want to take a chance on me falling and re-injuring myself because he might have to help for longer. His motivations are selfish."

"Uh-huh," she agrees, her tone deadpan. "He's gorgeous, can ride a bull, and is good with his hands. I can see why he wouldn't be a viable candidate for a dick appointment."

"There's also the part about him having no interest," I remind her through clenched teeth, then hold up a hand. "And before you read something into that, neither do I."

"Keep telling yourself that, girl. I'll pick you up for book club."

"Thanks, Avah." I hold her gaze for a moment. "For the record, no matter what you wear, you'll be a beautiful bride. Jon is lucky to be marrying you."

"Yep," she says. But I see her draw in a deep breath like my words resonated. I hope they did.

I enter the house and then let out a long sigh when I realize the scooter is on the other side of the living room. My armpits are constantly sore from the crutches.

Then I hear a noise from upstairs and freeze. I hope to everything holy some neighbor's cat broke in to terrorize Nibbles, Laurel's beloved pet gerbil. Because the idea of an intruder is not something my nerves can handle at the moment.

I reach for the purse I tossed onto the sofa, but when I look toward the steps again, my heart slams against my ribs as tanned feet come down the stairs. Then muscular calves sprinkled with light brown hair. And then a white towel and...my mouth goes dry as the rest of Chase comes into view.

His chest is damp and droplets of water glisten on his shoulders. Holy shit, his shoulders.

I mean, I knew they were broad, but seeing those muscles ripple underneath a sweaty T-shirt and witnessing the hard planes in all their naked glory are two different things.

He's securing the towel around his waist, and even though it feels like I'm incapable of it at the moment, I must make a sound because his gaze crashes into mine.

He misses his step and stumbles. And then, holy double shit, the towel drops.

And then I screech, and the crutches go flying.

I try to catch myself on the couch but miss, because—did I mention the towel dropping?

Talk about a man in all his naked glory.

I hardly have a chance to appreciate it, since I go down with a hard thud onto the hardwood floor.

A moment later, Chase is there, his arms extended like he's going to pull me to my feet.

But Lord have mercy—he's still naked.

And flying half-mast.

I've seen penises before and wasn't a virgin on my wedding night. I'd had sloppy, unsatisfying sex three times with a guy in my hometown. Then there was Teddy. Plus the self-care supplies in my nightstand. But nothing holds a candle to what Chase Calhoun has going on.

Not. Even. A. Flicker.

"You aren't supposed to be home," he barks.

"You aren't supposed to be running around my house naked," I shout back.

"I was wearing a towel."

"You aren't wearing a towel now."

"I was coming down to get my clothes. I accidentally left my bag by the front door."

I look down, realize that's what I tripped over, and shove it toward him. "Put something on. Please."

"You aren't supposed to be here," he repeats as he holds the duffel bag up to cover the family jewels.

"You need to leave." This earns a round of boos from my lady parts.

For another impossibly long moment, I've got a naked, wet, handsome-as-sin man who smells like fresh soap looming over me. Then he grabs the bag and heads out the front door, still naked as the day he was born. I should feel relieved. Instead, I'm left staring at the ceiling, my skin buzzing with electricity, wondering what might have happened if I'd asked him to stay.

12

CHASE

THE KNOCK COMES at my trailer door an hour later.

"Here we go," I tell my seventeen-year-old cat Princess—a grumpy, orange, former barn cat with the most impressive resting bitch face you've ever seen—as I move to open the door.

This is where Molly kicks me out, and Linda subsequently cancels our deal. Not that I'm feeling particularly excited about the deal anymore. I still haven't figured out how to get what I want without keeping my best friend's widow from getting what she wants. Hell, when did I become so invested in Molly's dreams anyway? I should be focused on securing my own damn future, not worrying about hers.

She's standing there with her red hair pulled back in a messy ponytail, balancing on her crutches, her cheeks still flushed pink from the effort of making it across the yard. The sight of her struggling just to get to my door makes something twist uncomfortably in my chest.

"I'll be off the property today," I tell her.

"I'm sorry for earlier," she says, ignoring my words.

"Why are you apologizing?" I ask. "You didn't do anything wrong."

"Neither did you. I told you to use the shower, and I got home earlier than I said, so..."

"I gave you an eyeful."

The look she gives me makes me think that could be the understatement of the year. Her gaze goes kind of dreamy, and the idea that thinking about my dick causes the reaction makes it twitch in my pants.

Not now, I command internally. I mean, it was bad enough that just the sight of her eyes on me sent the blood rushing south.

"Come in for a minute," I say, stepping back.

"You don't need to invite me—"

"I know I don't. But we need to talk."

"Talk," she repeats, like it's code for something else.

Is her something else anything like mine?

Which involves *not* talking.

"It's nice," she says as she looks around the small space.

One of her crutches catches on the top step, and she loses her balance, something I'm coming to expect and continue to find adorable. Also not complaining about an excuse to put my hands on her again.

Her cheeks turn a rosier pink as I lower her onto the small couch. Princess, who is not a fan of people in general, vacated the space when she heard another voice.

"Are those granite counters?" she asks, her eyes darting around the interior, clearly trying to look anywhere but at me.

I grin. "Were you expecting chipped Formica?"

She makes a face. "Along with pizza boxes, beer cans, and posters of women in bikinis."

"I'm not going to dignify that with a response." I take a bottle of sparkling water from the fridge and hand it to her.

"That's fair," she admits.

"I can go back to showering at my friend's place." I sit next to her, and when her eyes widen a fraction, I realize I should have sat a little farther away. There's not much space for *farther* in this trailer. "I don't want to offend your delicate sensibilities again."

She rolls her eyes. "My sensibilities are not delicate. You just caught me off guard."

"In a good or bad way?" I can't help but ask.

"I'm not answering that." Her eyes flash, a direct contrast to her tone.

"I'll remember to bring my clothes up next time."

"Why do you think I have delicate sensibilities?" She inclines her head like a teacher addressing a particularly recalcitrant student. "I was knocked up when Teddy married me. So you know I'm not that innocent."

I swallow back a laugh. "Did you just quote Britney Spears to me?"

"Not intentionally. But also, why do you recognize Britney lyrics?"

"My sister can take credit for that, too. Kind of the pre-Taylor era, you know?"

"Sure."

But the tilt of her chin tells me she's still bothered by the delicate sensibilities comment. "I didn't mean it in a negative way. I'm trying to be respectful."

Her brows furrow. "Maybe I'm not looking for respect," she murmurs, as much to herself as to me.

Heat shoots through me at her words, and I have to dig my fingers into the arm of the sofa to keep from moving closer.

"What are you looking for, Molly?" I pitch my voice low, making damn sure she knows exactly what I'm thinking about.

She's in the middle of taking another drink and starts choking on it.

I smile as I take the bottle from her and place it on the table. Watching her come undone might be my new favorite pastime.

"Don't do that," she tells me.

"I thought you were going to spill it."

"Not the water. I don't care about the water. Don't pretend to flirt with me."

"Who said anything about pretending?"

She wipes a droplet off her bottom lip and glares at me. "Do we need to go over the part where you'd have no interest in a woman like me one more time?"

"One more time, I did *not* say those words." I drag a hand through my hair. "Again, I was trying to be respectful. I didn't want your friends to get the wrong idea."

"Those aren't my friends. Those are school moms. *My* friends are desperate for me to clear away the coochie cobwebs."

I blink.

She blinks.

"Did you say *coochie cobwebs*?" My brain struggles to process the words that just spilled out of her mouth.

Molly covers her face with her hands and groans. "Why am I like this around you, and can I have a do-over on the last thirty seconds?"

"Hell, no," I interrupt, peeling away her fingers until she meets my gaze. "You can't say something like that and expect me to ignore it. My imagination is way too active."

She rolls her eyes. "I haven't been with a man since Teddy died. Since nearly a year before the accident, if I'm being completely honest." She laughs softly. "I don't know why I'm choosing this moment to be honest."

The explanation is almost as shocking as the term. "Was there something wrong with him?"

"Now you're just being mean."

I shake my head. "I don't mean to speak ill of the dead, but—"

"No, Chase." She lowers her hands to her lap. "Nothing was wrong with Teddy. There's something wrong with *me*. I know you know it. It's why you said what you did to the moms. I don't care that you wouldn't want someone like me. I swear I don't, but—"

"I. Never. Said. That." The words come out as sharp as a round of gunshots, which wasn't my intention. And when she looks like she's about to argue again, I lean over and press my mouth to hers.

The kiss is meant to be quick, but the moment our lips touch, something electric shoots through my chest and I pull her closer before I can stop myself.

I need her to know that what she thinks I think about her isn't true.

I can't *stop* thinking about her.

I also can't stop thinking that my best friend was an idiot. What a fool I've been to let his attitude and my baggage coalesce into judging Molly in a way she didn't deserve then, and certainly doesn't now.

"I'm trying to protect you," I say roughly, cradling her face.

"From what?" she asks, sounding curious but not concerned.

The way she looks at me, like I'm someone worth trusting, makes my chest ache with the weight of all of my many mistakes. She has no idea how many people I've let down. The broken promises left in my wake.

How easy it would be for me to hurt her without even meaning to.

"I'm not good for you, Molly." The whispered words come from some place deep inside me.

I expect her to take me at my word, because I mean every one. But this woman, who has surprised me at every turn, does it again. Instead of pulling away, she leans in closer and kisses me. As if her soft, willing mouth can fill the hollow places inside me.

I take everything she has to offer, then demand more.

Our kisses turn wild and unruly, and I don't know if the groan of pleasure comes from her or me, but it fuels my need.

Her hands rake through my hair, and I lower mine from her face to cup her generous breasts. Her nipples are hard beneath her thin shirt and the fabric of her bra, and I tweak one gently. But I want more. I want to drag my mouth over every damn inch, because I just know how good she'll taste.

Maybe it makes me a complete asshole, but I also want to crush any memory she has of another man's hands on her. I want to feel like something as beautiful and real as Molly could belong to me, if only for a few scorching moments.

I still don't know what the hell coochie cobwebs are, but I'll take care of those, too. I'll take good care of her.

I continue stroking her breasts with one hand and move the other toward the waistband of her leggings because—

"Chase."

Her voice trembles, and I pause but don't pull away. Not yet. I want her too much for that.

But I need to know she wants this, too.

Then it's like the fucking heavens sing out, because instead of telling me to stop, she whispers, "More." It's the answer to the prayer I hadn't even realized I'd sent up—to God, or the universe, or whatever entity I have to thank.

Her lips are soft and warm against mine. They taste like sunshine and something uniquely her. When I deepen the kiss, she responds with a hunger that matches my own, her fingers digging into my biceps as she pulls me closer.

The world narrows to only this moment. The gentle pressure of her mouth, the way she sighs against my lips, and the warmth of her body pressed against mine. Her breathing quickens, and when I trail kisses along her jawline to that sensitive spot just below her ear, she arches into me in a way that sends fire racing through my veins.

She lets out a little groan, then freezes like she's embarrassed by the sound.

"Sweetheart, you can make as much noise as you want. The louder the better as far as I'm concerned. There's nobody here but you and me, and my name on your lips when you're screaming in pleasure will be music to my ears."

But she does lean back slightly, her brows pulling together so tight I can almost see the thoughts pinballing through her mind. "Say whatever you need to, Molly."

"There aren't *actual* cobwebs," she says quietly.

Christ, the way she looks up at me through her lashes with that serious expression is so fucking adorable I want to kiss her senseless all over again.

"It isn't like I don't know how to take care of myself. I've got a whole nightstand..." She shakes her head. "Never mind."

"I will definitely mind," I counter. "Tell me more about the ways you take care of yourself. Pretty sure the best way to remove the cobwebs image from my brain is to fill it with the details of how you touch yourself."

Her cheeks turn rosy again. "I'm not telling you a thing."

I bite back a grin at that prim and proper tone as she tries not to talk about getting herself off. "You're something special," I say and then laugh. It feels so fucking good to laugh.

The things this woman does to me without even trying, I can't explain it. It's more than want or need, although that's part of it. She's just so damn *herself*, and while she may not be able to appreciate how amazing that is, I certainly do. There's no pretense or posturing. She doesn't want anything from me. And it makes me want to give her things I don't even think I'm capable of.

But I *damn* sure know I'm more than capable of dusting off some invisible cobwebs.

"This unwillingness to share your little nightstand kink only makes me want to get it out of you even more."

I kiss her again, slow and deep, savoring the way she melts against me. Her lips part under mine, and when I trace my tongue along her lower lip, she makes this needy sound that goes straight to my cock. Every kiss is deliberate, like I'm trying to memorize how she shivers when I graze my teeth along her pulse point.

When I feel her relax into me, I move my hands to the bottom of her sweatshirt and then up past the soft fabric of her leggings to her skin. I know it's smooth, but touching her under her shirt—putting my hands on skin that I haven't seen—feels like something sacred. Once again, she's trusting me, even though we both know she shouldn't.

She sways forward ever so slightly, and it's all the invitation I need. My fingers graze her ribcage, then trace the edge of her bra, but it's not enough. Not nearly enough.

I need to see her. I need my mouth on her. Whatever she's willing to give me, I'll take it all, greedy bastard that I am.

I start to tug her sweatshirt off, but I get only the barest glimpse of her creamy skin before she jumps away from me like I pinched her.

"Molly—"

Her chest is rising and falling like she's having trouble gathering air in her lungs. I know the fucking feeling, because when she whispers, "school bus," I don't even react.

Until—*oh, shit.*

The unmistakable wheeze of air brakes cuts through the afternoon quiet, followed by the low rumble of the engine downshifting as it approaches the farm's driveway.

"What time is it?" she asks, panic lacing her tone.

I point to the clock on the microwave. "Three-thirty. The twins are home." I'm already moving toward the door. "I'll run down to the end of the driveway. You—"

"I'll be right there," she says. "They can't see me in your trailer. Not like this."

"You look fucking perfect, but take your time." I can't help myself as I lean in and steal one last kiss from her full mouth. "We've got time, sweetheart, and we're going to make the most of it."

Her eyes widen, but she doesn't argue. That's enough for now. A small victory, but a victory just the same.

This isn't what I expected from my time at the farm, I think as I jog down the gravel driveway. It's not smart for either of us, especially not given that my deal with Linda and Molly's plan for her future are in direct opposition to each other.

But I'm a man who made his living climbing on the back of angry bulls. You don't get much more opposition than that. If I can handle the rodeo circuit, I can handle the complications of my growing feelings for my former best friend's widow. And there's no doubt that the risk will be worth the reward when it comes to Molly McAllister.

13

MOLLY

THE NEXT AFTERNOON, Chase is busy helping a friend move some cattle or a horse or something equally cowboy-coded, so I text my friend group to ask for a ride to The Roasted Sky, my favorite coffee shop.

I'm heading into town for a meeting with a bride who wants me to design a bouquet and the table centerpieces for her upcoming wedding. It's different than what I normally do with the flowers I grow, and my first inclination was to refer her to the local florist who handles almost all the special events in town. But apparently, they referred her to me because my aesthetic aligns with her vision.

I didn't even know I have an aesthetic, but who am I to deny it?

This is the new me. The one who will build a good life for my kids. Not just for them, but for me as well.

However, even new me can't pretend yesterday afternoon didn't mean anything, or that it's not a big deal that Chase and I kissed and stuff.

The good kind of stuff.

If I close my eyes, I can still feel the heat of his touch. And I want more.

I'm terrified that makes me a fool, but I can't seem to turn off my yearning. Last night and this morning, Chase did his best to keep himself busy with the kids and the farm without talking directly to me. Like he wanted to pretend yesterday never happened. So that's what I did, too. Because I'm very good at pretending.

Although he apologized profusely for being unavailable today, a little part of me thinks it was another excuse to avoid me.

But I don't have to pretend anything at my meeting. It's nice to be seen and appreciated. The bride, Mariel, shows me her inspiration board, and I share ideas for her bridal bouquet and the mason jars of cut flowers she wants on each table.

Mariel is from Nebraska and has flown in for a few days with her mom to plan the wedding. They have the kind of close relationship and easy camaraderie I've always envied.

Life with my mother wasn't easy. I was five when she overdosed, and I still wonder whether it was accidental, like my grandparents told me. Or did life—and me—become too much for her?

"Once you choose the date and secure a venue, we'll be able to plan in more detail." The bride is the same age as me, but seems years younger.

She offers a weak smile. "I hope I can find a venue that's both available and affordable. I didn't realize how expensive getting married would be, especially with a short planning window."

Her hand drifts to rest on her still-flat belly, and I understand. This isn't just about a wedding. They're getting ready for another new chapter of life. She mentioned earlier that she and her fiancé had been planning a long engagement, but finding out she was pregnant sped up the timeline. I remember that urgency, the mix of joy and uncertainty.

"I'm so grateful we found you. Your flowers are so beautiful and..." She laughs softly. "I can actually afford them."

"I'm getting an expanded version of my business off the ground," I tell her with a smile that comes easily. "So I appreciate you giving me a shot. If you need an affordable venue, you could host the ceremony and reception at the farm," I offer before I think better of it.

"You do events?" Hope brightens her eyes.

I swallow hard. "I've been planning to expand the business to include events." By plan, I mean the idea popped into my head a few seconds earlier. But it's still a plan. And Linda doesn't have to know.

"You'd have to rent linens and tables. I don't have a liquor license, so—"

"That's okay," she says.

Her mother seems less certain. "Do you have any experience hosting events?" she asks, one brow raised like she already knows the answer.

"I've been focused on the flowers," I say. "But I'm buying the property from my mother-in-law to more readily expand my offerings." I sound surer of myself this time. "The farm is truly beautiful. I think you'd love it."

"This would solve everything." Mariel shares a look with her mother.

"I'll need a couple of days to work up the numbers, but if you allow me to use the photos from your reception on my website and promotional material, I'm prepared to give you a discount."

Off rates I don't even have, but they don't seem to realize that.

"Of course," the bride agrees without hesitation.

"Sweetie, you haven't seen the space," her mother says, placing a hand on the girl's arm.

"I have pictures." I pull out my phone and queue up the album with the photos of the farm. "I've always loved taking photos of the flowers and barn through the seasons."

A flutter of pride bubbles up as I hand over my phone, like I'm showing these women a secret place in my heart. It feels as if some part of me took the photos because I knew this was meant to be.

"It's spectacular," Mariel whispers, and her mother's features soften.

"It does have the kind of rustic look you want."

"Daddy would have loved it, Mom." Her voice catches.

The two women explained earlier that they chose Colorado because Mariel's late father had always dreamed of living in the mountains. Just as the family was preparing to move, when Mariel was still a girl, he was diagnosed with ALS, and they stayed in Lincoln. Having the wedding here is her way to make it feel like he's part of the celebration.

"You're welcome to come check it out. The barn isn't quite reception-ready at this point, but you could get a feel for the space."

"I already know it's perfect. Thank you for such a generous offer."

I nod. "I think it's going to work out for both of us."

"We need to head to Denver to catch our flight," her mom says.

"Take your time deciding," I tell the bride.

Mariel shakes her head, smiling. "I don't need to look at any other venues. I know this is the right place."

When they leave, I sit at the table for a few more minutes, pretending to take notes on our conversation. In reality, my hand is trembling too much to put pen to paper.

I just pitched a new business idea and made the farm feel special to someone else. A step toward becoming more than the person I want to become.

Baby steps count.

When my breathing returns to normal, I glance at my watch. Avah is picking me up in five minutes, and I can't help but wonder when, and if, things will go back to normal with Chase. Do we even have a normal to return to?

He was as into the kiss as I was, I remind myself as I pack up my bag and wave to Sally, the coffee shop's owner.

I refuse to let my doubts creep in and ruin that moment with him. Because it was spectacular.

So what if it doesn't lead to more. At least I have confirmation that a mom whose perky breast days are behind her can get her groove back.

I hate that I let the issues with Teddy, and the distance that expanded between us, make me think less of myself. But, sheesh, old habits are hard to break.

I text Avah that I'm ready and walk out into the sunshine. I'm getting better with the crutches, even though I still feel like I could fall at any moment.

And I almost do when somebody runs into me.

"Oh, hey, Molly. Sorry about that." The tall man with a crop of thick brown hair and hipster vibes adjusts the messenger bag slung over one shoulder. His tone is equal parts distracted and friendly. "They say you shouldn't text and drive, but I guess you shouldn't text and walk down a sidewalk either."

I smile at Bryson Elias, who happens to be my mother-in-law's realtor. His father owns the company, but Bryson is doing more and more with the business.

Maybe this is another stroke of serendipity.

"I'm glad I ran into you," I tell him, offering a smile. "Or that you ran into me. I wanted to talk about the farm and Linda's plan for putting it on the market after her trip."

"Of course." He nods and adjusts the thick black frames perched on his nose. "Skylark's loss is the Albuquerque community's gain. My wife will be sad not to have your flowers on our table all summer."

I nod. "Thank you for saying that but—"

"For the record, Dad and I both told Linda that the farm

would sell quick. She doesn't need to make the deal with Chase Calhoun. I get that she has sentimental feelings, given his friendship with Teddy, but she's leaving money on the table. I'm sure of it."

I blink and glance up at the blue sky overhead, then blink again when spots appear in front of my vision like I've been looking at the sun for hours.

"I'm not sure I follow, Bryson. What deal with Chase?"

"The plan to sell it to him as a pocket listing." He looks at me like I'm slow on the uptake, and when I don't respond, he continues, "Because he's helping you and the kids while she's away."

My heart begins hammering in my chest, but Bryson's smile widens.

"You don't have to pretend with me. Linda made it clear Chase doesn't want to publicize their agreement because he's not ready for word to spread that he's retiring. I haven't told a soul."

I find myself nodding even though there's nothing remotely agreeable about the words coming out of his mouth.

"Chase Calhoun is retiring," I repeat. "And buying my—Linda's farm."

"It's hard to believe, right? I can't help thinking he's going to change his mind," Bryson says. "I guess even the best bull riders have to hang up their chaps or spurs or whatever they hang up at some point. It's a big get for Skylark that a hometown hero like Chase wants to settle here."

He leans closer. "If the wife and I got to choose, we'd pick you both. Have you considered leasing part of the farm from him for your flower operation?"

"We haven't discussed that." My voice is hollow because everything I considered is like crops decimated by a hailstorm after what Bryson just shared.

I don't know why it's such a shock, but Chase knows that *I* want to buy the farm. There's no guarantee I'll succeed, but he knows I'm trying. Here I am, finally pushing open a new door to walk through, only to have it slammed in my face. Chase must have gotten a big kick out of me sharing my dream, thinking that I'm as much of a fool now as I was when I first arrived in Colorado.

A white BMW SUV pulls to the corner, and I say goodbye to Bryson.

"Do you need help with the crutches or your bag?" he asks.

"I've got it."

I'm so sick of people thinking I need help.

Avah is halfway around the car, but I hold out a hand.

"I've got it," I repeat and open the back door to load the crutches inside.

"Alrighty then." She goes brows-up. "What's got your panties in a twist?"

I clench my hands into fists as I sink into the plush seat. "Chase isn't helping me because he owes the McAllisters. At least, that's not the only reason. Bryson just told me he and Linda struck a deal. If he helps me while she's away, she'll sell him the farm. The same farm I want to buy from her as part of my bucket list challenge."

"He can't buy it," Avah says as she pulls away from the curb. "Because you're buying it." She glances over at me. "Do not cry, Molly. There's no—"

"Crying in flower farming," I finish with a shaky laugh then dab a finger under my eye when a tear spills over. "You make it sound easy."

She points a finger at me. "You're making it too hard. Going after what you want doesn't have to be so difficult. I believe in you. We all do."

As much as I appreciate the support, it feels like climbing a mountain with my crutches might be easier. I hate the fact that I never truly learned to rely on myself. I went from the crappy one-bedroom apartment my mother and I shared, to the cramped attic spare room in my grandparents' house, to Teddy's cabin in the woods, to my mother-in-law's house.

How pathetic is that?

I've never once lived on my own. I've never paid a utility bill. So maybe this was bound to happen all along. Whether it was Chase or some other buyer, I'm not sure why I ever thought I could make something of myself alone. We don't talk on the way back to the farm. Avah seems to realize I need a few minutes to process this new piece of information.

"We're going out tonight," she says into the silence as she turns down the long driveway.

"I'm not asking Chase to babysit," I mutter. "I'm going to text that I don't need his help for the weekend."

Except I do. But I'll pull up my big girl panties and figure it out.

Avah stops in the middle of the gravel drive and grabs her cell phone from the console. She punches in a number, and a moment later, Sadie's voice is on speaker.

"Hey, what's up?"

"Do you and the Playmaker have plans tonight?" Avah asks without preamble, even as I shake my head.

Sadie laughs. The Playmaker was her husband Ian's nickname when he played in the NFL, and while she doesn't usually call him that, the rest of us still enjoy it.

"Riva's going to a school dance, so our night will involve Ian pacing the front hall. We offered to chaperone, but that was a hard pass from her."

"How do you think he'd feel about Luke and Laurel pacing alongside him?" Avah asks. "Molly needs a babysitter."

"I don't," I say quickly. "It's fine."

"We'd love a twin sleepover," Sadie answers Avah, ignoring me. I get that a lot.

"Seriously," I protest. "You don't need—"

"You need a night out," Avah insists.

"Ian has been looking for an excuse to make his famous—according to him—bananas foster waffles," Sadie offers, and I hear the smile in her voice. "You're doing me a favor."

"I need to deci—"

"We're going axe throwing," Avah says into the phone.

Sadie laughs. "That's a brilliant idea. Text me when the kids are home from school, Mol, and I'll swing by to pick them up."

Okay, I have to admit that in my current mood, a night off while hurling weapons through the air might be just the ticket.

"If you're sure—"

"One hundred percent," Sadie says before her voice is drowned out by the sound of barking in the background. "I need to run. Text me later."

"That was bossy, even for you," I say with an eye roll as Avah disconnects the call. "Axe throwing?"

"You have some aggression to work off. I can't think of a better way to do it than with beer and axes. I'll even print a picture of Chase to hang on the target."

"I think I'll be able to imagine him in my brain just fine," I assure her.

"This isn't over, Molly. Not if you don't want it to be," she says.

I want to believe her. Almost as much as I want to believe in myself.

14

MOLLY

SOFT LIGHT SPILLS out from the windows of Chase's trailer as Avah pulls down the driveway later that night. "Looks like somebody's having a low-key Friday."

"That's weird. I texted that I wouldn't need his help again until Sunday night." Awareness flutters across my middle, but I blame it on the drinks I had between rounds of axe throwing. Still not sure axes and liquor go together, but I'm feeling way less stabby than I was earlier.

She gives me a funny look. "I thought the sardine can on wheels was his house."

My snort can by no means be described as delicate. "I'm sure Chase can find a warm bed to spend a weekend in. One that would give him easy access to indoor plumbing."

Her laugh is husky. "As well as easy access to a warm body."

I force a tight smile. "I think the official term is buckle bunny."

"Oh, yeah." She gives an exaggerated nod. "A staple of the rodeo circuit. I feel like there were dozens of them at the fairgrounds last fall before his accident."

Those flutters hit my gut like a truckload of bricks. "Exactly," I agree with a sigh. "The man has way better options than spending the weekend holed up in an Airstream." I lean forward like I'm suddenly going to develop x-ray vision. "Why isn't he taking advantage of them?"

She hits the brakes. "You want to knock on his door and ask?"

"Of course not." I smack her arm. "Don't slow down. Remember, I'm back to hating him."

"Back to," she repeats as she pulls to a stop in front of the house. "Which means there was a period, however brief, when you didn't hate him." She grins. "I knew it."

"To be clear, I didn't ever *like* him," I say, amazed I sound so composed.

"Girl, I'm on your side no matter what. If you hate him, I hate him. But..." She shifts the car into park, and the quiet of the night settles over us.

"I know I'm going to regret asking this," I tell her with an eye roll. "But what?"

"Hate sex can be flippin' hot."

"It doesn't sound hot."

"Trust me."

My mouth drops open. "Do you and Jon have hate sex? You're engaged, which means you love him."

"Of course. But in the early days of our relationship, things were...tumultuous." She shrugs. "I'm not sure if you've noticed, but I occasionally rub people the wrong way."

"I suppose that's true," I answer with a soft laugh. "But never me, and not Jon, right?"

"Not anymore," she says, but I notice the smile doesn't reach her eyes. "Now things are...comfortable."

"You say that like comfortable is a bad word."

"It's not." She tucks a strand of blonde hair behind her ear. "But being out of your comfort zone isn't bad either."

"I'm getting used to being way out."

"It's a good look," she says, her tone earnest. "I'm proud that you aren't letting a setback derail you."

Yep, that's right. One night of axe throwing with my bestie, plus a little bit of harmless flirting with a guy I'll likely never see again, and I've recommitted to my bucket list goal of building a life for myself and my kids on my terms.

My mother-in-law made her arrangement with Chase before she knew I wanted to stay in Skylark. I can't fault her, given that I never spoke up about my dream. Heck, I barely let myself acknowledge I had one before my book club friends challenged me to claim it.

Linda told me her plan to sell the property, and the twins and I moving to Albuquerque with her was part of that decision. There was no discussion about what I wanted, which is on me. I didn't feel like I could talk about my dreams because I hadn't done enough to earn them.

Now I know the quickest way to make a dream come true is by becoming the person who lives that life. I'm becoming that person.

I flash a smile that only wobbles a bit at the corners. "Thank you for kicking my ass into gear and being my best friend. I wouldn't want to do life without you."

"Samesies, girl," she says with a wink. "You're my ride or die, Mol."

The first words that pop into my mind are a denial that she needs me like I do her, but I don't say them. Because half of the problem is that I've spent too long selling myself short. I'm not going to do that anymore.

At least I'm going to try not to.

"Do you want help getting into the house? I feel like that shot might have pushed you over the edge."

I laugh softly. "Why did I let some rando guy convince me to do a shot?"

"It was the dimples."

I laugh again. "I think my coordination improves when I'm drinking."

"That's not a thing, hon," she answers. "It's the Wild Turkey talking."

"Gobble gobble," I tell her, and climb out of the car, suddenly not looking forward to a night alone in the house. "I promise I'll take it slow."

I grab my crutches from the back seat once again, looking forward to a time when I'm back on two feet. My ankle isn't hurting as badly as it did right after the accident, but a couple of hours standing while we chucked axes at a target hasn't helped.

Once I'm out of the car, crutches tucked under my armpits, I wave and watch her drive away.

"Why are you trying to get rid of me?" a deep voice asks.

I let out a yelp, then spin around, one crutch swinging wildly while the other catches my shin.

As I'm coming to expect when Chase is around, I fall flat on my butt.

In a couple of quick strides, he's down the porch steps, where I did *not* see him sitting. He grabs the crutches, then yanks me to my feet before I can protest.

"Why are you lurking in the dark outside my house?"

"I was sitting on your porch swing," he says with an amused scoff. His gravelly voice slides across my skin like velvet.

I blame my reaction on the shots and shoo him away before he can scoop me into his arms. My body would like to throat punch my brain in protest.

The porch light is off, leaving us in near darkness, and the pale moonlight casts shadows across his face. I can barely make out his features, but I can tell his gray eyes have gone dark.

"We need to talk," he says. I almost lose my footing again when he follows up with, "About your...you know." He flaps a hand. And I don't know how hand flapping can look manly, but somehow Chase manages it. "Your cobwebs."

"Coochie cobwebs," I clarify, narrowing my eyes and trying to ignore the flush that rises to my cheeks. Humiliation wipes out my buzz in one fell swoop. Will I ever live down that moment of verbal indiscretion? "I'm not talking about my cobwebs with you. Or with anybody. But definitely not you."

"Come on, Molly." He runs a hand through his hair like he does when he's frustrated or discombobulated. "I don't want things to be awkward between us. I won't apologize for the kiss, but I'm sorry if it made things weird between us."

I feel my mouth drop open. "Do you seriously think I'm mad about the kiss?"

"Yeah. No?" He shakes his head. "You know it was more than a kiss. Just like I know I have no right to you. You're my best friend's woman and—"

"Hold up, cowboy. In case it's unclear, we're not role-playing some testosterone-fueled *Yellowstone* knock-off. This is real life. Calling me your *best friend's woman* makes it sound like Teddy owned me." I jab a finger into Chase's chest. "He didn't. And besides, he's been gone for over two years. I don't belong to anyone except myself. I'm the one who chooses who I kiss and when."

"Got it," he says, hands up, surprise and respect flickering in his expression. "You were the one who brought up cobwebs, Molly. What was I supposed to think?"

It's a fair point, but not one I'm willing to concede to at the moment.

"That I'm a single mom of twins living with my late husband's mother?" I roll my eyes and let out an exasperated sigh. "I have priorities other than hooking up. Or maybe I was waiting for a night like tonight and the cute guy at the axe throwing place who—"

His eyes flash with an emotion I can't decipher. "What axe throwing place?"

"The Max Axe." I tilt my head defiantly. "It opened at the beginning of the year. Turns out beers and blades are cathartic." I don't mention the shots.

"Were you on a date?" His words are growly and low, and

damn if it doesn't make my stomach do a bunch of unwanted flip-flops.

"None of your business."

I slowly make my way up the ramp he built, unable to continue holding his gaze. Not with the intensity in his eyes.

"We kissed," he says, and even though his voice is barely above a whisper, the words stop me in my tracks.

"That doesn't make us Instagram official," I say over my shoulder, proud of how casual I sound.

"I don't have a fucking Instagram account," he shouts.

"No need to share it with the whole neighborhood."

"We *are* the neighborhood, Molly. Would you please—"

"But while we're on the topic of sharing," I interrupt from the top of the ramp, "perhaps you'd like to explain the secret squirrel agreement you have with my mother-in-law."

His head snaps back like I've slapped him. "I don't—"

"In exchange for babysitting me," I say with a tight smile, "she's going to sell the farm to you."

"Who told you that?" His voice goes from shout to whisper in the span of seconds. "No one was..." He closes his eyes for a moment and I see his chest rise and fall in an unsteady breath.

"Chase, I'm not just anyone. I told you my plan to approach Linda about buying the farm. You knew something about me, and you didn't think to mention that I can pound sand because you've already worked out a deal with her."

He walks up the steps until he's standing on the one below me, putting us at eye level. "I'd never tell you to pound sand, and nothing with Linda is a done deal. When she and I discussed a sale, I didn't know you wanted the farm."

"Are you going to back out now that you do?" I ask.

When he just stares at me, I roll my eyes. "That's what I thought. I hope you get why I don't want to be around you." Liar, my body chants, and I mentally shush it. "It's not at all about the kiss."

I turn toward the house, wishing I could stomp or flounce away, but the crutches make that impossible. He follows me, and although I could tell him no, I don't.

Despite my anger and frustration, I want him here.

"If I'm going to make a go of my plan for a cattle operation," he explains, "I need to add the acreage from this property to my family's land. It will give me access to the public land beyond it for grazing. It's not as simple as walking away, Molly."

Don't I know it. But complications don't seem to hold as much weight when it's just the two of us in this quiet house. A place that doesn't belong to me, but still feels like home.

Avah's words spin through my mind.

Hate sex.

Do I hate Chase? No. It would be easier if I did.

I stop before I get to the stairs. "Do you know what *is* simple?"

I don't even realize I've asked the question out loud until Chase answers.

"Tell me," he says, his tone coaxing. "Because I could use a little simple and straightforward about now."

He's staring at my eyes, but I'm staring at his mouth. There's a shift in the energy between us, and he has to know where my thoughts have gone. Following my needy body down a dangerous path that could end in me falling off a cliff.

I can't seem to bring myself to care.

It's not hate. *Tumultuous* was the word Avah used. It fits the mood.

I expect Chase to step forward and take control. It's what I expect from the people in my life, and it's what always happens.

He continues to watch me without moving. I can practically feel the tension vibrating from his body.

"Tell me," he repeats, his tone rough but also tender.

Ignoring the warning from my better self and tossing good sense straight out the window into the dark outside, I reach for him, cursing how awkward the crutches make me feel.

But I love that he comes without hesitation, like I'm somebody he'll let command him.

And damn, I want to.

"This," I whisper and press my mouth to his.

Chase kisses me like he didn't think he'd get the chance to again and wants to make the most of it. He keeps his hands fisted at his sides like he's fighting every instinct to grab hold of me. The restraint only makes me want him more.

I plunge my tongue into his mouth and tangle my fingers into the soft fabric of his shirt as if he truly belongs to me. As if I'm the type of woman confident enough to claim a man like him.

The tension between us flames like a match. Yes, I'm angry. And yes, I want him anyway.

He groans low in his throat, and the sound sharpens the ache between my thighs.

I break away, breathing hard. "Bedroom. Now."

His brows furrow. "Molly—"

"It's simple and straightforward, Chase." Pretty sure I'm reminding us both. "Either you're with me or not."

He blinks, and I almost smile at his expression—like I just knocked the air out of his lungs. It's a heady sensation, one that makes me feel powerful in a way that's both unfamiliar and inherently right.

"I'm with you." He steps aside so I can pass, as if he knows I'm not going to be able to handle his touch. "Let me help—" he starts, reaching for my crutches.

"I've got it." I adjust the grip and make my way toward the staircase. My ankle throbs, but it's background noise to the electric buzz in my veins.

I can feel him at my back. "Please," he whispers, and I sigh as I lean the crutches against the handrail and turn to him.

"Fine, but only so I can save my energy for the good stuff."

His lips twitch as he lifts me into his arms. "So much good stuff."

He takes the stairs two at a time and gently places me on the bed, towering over me but still waiting for permission.

I stretch out and look up at him from underneath my lashes. "If you're going to act like you're scared to touch me..." I gesture toward the nightstand. "I have a drawer full of toys to take care of this myself."

That earns a low laugh. "Tell me what you want."

I lean back against the pillow. "I want to be in this moment."

"Just us," he agrees.

The air between us shifts again. It's less volatile now, but more charged. His gaze trails down my body, lingering on my injured ankle.

"I don't want to hurt you," he says softly.

"You won't."

He kneels in front of me, and his hands go to the strap of the orthopedic boot. He slides it off like I'm made of glass, then leans forward and kisses the skin just above my ankle. It's tender and intimate and steals my breath.

I reach for him and pull his T-shirt over his head, my fingers skimming across smooth skin and taut muscle. He helps me tug it off, and then his mouth is on mine again, deep and searching. His hands cradle my face, and mine drift over his muscled chest and stomach, savoring the way he shudders under my touch.

"I want to see you," he whispers.

He helps me peel off my shirt and then my bra, flinging them to some far off corner of the room, then follows me when I shift back on the bed, maneuvering carefully to protect my ankle. He trails kisses down my neck and collarbone, then over the curve of my breast. There's a quiet reverence in the way he touches me that makes my eyes sting.

Forget cobwebs. It's as if my heart has been frozen for years, and every kiss is melting the ice around it.

I don't stop him as he slides his hand beneath the waistband of my leggings, lifting my hips to give him full access. Because I trust him with this.

With me.

His hands find the curve of my waist, the swell of my hips, his caress sending shivers along my skin even as he claims more. "Christ, you're so wet," he says as his fingers dip into me.

I bite back a moan as he grazes his thumb across my clit, the sensation almost too much to bear. It's not as if I don't know what it feels like for a man to touch me, but everything about Chase makes this moment feel different. More.

"Wait."

He goes still, and I watch as his chest rises and falls in ragged breaths. I'm glad I'm not the only one with that reaction.

"Take off your clothes," I command gently.

"Kind of busy here," he says with a tight laugh.

"We're in this together," I remind him, cupping his jaw.

My breath catches as he stands and begins to strip, eyes locked on mine. I drink in every inch of him—those broad shoulders, abs that flex with each movement, thick thighs I can imagine between mine. His cock is already hard, and my mouth waters at the sight of him.

"You're staring," he murmurs as he places his wallet on the nightstand.

"Of course I am." My voice is so thick I barely recognize it. When I sit up straighter and drag my nails down his stomach, he hisses between his teeth, but doesn't stop me. "I want to be on top."

His brows shoot up. "Your ankle—"

"Can handle it," I tell him. "Trust me."

He pulls me to my feet, pulling me close for a long kiss before he takes my spot on the bed. He looks like every forbidden fantasy I've ever tried to suppress. "Molly, are you sure..."

I bite down on my lip, then draw in a long breath. "I'm done pretending I don't want you."

"Thank fucking God," he murmurs.

It takes an awkward minute to shimmy out of my leggings without putting weight on my right foot. I make it work and climb onto the bed, straddling him with my good leg tucked around his hip, the other extended slightly off to the side.

He's careful with me, his hands gentle at my thighs, but his gaze is raw.

I slowly grind against him as he grabs the wallet and pulls a condom packet from it.

"Jesus," he groans. "You're killing me."

"Paybacks are hell."

He sheaths himself, then reaches up to brush his thumbs over my nipples, and I gasp at the spark it lights in my belly. Our next kiss is wild, all teeth and tongue as I reach between us to stroke him. He's so hard and thick, and I love how he tenses under my touch.

I lift up and then slide down onto him, and it's like slipping into a part of myself I've never known before. We both freeze for a second. He's buried inside me as I hover over him, our breathing ragged.

"Fuck, Molly," he groans. "You feel..."

"Don't talk," I whisper against his mouth. "Just be here."

I deliberately roll my hips, watching the way his jaw clenches. His eyes go half-lidded, but he lets me set the pace, even as his hands roam my body like he's trying to memorize every curve.

I ride him like he never belonged to anyone else. Like he's mine, and I'm not breaking every rule I set for myself.

He sits up and buries his face in my neck, and we move together. The world narrows until it's just the two of us in this moment. My body's already close. Years of frustration, powerlessness, and grief transformed by lust and heat and pleasure.

I finally allow myself to let go, and when Chase grazes his teeth against my fluttering pulse, I come. A wave of stardust shimmers through me, and he follows with a strangled groan, pulsing inside me as he holds me tight.

We stay tangled together, his forehead pressed to my collarbone, as sweat cools on our skin.

"You okay?" he murmurs.

"I just took what I wanted." I smile, still breathless. "I'm more than okay."

He kisses me, slow and sweet like a promise.

And for the first time in a long time...I feel more than okay. I feel beautiful and powerful in a way I didn't know was possible.

15

CHASE

I'VE NEVER BEEN the kind of guy to lose my head or heart over a woman, and that's not changing any time soon. Yet after one night with Molly, I'm floating on some orgasm-induced cloud.

It's not like I took a vow of celibacy or anything, but I outgrew wasting my time with buckle bunnies years ago. I'm choosy about the women I sleep with, especially since the accident. Recovery gave me an excuse, but the truth is, no one's lit me up like that in a long damn time.

Everything was different with Molly. The way she let go and gave herself over to the connection between us fed something in me I didn't know I was hungry for.

I've also never been much for sleepovers. But I couldn't imagine a better way to wake up than with her warm, sweet-scented body curled into mine. When I fitted myself along her back and took her slowly from behind, it was like the rest of the world didn't exist. Just us in our own little bubble of need and desire. And for the first time in forever, I didn't want to be anywhere else.

She felt it, too. I know she did. We didn't talk about what it might mean going forward, but I saw it in her eyes before the kids got home.

Her friend Sadie dropped them off Saturday morning, along with Ian Barlowe, the football legend himself. I knew he lives in Skylark, married to Sadie, but this was the first time I shook his hand, and the guy's got a grip like he was born to break bones.

They hung around for a bit, and Laurel must have talked up Fancy, because Sadie was eager to meet her. Apparently, she's a sucker for anything with four legs. The whole group ended up following me to the barn, which shouldn't have made me nervous, but it did. As if I were on display in a different way than I am on the back of a bull.

Sadie and Ian didn't mention the circuit or ask what I'm doing next. For once, no one wanted something from me. There was no angle or pressure, just real conversation. It was refreshing as hell.

If Molly shared anything with Sadie about the deal I made with Linda, she kept it close to the vest. They talked flowers and building plans like nothing was off-kilter. And I loved that for both of us, even if I can't wrap my head around how to make this work.

After they left, Molly, the kids, and I had the most uneventful, ordinary, and, in my opinion, amazing day. We did chores, worked in the greenhouse, made dinner, and then played rounds of Uno for hours. It felt like the most natural thing in the world to hang out together—almost like we were an actual family.

Yep, my idea of a perfect Saturday has switched from the bar scene to getting my ass kicked in cards by two first graders, like I was auditioning for Dad of the Year or something.

Yesterday, I took them over to Ray's ranch. He and Janice are fostering a litter of shelter kittens, and I figured if I'm already playing the part, I might as well bring in the big guns. Kids and kittens? Game over.

I could tell by the looks Ray kept giving me that he'd picked up on the fact there might be something going on between Molly and me. The strangest part is that I have no desire to deny it.

Molly doesn't exactly share that sentiment and only lets me steal a couple of quick kisses while the kids are upstairs getting ready for bed. I respect her boundaries, even though I'd rather ignore them and pull her into bed again. And again.

But for now, I'm keeping my dick in my pants and hoping— hell, maybe even praying—she decides another round or two (or twenty) is what she wants.

In the meantime, I've been mulling over ways to handle the situation with the land. I want to buy it, but I also want Molly to be able to keep her flower farm running. If she wants the farmhouse, I'll build another one. No hesitation.

Sure, I keep telling myself this is all for Teddy. I'm looking out for his widow and kids because he was my best friend.

Yeah, I think we all know there's more to it than that.

By this morning, the golden haze of the weekend with our shared chores, quiet laughter, and soft kisses has burned off like morning fog. The kids are at school, and Molly is back to treating me like the hired help. Just a guy lending a hand until her ankle heals.

"You're welcome to drop me off at Sunnydale," she says, like she thinks I've been quiet on the drive into town because I've got someplace I'd rather be. "I usually visit with a few residents after my weekly flower delivery. Monday mornings are sing-along time."

I nod as I pull into the assisted living facility's parking lot. "I know. My mom lives here."

Molly draws in a sharp breath. "Were you going to mention that to me?"

I grip the steering wheel tighter. "I just did."

"Alright then." Her voice gentles, like she's reading the tension radiating off me. "What's her name?"

"Brittany Lynn."

Her eyes brighten. "I've brought her flowers a couple of times, but we haven't spoken much."

"She's not very social." I shrug. "Or communicative."

"Huh. Is that where you get it?"

I breathe out a small laugh because I know she's trying to lighten my mood. "Mom has early-onset dementia. She's always been quiet, but now even more so."

"I'm sorry, Chase." She reaches across the seat, her hand brushing mine, and it feels like more comfort than I deserve.

"She's doing okay, and my sister—" Damn. Why is there a stupid catch in my voice? I clear my throat and try again. "My sister handles most of it, getting her to appointments and making sure she has the right snacks. I'm more involved now that I'm here, but my sister's a better caregiver. Mom..." I trail off, swallowing hard. "There was never any question who was her favorite growing up."

"I'm sure she's happy to see you more often," Molly says. But there's an undertone I can't identify in her tone. I have a feeling she knows what it's like to hope for something not meant for you.

"Yeah, maybe."

She glances at me as I pull to a stop in front of the building. "Does your family know about the arrangement to buy the farm?"

"Tentative arrangement," I clarify.

"It's your plan for staying in Skylark." She takes her hand back, and I have to clench mine into a fist to resist the urge to reach for her again.

"No one knows except you, Linda, and the realtors." I rub a hand along the back of my neck. "It's not a done deal."

"I know," she says, far too brightly. "Like I told you, I'm going to find the money to make a better offer than whatever you're giving her."

When she'd said it in bed, naked and fierce, her eyes dancing like she wanted nothing more than to best me, I'd found her competitive spirit incredibly attractive. I'm not sure she truly believes it, but hell if it doesn't make me smile.

We get out of the truck and circle around to the bed, where her scooter's loaded. I've made a few modifications, adding a basket for her supplies, and attaching a wagon with a makeshift hitch so she can haul more without overtaxing herself.

"I'm happy to carry everything in," I say.

"I want to practice maneuvering with weight in the wagon."

"But I'm right here." I hold out my hands. "Cheap labor."

"You sell yourself short, Calhoun."

Something about the way she says it makes me want to believe her. To lean into her confidence the same way I leaned into her touch.

The way she so easily shifted past her anger about keeping the deal quiet bothers me. It's clear she's accustomed to being left out of decisions that affect her, like being brushed aside is par for the course.

We load the wagon with flowers, and she lets me carry the two biggest. It's a slow trek through the parking lot, and even though I can see sweat beading on her brow, I also know she needs to feel like she's handling things.

I get that better than most. I built a career out of being self-reliant. Just me, a bull, and eight seconds on the clock.

What I don't understand is why Molly keeps downplaying her own value. Within a week of spending time with her, it's abundantly clear that everybody who knows her loves her.

Not me, of course. I don't do love.

But I *like* her. More than I've liked anyone in a long while.

I hate how easily I bought into Teddy's bullshit before the wedding and believed that she'd trapped him with a pregnancy. That he was some kind of hero swooping in to save her reputation. I should have known better, and he should have, too. It's clear that my old friend failed to appreciate how luck had smiled on him when Molly came into his life. Teddy had a family most people only dream about, and he didn't just take it for granted. He threw it all away.

Not just the day he took out a raft when the water was running dangerously high. Based on everything I've witnessed and the little she's told me, he made her feel like less at every turn. Like she was lucky to have him instead of the other way around.

I'm ashamed to admit I wasn't much better. I told him she wasn't good enough based on nothing but the kind of assumptions I should have known better than to trust. I knew how captivating Teddy could be when he wanted something. If he'd decided he wanted Molly, he would have charmed her without thinking about the potential consequences of that one night stand.

Once she got pregnant, he should have stepped up completely. She and the twins had been counting on him to be the man they needed. To put their safety and security above everything else. He never should have taken that risk on the river.

If a person wanted to, they could argue that the choices I made for most of my career were just as dangerous. But I didn't have anyone depending on me. If I got trampled or paralyzed, broke bones or suffered head trauma, who would care? My sister? Ray and Janice? Not my mom or dad, that's for sure.

I scrub a hand over my face and give myself a mental shake. Look who's running for Mayor of Maudlin Town.

The ladies at the front desk greet Molly with hugs and cheerful chatter, talking about how impressed they are with her stamina. I sign in as well, my own greeting less enthusiastic, which I understand. It has more to do with my mom than me.

My mother isn't a staff favorite. She's difficult, stubborn, and not particularly kind. Ada and I try to make up for it with generous holiday gifts and contributions to their fundraisers, but it's still tough.

"I'll come by your mom's room when I'm done," Molly says. "Unless she decides to join the sing-along."

I don't miss the look that passes between the two women behind the desk.

"I'll ask," I tell her, ignoring the way my gut churns. I should start bringing donuts. Or sandwiches. Or maybe a damn case of wine. Bribes—whatever it takes to get the staff to look at me the way they look at her.

"Do you need help?"

I hope she says yes.

"I'm good. Have a nice visit with your mom."

"Right."

I tap my palm on the counter and turn toward the hallway, my stomach twisting with a familiar mix of guilt, dread, and resignation.

I walk down the hall, straighten the cheery spring wreath my sister has hung on her door, then knock.

"What do you want?" a sharp voice calls out.

The visit is already off to a stellar start.

I open the door and peek inside. "Hey, Mom. You up for a visit?"

"You bring chocolate?" she snaps from the recliner in the corner.

I reach into my vest pocket and pull out a salted chocolate bar. It's her favorite, and I quickly learned not to show up without one. "Sure did."

"Bring it over," she says, waving me in.

My mother was never what you'd call soft, but she used to be gentler. Those days feel like a long time ago. Still, I was probably due more tough love than she gave me growing up, so this version of her feels right.

"There's a sing-along in the rec room," I tell her as I break off a piece of chocolate and hand it over. Her eyes close as she takes a bite. At least I can bring her a little bit of happiness. "Should we check it out?"

She lets out a sharp laugh. "You can't carry a tune."

For all the memories dementia's stolen from her, that one stuck.

"True," I agree. "But *you* have a nice voice."

Her gaze softens, and she smiles, just slightly. "I do have a nice voice."

"You used to sing while you cooked. I always knew we were having meatloaf if I heard Reba coming from the kitchen. Reba was for meatloaf. Toby Keith meant chicken-fried steak."

"Chicken-fried steak was your favorite."

The breath whooshes out of me.

"It was," I say. "Nobody makes it better than you."

She nods and holds out her hand for more chocolate.

There's a knock, and Molly peeks in.

"I was wondering if you'd like some fresh flowers in your room, Brittany," she says gently, like they've known each other for years.

"Daffodils," Mom says, pointing at the bouquet. "I like those."

"I remember," Molly says, her voice like spun sugar.

God, she's sweet. Sweeter than I deserve. I didn't even know Mom liked daffodils, and I definitely never thought to bring her flowers. Only chocolate as a bribe for a better mood. But I *could* do more. I *should*.

"I'll put them here on the end table." Molly moves closer then gives me an encouraging smile.

As Mom stares at the flowers, her brows furrow and her mouth pulls down into a frown.

"He hates flowers," she mutters. "Says they make him sneeze. He thinks I buy them on purpose to make him miserable." She shakes her head. "I just want something pretty in the house."

My heart stills, then thumps wildly against my ribcage. "Mom, you're the only one here. You can have flowers whenever you want."

I figure she's talking about my father. I don't remember his allergies, but I *do* remember how much he hated joy. Hated anything that made us happy. Whether it was flowers, bikes, or birthday parties, it didn't matter. He'd find a reason to ruin it.

"If the flowers start bothering you, let one of the aides know," Molly offers, gentle as ever.

But Mom's not looking at her anymore. She's staring at *me*. And there's no recognition in her eyes.

I offer her what I hope is an understanding smile, even though my cheeks feel frozen. "Mom, if you don't want—".

"Why are you here?" she snaps. "I don't want to see you. Haven't you done enough?"

"Mom..." I hold up the chocolate like it's a peace offering. "It's me. Chase. I brought chocolate."

I try to hand her another piece, and she flinches.

"Don't touch me. You can't be here."

"I'm not—"

I start to move closer, but step back the moment she cowers.

"Call the police," she tells Molly, her tone frantic. "There's no telling what he'll do."

My gaze locks on Molly's and the understanding swirling in her green eyes nearly brings me to my knees. "It isn't me she's..."

My mom has gone completely still, almost catatonic, staring through me like I'm not even there.

"I know." Molly lays a hand on my arm, her touch grounding me in a way that feels like it's the only thing keeping me tethered to this world.

"I've got this," she says. "Go find someone on staff. It's not your fault."

I want to believe her.

But I've done enough. Just by looking like the old man. Just by being here.

"I'm sorry, Mom," I whisper.

But she doesn't respond. I'm not even sure she can.

At the door, I glance back. Molly's kneeling in front of my mother, holding her hands and speaking so softly I can't make out the words. But Mom is nodding.

That's something.

I stop the first staff member I see and explain that something's upset my mom, and she needs help. The woman gives me a strange look when I don't follow her down the hall.

"Someone's in there with her," I say. "I'm part of the problem. She thinks I'm my father," I add, because I *have* to say it out loud, not willing to allow anyone–even a stranger–believe I would elicit that sort of reaction in my mother.

"That happens," she says kindly. "We'll take care of her."

And I'm left standing there alone. Shut out. Turned away again.

I'm too old to be wondering when someone will take care of me. I'm a grown-ass man, but I feel like a kid again. The boy who used to lie awake in bed listening for the sound of breaking dishes or screaming. The one who hated himself for not being able to protect her. For still loving a man who hurt him.

The part of me that hated my father eventually won out. But back then? I just wanted to figure out the magic formula that would keep things calm and my mom, sister, and me safe.

Because the good times were good. My little boy brain thought maybe, just maybe, if I behaved right and said the right things, the good times would stay.

They never did.

The same darkness that consumed my father is inside of me and always has been. I can feel it pulsing through me now, sticky and black as tar. Riding bulls was how I kept it from eating me alive. I took my life in my hands for eight seconds at a time and, somehow, that made me feel like I had control.

My dad hated that he wasn't good enough to make it on the circuit and I was. Sometimes I wonder if he'd had an outlet like that, would it have been enough? Would we have been safe from his darkness?

And if I'm really done—if I retire for good—where does that leave me? Where does that leave the darkness and what happens when there's no place to ride it out?

16

MOLLY

CHASE HADN'T WANTED to talk about the visit with his mom, or much of anything, on our way back to the farm. He played it off like it hadn't rattled him, but I noticed the muscle tic in his jaw as he kept his eyes fixed on the road.

I didn't push because I understood he needed space to process what had happened, and I respect him enough to give it to him. I also trust that he'll share when he's ready. Or maybe he won't. Does great sex mean he owes me his emotions? I want to be the person he turns to, even though I have no real claim on him. Isn't that the story of my life, craving more than someone is willing to give me?

We drove home in silence, and he spent the afternoon in the flower field, met the kids at the bus stop, and then took off on horseback like he was chasing something only he could see.

I hugged both my babies and sent them inside for snacks, then finished up in the greenhouse. Laurel is sitting at the kitchen table when I hobble through the front door, pencil in hand with an all-too-familiar crease between her brows.

"Where's your brother?" I ask when Luke doesn't answer my calls up the stairs.

"He went outside," she replies without looking up. "Mom, why can't he be normal?"

I whirl around on my crutches so fast I nearly land on my butt again. "Your brother is perfect just the way he is. Why would you say something like that?"

"He's not perfect." She rolls her eyes. "He's...weird."

"Laurel Marie."

She lets out an exaggerated sigh. "He's always trying to hang around me and my friends because he doesn't have any of his own."

"You're his sister. He loves you. You have a twin bond." I say it with conviction, but my gut twists because I know what it's like to feel pressure to act a certain way.

I also understand that my kids are very different from one another. Things come easily to Laurel, just like they did for Teddy. She's confident and social, the kind of kid people naturally gravitate toward. Luke reminds me of myself. Quiet, tender, and unsure of where he fits.

I don't want Laurel to resent her brother for needing more, and I know with enough time and patience Luke will find his place in the world. I've found mine here in Skylark, and I'm holding on to it with both hands. This town has healed something in me, and I want it to work that same magic on my sweet son.

"The other kids need to give him a chance." I'm not sure if I'm trying to convince her or myself.

"The Chase hype helped," she says with a shrug.

"The what now?" I blink. "What's the Chase hype?"

Laurel looks at me like I'm a few Draw 4 cards short of a full Uno deck. "Everybody knows Chase. He's famous—not like Taylor Swift or Ian Barlowe famous, but he's a big deal around here. When he came to school and was nice to Luke, it made Luke a big deal for a second."

"Is that for real?" My mind boggles at the idea that one visit to the classroom from Chase did that much for Luke.

"Totally," she says. "You saw how they picked him when we played the shower games. Luke never gets picked for a team. He should have acted like us knowing Chase was a bigger deal."

"Why should he *have* to?" I ease down into the chair across from her. "Why are kids so mean?"

"I don't know, but they are. I try to help him, but it's not easy. I guess it's gotten a little better, but next year we'll be starting over again, and I can't be his blankie."

I offer her a soft smile. "Not even a corner square?" I shake my head before she can answer. "Forget I said that. You aren't responsible for your brother."

Luke still sleeps with the fleece blanket someone gifted the twins as babies. When he started elementary school, we battled daily over whether he could bring it with him. Finally, we compromised, and I cut a square from the worn fabric and tucked it into the front pocket of his backpack.

It's still there. Sometimes when I volunteer, I see him wander over to his hook, unzip that pocket, and run his fingers along the fabric like he needs the comfort.

"What if we could stay in Skylark?" I ask quietly.

Laurel looks up, wide-eyed. "Can we? I don't want to go to Albuquerque with Nana. I like it here." She tucks her hair behind one ear. "I'll never make friends like the ones I have in Skylark."

"Sweetie, you'll make friends wherever you go." I pause. "But I'm working on a plan. I want us to stay. I'm going to try to buy Nana's farm. Things might be tight for a while..."

She bolts from her chair and wraps her arms around my neck, climbing into my lap like she's little again. "Please, Mommy. I want to stay so bad."

"Oh, sweet girl..." I cradle her face in my hands and brush my thumbs across her cheeks when tears spill down them. "Why didn't you say something when I told you Nana wanted us to move with her?"

135

"Because I thought *you* wanted to, and she acted like we had to come with her."

I want to cry right along with her. Because my brave, bold, beautiful daughter has learned from me what it looks like to stay silent to keep the peace.

"I'm grateful to Nana for everything she's done," I tell my daughter. "But she wants us to be happy. Daddy would want us to be happy. I think he'd love knowing you're happy here."

"I want to stay on the farm," she whispers. "Do you think Nana will let you buy it? Or maybe we could just live here, like we do now?"

I've considered asking Linda if she'd rent the house to us until I can save up enough to buy it. But I don't know if she'd say yes. She wants her grandkids close, and I tentatively agreed to follow her to Albuquerque, but we need a place that's ours.

Maybe it's finally time I stop doing what everyone else expects and start doing what's right for us.

"Laurel, I can't promise I'll always be able to give you everything you want. But I *do* promise to always listen. You never have to hide your feelings from me. We'll figure this out together. And I'll help your brother too. You're allowed to have your own friends."

"Thanks, Mommy," she whispers.

We talk a little longer as I turn over the possibilities in my mind. What happens if I can't buy the farm? Or if Chase changes his mind and decides not to step aside after all? After watching his mother mistake him for the man who once terrified her, and seeing how deeply it shook him, I get it. He needs peace and a place to start over that doesn't carry shadows. Just like I do.

But this farm has become more than just a house for the kids and me to live in. It's our home.

I've spent so long doing what's best for everyone else. Now, for the first time in years, I feel like I'm building something that's mine. I've made a life here, one where I can finally stand on my own two feet. I don't want to walk away from that. I don't want to pull my kids from the house where they finally feel happy, or give up the flowers I planted with my own hands. They're blooming now, and so am I.

"I'll be nicer to Luke." Laurel sniffs as she steps out of my arms.

"We'll help him find his own place. He's got a good heart, and he just needs to be around people who see him for who he really is. People who won't make him feel like being gentle means he's weak or weird."

She bites her lip and turns away, like she's holding something back.

"Remember what I said. You can tell me anything, Laurel. Even if I can't fix it, I want to know what—"

"Daddy used to make fun of Luke," she blurts.

My mouth goes dry. My stomach knots and a dull pressure creeps up the back of my neck. "What do you mean?"

"He used to call Luke his little freak show to his friends because Luke was so shy and awkward. I tried to make it better, Mommy. I talked enough for both of us. But when we had to go places with him, he'd make Luke stay in the car. He'd tell people he had a daughter, but not a son."

I can't breathe. It's like the air's being sucked out of the room. A slow, cold fury settles in my chest. I want to go back in time, pull my son out of that car, and hold him tight so he never hears those words.

"Are you sure that's what happened? You were both so young. Maybe—"

"I remember," she says firmly. "He told a group of rafters Luke got dropped on his head, and he wasn't joking." She swallows hard. "I loved Daddy, but he wasn't very nice sometimes."

I pull her back into my arms. "Of course you love him. He was your dad. He wasn't perfect, but he loved you *and* your brother."

She leans her head on my shoulder. "He loved you too, Mommy."

That nearly shatters me. Because if Teddy were alive right now, I'd want to kill him myself. How could he have acted that way about his own son?

Laurel returns to her homework, humming softly under her breath. I swear, I can tell that something has lifted off her shoulders, the invisible weight she's been carrying transferred to me. I'll take that burden from her every day, even though I have no idea how to fix the damage my late husband has caused by his callousness.

I finally pull myself together enough to go looking for my son. Sometimes Luke likes to dig in the dirt behind the greenhouse, but he's nowhere to be seen. I glance at Chase's trailer, wondering if he's gone to visit Princess. The grumpy cat who hisses at me every chance she gets has taken a shine to my son, contentedly purring every time he curls up next to her on the small sofa.

Despite everything with Chase—the mess of our past—I'm grateful he's here. Not just because he seems to really see Luke, but when the weight of everything threatens to crush me, his presence makes it feel a little more bearable. As if having Chase close means I don't have to hold it all alone.

A soft whinny draws my attention to the barn. The doors are wide open, and the air still holds the warm kiss of late spring, even as the sun slips behind the Flatirons. I stop just before the entrance when I hear Luke's voice followed by a low, familiar chuckle.

My first instinct is a gut punch of panic, terrified that Chase is laughing at my son the way his dad used to. Suddenly, I'm back in a different life. One where I confused cruelty for teasing and tried to convince myself we were happy.

My feet feel rooted in place as a wave of nausea rises. What if Chase is no different than Teddy? What if I let my guard down and brought another man into Luke's life who might hurt him?

No. I won't let that happen again.

17

MOLLY

HEART POUNDING, I step closer, ready to face whatever I've just walked into. But I freeze as my son's sweet laughter cuts through the dusty air.

"Her mouth tickles." He giggles again.

"That's because she doesn't want to hurt you," Chase replies, his voice low and easy. "She just wants those carrots in your hand."

"Why didn't Daddy keep riding?" Luke asks.

There's a pause, then Chase says, "That's a question I don't know the answer to. Your dad and I grew up trail riding. Your nana kept an old horse here, not good for much but slow rides into the hills. Your dad could have been good at bull riding, roping, barrel racing...anything he put his mind to. He had a way with animals, like you do, but they didn't give him the adrenaline rush he was looking for."

I inch forward and pause at the edge of one of the wide doors. Luke is looking up at Chase like the guy hangs the moon and stars. I know the feeling.

"I was with him," Chase says softly, "the first time he went over a class five rapid. Do you know about class fives?"

Luke nods. "They're the most dangerous."

"Yep. We were young and stupid, and your dad had made friends with this guy who worked on one of the ski mountains but guided rafting trips in the summer out of Buena Vista. He invited us to go with him, and since your grandma was out of town, Teddy borrowed her car. Neither of us even had a license." Chase chuckles, but there's no humor in it. "We drove down early in the season, after a heavy snow year, so the runoff was wild. We had no business being on that river, and it scared me in a different way than a bull does. But your dad? He was hooked."

"He fell out of the boat the day he died," Luke whispers. "On a class five." His voice drops. "He was out there because of me."

I feel my lungs lock up, like someone's cinched them tight. I want to burst in and scream that it wasn't Luke's fault. Teddy made his own reckless decision. We'd been fighting about whether to force Luke into another miserable season of rec league soccer. A sport he hated and wasn't any good at, but Teddy wouldn't let it go. He was determined to make our son into something he wasn't.

Still, I don't move. My knees won't let me.

"Your dad and I were a lot alike," Chase says. "Not very good at dealing with our feelings. We found other ways to clear our heads. But your dad wasn't thinking straight that day he took the raft out in those conditions. That's not on you."

My breath catches. I haven't talked to the kids in detail about Teddy's accident. I didn't think they were ready. I didn't think *I* was ready. I never imagined Luke might be carrying a weight he was never meant to hold.

"You don't know." Luke says the words like an accusation.

"Your dad knew better than to be on that river at that level. He also knew he need to be wearing a life vest and helmet, but he wasn't that day. Those were his choices, not yours."

Luke sniffs, and it feels like my heart is shattering into a million pieces. "But if I was more like Laurel or liked soccer..."

Tears stream down my cheeks. I swipe them away, blinking

hard because I can't let him see me like this. Then I hear Chase's steady voice again. It feels like a lifeline, and not just for my son.

"You're doing fine just the way you are, Luke. You're a good kid with a big heart. Heck, even Princess likes you, and she doesn't like anyone but me."

That earns a smile. "She scratched Laurel the other day," Luke says, then shifts his weight like he's guilty of something. "We went into the trailer when you were gone, but we didn't mess up anything. We just wanted to pet the cat."

"You're welcome to visit Princess anytime." Chase doesn't sound mad, and my already gooey heart melts a little more. "She's got a soft spot for you." There's a pause before he adds, "For the record, there are a lot of things you can do in life besides soccer."

"I hate soccer," Luke blurts. "What's the point of playing a game with a ball if you can't touch it with your hands?"

"I'm with you on that one," Chase agrees, and they both laugh.

"Hey there, kiddo," I say gently as I step inside the barn. "Your sister's working hard on her homework. You got yours done?"

He turns, squinting at me in the afternoon light spilling into the barn. "Mommy, when are you gonna let me ride Fancy?"

I blink. "I didn't know you wanted to ride Fancy. I thought that was your sister's thing."

He shrugs. "I could try."

"I thought you were scared." The words come out before I can stop them, and I instantly regret it.

He glances at Chase, then back at me. "I'm kind of scared. But I still want to try."

My chest tightens as the bravery of my seven-year-old son levels me.

Chase steps in smoothly. "When your mom says it's okay, you and your sister can start lessons."

Luke's face lights up, a soft, hopeful glow I don't often see in his gaze. It's enough to make my heart catch.

"Riding *lessons*?" Luke repeats, putting extra emphasis on the last word. "The boys in class asked if I was taking lessons from you."

Chase winks. "I'm not the one you've got to convince, kid."

My son spins and bolts toward me.

"Please, Mommy. I'll do all my homework and help you in the greenhouse without complaining. And clean my room."

"You already keep your room clean," I remind him.

"I'll keep it cleaner."

I tip his chin up, and his big eyes lock on mine. "If Chase is willing, riding lessons sound like a great idea."

"Thank you, thank you." He throws his arms around me, my crutches clattering to the ground as he hugs me tight. "I gotta tell Laurel."

He pulls back, his eyes shining, then glances toward Chase. "I'll clean the stalls, too."

Chase smiles. "That's a solid offer. A lot of cowboys started out mucking stalls."

"Cowboy," Luke whispers, like it's the most magical word in the world. "I'm gonna be a cowboy."

And just like that, he takes off, footsteps echoing as he disappears out of the barn.

"I think seven's a little early to lock in a career path," I say as I bend to retrieve the crutches.

"Don't worry," he tells me. "He'll grow out of it." He's absentmindedly stroking Fancy's neck, the horse leaning into his touch like she was made for it. How pathetic am I that a little part of me is jealous of a horse?

"Do you want riding lessons?" he asks, his voice low and full of suggestion.

I laugh. "I don't think that came out the way you wanted it to."

He grins. "It came out exactly the way I meant."

"Really? Because you're blushing."

"I am not." He takes off his hat and runs a hand through his hair. "Cowboys don't blush."

"The tips of your ears are pink."

"They're sunburned. From all my hard work in the field." He holds up a hand. "I even got a new callus today."

"Impressive," I murmur. "Thank you, Chase, for everything." When I'm close enough, I take his hand and press a kiss to his palm. "Even the riding lessons," I add with a wink.

He groans. "Just to be clear, that was beginner level. We've got a lot more ground to cover if you want to make it to advanced lessons."

I do, more than I'm willing to admit. Fancy snorts and shifts like she's not thrilled with me getting so close to her man. Honestly? I don't blame her.

"Want to give her a treat?" Chase gestures to a bag of carrots sitting on a hay bale nearby.

"Are you joking? You know she has teeth, right?"

He considers that, lips twitching. "Most animals do. Maybe all animals. I'd have to look that one up, but she's not going to bite you."

"She looks like she wants to bite me, knock me flat, then stomp me for getting too close to you."

"Fancy's not the jealous type." He scratches behind the horse's ears. "Except for that one buckle bunny up in Cody a couple of summers ago. But those days are long gone."

And stupid, sentimental me wants to believe that.

"Come on," he urges. "Give her a carrot. If Luke can be brave, his mom can, too. Kid needs a role model, right?"

The words hit harder than they should. I try not to let it show, but Chase sees right through me.

He gently cups my face in his rough hands. "It was a joke, Molly. You're a damn good role model."

I shake my head. "I haven't been. But I'm trying."

"The twins are lucky to have you."

I rest my hands over his and broach the subject that's been on my mind. "Do you want to talk about what happened with your mom today?"

"Not even a little," he says.

I feel the tension coil through him, but I can't help pushing a bit. I hate how he looked earlier, all that hurt simmering just under the surface.

"She didn't know it was you."

Chase exhales sharply and scrubs a hand down his face.

"It just about killed me that she thought I was the man who hurt her."

"That was the disease talking," I say gently. "Not your mom. I know you'd never hurt her. And somewhere deep down, she knows, too."

"He's still alive." His jaw tightens, and he takes a half step back. Like he's trying to put distance between himself and the memory. "He lives here in Skylark. He was at the rodeo when I got hurt, but only came to the hospital one time. Mainly to give me shit for getting hurt."

"He's a jerk," I say, moving closer to Fancy's stall.

"You don't know him."

"No. But I know you."

The way he looks at me, I can feel how much that means. Or maybe it's just how much I want it to mean.

"I know your horse loves you," I say with a soft smile.

That earns a real laugh, and God, it's good to hear it.

"Give me a carrot," I say, propping my crutches against the stall. "And if she bites me, I'm biting you."

He laughs again. "That sounds like a promise."

"Hardly," I mutter, but a shiver runs up my spine.

He takes a carrot from the bag, breaks it in two, then gently places the pieces in my hand.

I stretch my palm out, but as Fancy leans in, I flinch and yank back. The carrot drops to the dirt.

"Easy there," Chase says, his voice warm and calming.

He could be talking to the horse or me. Either way, the words seem to settle us both.

"Let's try again." He bends down, dusts off the carrots, and returns them to my hand.

"You could just give them to her, you know."

"Oh no," he says, grinning. But this time, he wraps his hand around mine and guides it forward.

Fancy's breath is warm on my skin. Her teeth graze my palm— more tickle than bite—and I let out the breath I didn't realize I was holding.

When I lean back and settle against Chase's chest, his solid weight grounds me in the moment.

"I did it," I whisper.

"One more. On your own."

He places another carrot in my hand, but doesn't move. He just lowers his arm, as if he trusts me now.

"You can pet her, too," he says. "Talk to her. She likes it."

I glance at the horse. "I don't know if you'll like me talking to you as much as you like Chase talking to you. I get that."

Fancy snuffles, then gently takes the carrot from me.

"Good girl," I murmur. "Thanks for not biting me. And thanks for being sweet to my kids. I don't want them to be afraid of life the way I've been. Maybe that starts with not being afraid of a really nice horse."

She finishes chewing, then turns away like we're done here. Chase is watching me with an expression so tender, it makes my heart ache.

"You didn't even flinch," he says softly.

"I kind of wanted to."

He moves closer, and the world narrows to just the two of us. His gaze drops to my mouth, and my breath catches.

I want to lean in, but step back instead.

As much as I want this, I can still hear Luke's voice in my head,

MICHELLE MAJOR

see the hurt in his eyes, and feel the weight of all the things we're still figuring out.

"I should check on the kids." My voice is barely above a whisper.

Chase doesn't move. He gives me a small nod like he understands.

"You know where to find me," he says.

I tuck the crutches under my arms and start toward the door, the scent of hay and cedar and something strangely hopeful trailing behind me.

I don't have to look back to know he's watching me go.

146

18

CHASE

"You don't need to help me," Molly says the following Saturday as I load the last tub of flowers into the back of the truck. "Iris said Jake's available for any heavy lifting I need—"

"I can handle your heavy lifting," I cut in, sharper than I mean. She's been trying to get rid of me all morning, and I'm damn tired of it.

"It's the weekend. I'm sure you've got better things to do than—"

I slam shut the tailgate. "Why are you still doing this?"

The morning sun filters through the cottonwoods lining the driveway, casting dappled shadows across the gravel. The air is warm under a cloudless sky, one of those perfect spring mornings in Colorado. It *should* be perfect, but all I can focus on is the way she keeps trying to push me away.

She stares at me like she doesn't understand the question. "Doing what?"

"Refusing to accept help. God rest Teddy's soul, but I'd like to knock his teeth out right now."

She hesitates, chewing on her bottom lip. "It's not his fault," she says quietly. "I was pretty much fully formed when I met him."

"I don't understand." I'm angrier than I have a right to be and frustrated that she insists on downplaying her worth at every turn. She's strong and capable and deserving of every good thing this world has to offer.

"When you grow up feeling like the people who were supposed to love you are only there out of duty, like you're a burden instead of a blessing, that feeling gets into your bones."

There's a hollowness in her voice that burrows into my chest. I want so badly for her to see herself the way I do. "It's time for a change, Molly."

"I'm trying," she says, eyes flashing. "But every time I do, something gets in my way." She lifts a finger, pointing straight at me. "*Someone* gets in my way."

"I'm helping you," I argue. "Heavy lifting and..." I take a step closer. "Dusting off the cobwebs. Whatever you need."

She rolls her eyes. "I'm not a charity case."

"I know that, but—"

"If you really want to help me..." Molly says, her voice low. "Back out of the deal with my mother-in-law."

I freeze. It doesn't sound like a challenge, more like a plea she hadn't meant to let slip.

"Fine," I say before I can think better of it.

Her eyes flick to mine. "Just like that?"

"Just like that." I shrug, not wanting her to see the weight behind it. The way I'm already half gone for her and her kids. How the three of them are quickly becoming the family I never knew I was looking for.

"Nothing's finalized," I remind her. "Linda knows I'm interested. That's all. Have you talked to her about your plan?"

Molly looks out toward the gentle slope of the pine forest that borders the property. "Not yet."

"Why not?"

"This is her dream trip. The first thing I've seen her truly excited about since Teddy died," she says. "I don't want to mess it up. Besides, I need to know I can afford it first. That it isn't just a fantasy."

"It's not a fantasy."

"If she agrees..." Her gaze crashes into mine again, and her expression looks both defiant and vulnerable. The combination steals my breath. "It means you don't get what you want."

"But if I don't step back, *you* don't get what you want. So here we are."

It's quiet for a second. The air between us is charged, but there's something more underneath. A thread of connection I still can't explain, but also won't try to deny.

"I never wanted this to be a competition," I tell her. "Not with you."

"It's kind of a mess," she says.

"I like making a mess with you."

She laughs softly, and the tension between us eases.

"If you talk to Linda and she agrees to sell it to you, I'll step aside. No hesitation."

She looks like she wants to argue, but I lift a hand.

"I'm not saying that because I don't want the land, but I'll keep looking if I have to. You've got kids and a dream. If you can make this happen, you should. I won't stand in your way."

She swallows, her eyes shining just a little. "Do you mean that?"

"I do."

"What if I can't make it work?"

"Then I buy it," I say gently.

Her brows knit together. "I'm going to do it."

"I believe you." There's still so much unspoken between us, but right now we're just two people trying to figure out how to want the best for each other without losing what we want for ourselves.

"What's your backup plan?"

"I'll get hired on at a ranch somewhere," I say like it's no big deal. "Or go back on the circuit for a year or two until I figure things out."

"I thought the doctors said you shouldn't ride again."

Christ, I regret mentioning that to her in an unguarded middle-of-the-night moment when the darkness made everything feel safe.

"It was a suggestion."

"It's too dangerous," she whispers.

No more dangerous than staying here and falling harder every damn day for a woman I have no right to claim.

"I'll figure it out."

She frowns like she wants to argue again, then asks, "You're truly willing to walk away?"

I want to tell her the truth. That I can't stop thinking about her. That every part of me wants her to be happy. Sometimes I think I'd burn down everything I've built if it means she gets to keep what matters most to her.

"It's what Teddy would have wanted."

The light in her eyes dims. The answer was the safest, and clearly the wrong one.

She crosses her arms over her chest, and I try not to notice how the soft cotton of her T-shirt pulls across her gorgeous chest. Or the strand of bright copper hair that's escaped her ponytail to frame her face. She's the most beautiful thing I've ever seen, even when frustrated and guarded. It takes everything I have not to reach for her.

"Is that why you had sex with me?"

The question knocks the wind out of my lungs. "Are you fucking joking?"

"Do I look like I'm joking?"

"Of course it wasn't about Teddy. Is that why *you* slept with me? To scratch some twisted itch for your late husband's best friend?"

I see the blush spread across her neck and color her cheeks, but she tilts her chin and holds my gaze. "Not my kind of kink."

"Where the hell is this coming from, Molly?"

Uncertainty flashes in her green eyes. "Nothing has happened since last weekend. Why are you keeping your distance?"

I keep my jaw from hitting the ground, but just barely. "I'm trying to respect you. I don't want you to think I expect to end up in your bed every time we're alone."

She inclines her head like she's never actually considered that as an option. "Do you want to be in my bed again?"

"Sweetheart, is the Pope Catholic?"

She breathes out a laughs. "Is papal kink *your* thing?"

I step toward her with a growl. "You're my thing." God help us both how much I want her. I want to kiss the laugh off her lips, to feel her come apart in my arms again. To wake up every morning with her warm body pressed against mine.

She glances toward the house. "The kids will be coming out any moment," she whispers, but she's already leaning closer. "I can't let them see me with you."

Another growl rises up in my throat, but I tamp it down. "I get it." She wants me, but she's smart. Smart enough to keep what's happening between us a secret, which is fine with me.

I *almost* believe that lie. I do want more, but I'll take what she's willing to give.

"Tonight," I tell her.

"I'm not sure I can arrange sleepovers for the kids."

"Then we'll be quiet."

I see her draw in a shaky breath. "After last time, I don't know if I *can* be quiet."

"Call it a challenge." I lean in closer. "You up for it?"

She blinks, eyes softening. "Yes."

I almost kiss her right then and there. But this isn't permanent, and she's the one setting the terms.

"Mom," Laurel calls as the screen door slams. "Can we have money for the crepe stand?"

Molly jerks back as Laurel and Luke barrel toward us. "You bet."

"Are you sure about staying for the market?" she asks me as the kids pile into the old truck.

"You're not getting rid of me that easy."

"Not yet, anyway," she whispers. And just like that, we're both reminded this has an expiration date.

The weight of those words settles between us as we finish loading the tubs of flowers then head toward town and the first weekend market of the spring season. The kids are talking a mile a minute, which is a nice distraction, but I won't lie, part of me wants to skip the farmers market altogether. Since the accident, I've kept my distance from crowded town events. It's the easiest way to avoid questions I don't want to answer.

Maybe it's time to stop hiding. Being with Molly and the twins, their unbridled excitement over everything from the perfect parking spot to whether Mrs. Henderson will have her famous strawberry jam—it's infectious. The back of the truck is loaded with Molly's arrangements: cheerful daffodils and tulips, fragrant purple hyacinths, and delicate branches of flowering cherry she must have coaxed from somewhere. The sweet, hopeful scent of spring fills the cab, and for the first time in months, I feel like I'm part of something that adds beauty to the world instead of just taking up space in it.

"Sadie and Piper are volunteering at the Humane Society booth," Luke says as we pull into one of the vendor parking spaces. "Can I go help with the animals?"

"Sure," Molly says. "Laurel can go with you."

"I want to hang out with my friends," Laurel says quickly.

Molly looks like she's holding back a frown. "Sure. Luke, maybe you should see if any of your friends are here before you—"

"I want to help with the animals," he insists.

"Before either of you run off," I tell the kids. "How about you help your mom and me unload the flowers and set up the booth?"

They two kids stare at me like I just asked them to donate a kidney.

"Mom doesn't want our help," Laurel says matter-of-factly.

I glance at Molly.

"That's not true, sweetie," she says quickly.

"Last year you told us not to hang around your booth," Luke adds.

"I..." She shakes her head. "I didn't want you to feel obligated."

"What does oblivated mean?" Luke asks.

Molly ruffles his hair. "It means feeling like you have to help me because I'm your mom."

"They *do* have to help you because you're their mom," I chime in.

"We *want* to help you," Laurel says, like it's the most obvious thing in the world. "Because you're our mom."

"Not cuz we're oblijaded," Luke adds.

Molly blinks like it's a thought she's never quite let herself believe. And I get it. Because when you feel like a burden in your soul, it's hard to turn that off even with the people closest to you. "Of course I'd love your help, especially now." She rests a hand on Laurel's shoulder, clearly overwhelmed but smiling. "But not just because of my ankle. I always want you involved."

Both kids nod. "We'll be careful," Luke says, already bouncing on his toes. "We won't mess anything up."

"I have total faith in both of you." Molly's expression softens as if she realizes she may have kept her kids at arm's length for all the wrong reasons.

"Okay then, it's settled," I say when she gives me a teary-eyed smile that does funny things to my insides as we step out of the truck. "Do you guys know where your mom's booth is?"

"Same place as last summer?" Laurel asks.

Molly nods. "End of the second row."

"Luke, think you can carry this bucket of tulips? It's heavy."

"I'm strong," he says. "Real strong."

"I know you are." I pass it to him, then hand Laurel a box of dried flower bundles. "Drop those off and come back for the next load. We'll get everything set up, and then you can roam the market."

"Or help me sell flowers," Molly adds, earning wide grins from her son and daughter.

"I bet I can sell more than you," Laurel tells Luke as they walk away.

"Well, I bet I can wrap flowers faster than you can," he shoots back.

Molly watches them go, shaking her head. "Have you ever thought you were doing something right only to find out you've been making big, fat mistakes all along?"

I load her cash box, business cards, and spools of twine into the basket on her scooter, then grab two more buckets of tulips before looking at her with a smirk. "I made a career out of getting on the backs of angry bulls. Every decision I made for about a decade was a calculated risk, if not a flat-out awful idea."

She rolls her eyes. "When my mom died and I moved in with my grandparents, it was made very clear that I wasn't wanted. They'd already raised their kid and weren't looking to do it again. So I became useful. I helped on the farm and stayed out of the way. Never had much of a social life, but I had a roof over my head and a hot meal every night. When I started this flower business, I didn't want my kids to feel obligated to carry the load just because I couldn't."

"I don't think you're in danger of turning them into indentured servants," I tell her. "They want to help. You're not forcing anything. Someday soon, they'll be way too cool to be seen selling flowers with their mom. Take the labor while it's still freely given."

She gives me a sidelong glance. "Like yours?"

"I'm an indentured servant."

"Stop pretending to be an asshole when we both know you're not."

"Wow." I clasp a hand to my chest. "As compliments go, that was weirdly touching."

"High praise indeed." She shakes her head, but there's a brightness in her eyes that makes them shine like emeralds. "Let's sell some flowers."

She looks at me from the corner of her eye, like she's waiting for the moment I'll change my mind. Like she's still bracing for the part where wanting the same thing she does turns us into enemies.

I don't say what I'm thinking—that I want her dream to come true more than I want my own. I'm not there yet. Or maybe I am, but I know she isn't ready for that kind of risk. Not with someone like me. Someone who's spent years keeping people at arm's length because getting close means they can get hurt when the darkness I inherited from my old man decides to surface, like it has before. She's already been through enough, and her kids don't deserve a man who is bound to leave wreckage in his wake.

So I just carry the buckets and walk beside her, hoping she knows I'm not going anywhere.

Not yet, anyway.

19

MOLLY

I STILL DON'T UNDERSTAND why Chase is so dedicated to helping me. Maybe I'm a fool for trusting him. But my heart, not to mention my body, refuses to believe that.

He remains close while the kids flit about the market, making sure I stay off my feet while he gathers blooms and wraps bouquets. The three hours go by in the blink of an eye, and during that time, more than a few people stop by the booth to talk to him. They all ask about his career or the latest rodeo, inevitably circling back to the same question: when is he getting back in the proverbial saddle?

I can see how much he hates those conversations. He tries to steer them back to me and the flowers, but it's not easy.

An older man with a bushy gray mustache and a weathered ball cap shading his leathery face strolls up to the booth and plants himself right in front of Chase.

"Calhoun, what the hell are you doing here?" He shakes his head and adjusts the hat. "Why is one of the best damn bull riders in the country slingin' daisies?"

Chase gives a tight smile. "Helping out a friend, Uncle Walt."

Walt—as he quickly informs me—is not an actual uncle, but

an "honorary" one, whatever that means. My hands curl into fists at my sides as he fires off questions like he's been saving them for months. Chase is clearly uncomfortable. He keeps his tone polite, but his answers are short, and his eyes flick to mine more than once, like he's hoping for an escape.

The mother bear instinct that normally only shows up when someone messes with my kids roars to life. For this man, who has been helping me without asking for anything in return.

I stand and use the scooter to move a few steps forward, clearing my throat until the older man turns to me, thick brows furrowed like he can't understand what I could have to add to the conversation.

"Walt," I say, voice calm but firm, "if you're not planning on buying any flowers, it might be time to move on. I'm running a business here, not hosting an honorary family reunion."

He blinks at me. "Well now, I didn't mean—"

"Of course not," I cut in gently. "But I also need Chase to be able to give his attention to our paying customers."

Walt rubs his thumb and forefinger across his mustache and gestures toward a bouquet of wildflowers like it's a peace offering. "Uh...these'll look nice on the table. For my wife."

"Lovely choice." I pluck them from the bucket and then wrap them in brown paper with more enthusiasm than necessary. I see Chase's lips twitch as he watches the interaction.

Buying the bouquet gives Walt an excuse to linger, but fate throws me a bone in the form of Sadie and Ian. Nobody soaks up attention better than a former NFL star with a movie-star smile. I lock eyes with Sadie then tip my chin toward Uncle Walt, shooting her a silent plea for help.

Without missing a beat, she nudges Ian, who steps forward and claps Walt on the shoulder. "Hey there, buddy."

Walt turns, delighted to have the attention of Skylark's resident football legend. They talk about the upcoming season, and Ian's younger brother, Felix, also a football legend, being traded to

Denver. I don't really follow professional sports, but I do know that people around here are delighted to have both Barlowe brothers calling Colorado home. A few minutes later, Ian steers Walt down the aisle and away from my booth.

I let out a slow breath and subtly shift to block Sadie's view of Chase, who's now helping another customer. He glances toward me for a moment, and I notice how his shoulders relax as the tension releases from his body.

It's not like I needed to protect him. Chase is more than capable of handling himself. But there was something about seeing him cornered that tugged at a place deep in my chest.

Sadie watches the two of us with quiet curiosity, but doesn't comment. She's known me long enough to read between the lines, and seems willing to wait until I'm ready to spill.

Still, I find myself avoiding her gaze. "So," I say, trying to sound casual, "do you, um...have plans tonight?"

She quirks a brow. "Why? Are you thinking of sending the twins my way?"

"I haven't told them yet, but I was hoping you'd say yes to a sleep over." Chase is now talking to a middle-aged couple who've approached the booth. "I don't want to take advantage of you guys."

"You never take advantage, and we love having Luke and Laurel. Riva's with her mom in Aspen this weekend. Ian always misses her, even when it's just a couple of days, so they'll be a welcome distraction. They can come home with us after the market. We'll stop by the store, grab the ingredients to make pizza and you can bring PJs and stuff over later."

"You're the best, Sads." I reach over the table to hug my friend as something soft unfurls in my chest. This town and the people in it who have become my family are why I can't imagine leaving Skylark. "I'm surprised Ian hasn't convinced you to pop out a whole football squad."

Her smile dims slightly. "We have plans," she says quietly. "They're just not working out yet."

"Oh, honey." I wrap my hand around hers. "That was a dumb thing for me to say. I'm so sorry. I didn't know."

"It's okay. We haven't shared it with anyone."

"It's going to happen," I say, knowing full well I have no business making that promise. But I can't help it.

She turns her hand in mine and squeezes. "I think so, too. Until it does, I love being a dog mom and honorary aunt."

"You're the best." I pause and then add, "I truly believe, Sadie. With all my heart."

Her eyes glisten just a bit. "Thanks, Mols. It feels like you and Chase have things under control here, so I'm going to head back over to the Humane Society booth."

"I'm sure Luke is still there with Piper."

"He's got a way with animals," Sadie tells me, and I know there's no greater compliment from her.

"Thanks again for tonight."

"Anytime." Sadie slips away just as I turn to face two new customers, a woman who looks a few years older than me and her mother.

The daughter's gaze snaps to Chase, which shouldn't surprise me. I'm used to women needing a moment to process him—that thick hair, the Clint Eastwood jawline, and the cowboy swagger that's as natural to him as breathing.

"Chase," the woman breathes, like she actually knows him.

His eyes go wide as he glances up, and it looks like he wants to bolt. "Hey, Mariah."

"Chase Calhoun, where have you been hiding?" her mother exclaims.

"Hello, Mrs. Crawford."

"Gone from taming bulls to selling flowers, huh?" Mrs. Crawford teases. There's something about the exchange that I don't understand. The words are straightforward but the sudden tension pulsing in the air is anything but.

Chase gestures toward me. "Have you met Molly McAllister?"

Both women pause for a beat.

"Teddy's widow," the mom says, her voice dipping slightly.

"Hi, Molly." Mariah gives me an almost apologetic smile. "Teddy, Chase, and I went to high school together."

"Ran wild together is more like it," her mom adds. "I thought my baby and Chase were gonna end up hitched right after graduation. They were—"

"That was a long time ago, Mom," Mariah cuts in, a blush creeping up her cheeks.

If Chase seemed uncomfortable before, now he looks like he'd gladly disappear completely. Mariah seems just as flustered. Meanwhile, a completely oblivious Mrs. Crawford beams like she's ready to mail out engagement announcements.

"Chase is doing a favor for my mother-in-law," I say evenly, keeping my tone light and trying not to notice how his shoulders tense at the explanation. "He's been kind enough to pitch in with the flower business while I'm recovering from a sprained ankle."

"He always was a good boy, this one," Mrs. Crawford says with a wink. "The kind you don't want to let slip away."

Subtle as a sledgehammer, that one.

"Mariah is back in Skylark, too," she tells Chase. "Living with me. You'll have to come for dinner to catch up." She pats her daughter's arm. "Just like old times."

"I'm just living with Mom temporarily," Mariah offers quickly. "I moved back last month after my divorce was finalized."

"I'm sorry to hear that," I say automatically, though the words feel small based on the devastation in her eyes.

"It's for the best," she assures me, and why does it feel like we're both avoiding making eye contact with Chase?

"Were you looking for anything specific?" I manage to keep my tone warm, even as something tight coils in my chest.

Mariah is everything I'm not. She's petite and classically beautiful with shiny blonde hair and bright blue eyes—the kind of girl whose homecoming queen crown is probably still sitting on the dresser in her childhood bedroom.

"You know," Mrs. Crawford says, eyeing the blooms, "these are a lot more expensive than the bouquets at the grocery store off the highway."

"Mom," Mariah mutters.

"The market's almost over," I say, keeping my smile in place. "Why don't you pick your favorite and consider it an early Mother's Day gift from Meadow Blooms."

"You don't have to do that," Mariah says, shaking her head.

"I want to." I catch her eye and nod. Her mother's obvious re-matchmaking seems to be making Mariah almost as uncomfortable as Chase.

Mrs. Crawford takes her sweet time, but finally settles on a simple bunch of daffodils.

"These will look lovely on the dining room table." She focuses her calculating gaze on Chase. "I expect you to come by for dinner this week."

"I appreciate the offer," he replies, and I don't think she notices the noncommittal answer. "Good to see you again, Mariah," he adds with a tight smile.

"You too, Chase." Mariah loops her arm through her mother's and hustles her away before any more awkwardness can escape Mrs. Crawford's mouth.

"We should pack up," I say, already moving to consolidate the leftover flowers into one bucket. "We've sold out of almost everything. Who knew cowboys were so good at selling flowers?"

Chase steps closer, his presence warm at my back. "You should sit down again. Let me pack up. You've done more than enough today."

"I need to stand. My other leg was starting to cramp." I shoot him a crooked smile. "Avah gets regular massages. I should probably get on that train one of these days."

"I could do that," he says, voice low and smooth. "If you want."

The air under the white canopy covering us turns hot enough to make me dizzy, and every rational thought in my head turns to vapor as I realize I'd happily let this man do just about anything.

Trying to play it cool, I focus on the flowers, even as my fingers tremble. "Sooo...the twins are having a sleepover tonight at Sadie's."

He nudges me with his elbow. "I heard. Thought maybe you were planning another girls' night out. Maybe you switch from axes to nunchucks?"

I laugh even as my cheeks heat. "I was actually hoping for a you-and-me night in." Where did that husky note in my voice come from? "I mean..." I pretend to shrug. "Unless you have other plans."

"Not even close," he says roughly. "Nothing in this world could keep me from you tonight, Molly."

Before I can respond, another couple approaches the booth and buys the last three bouquets. I give them a discount they didn't ask for, mostly because my mind is spinning. Because I know exactly what inviting Chase into my bed means. The pleasure and the push and pull between us. The way he makes me lose control. The way I let him.

But it's not just about tonight. If this keeps happening, it won't just be my bed he ends up in. He'll be a part of my heart, too.

I don't know how to stop that. And I'm not even sure I want to anymore.

"Mommy!" Luke's excited voice pulls me out of my spiraling thoughts. "Ian bought me a puppy!"

"It's a stuffed animal," Ian clarifies immediately. "Luke, you're going to get me in trouble."

Luke grins, clutching a soft brown-and-white plush dog to his chest.

"We could get a real one," he says, his tone hopeful.

"You know the answer to that," I remind him gently.

My mother-in-law has lived on a farm for most of her life, but claims to be allergic to dogs. I've often wondered if Linda gave us that excuse because she didn't want one more thing to care for. But I want to adopt a dog, maybe two. I want the whole package of childhood happiness for my kids–as much as I can give them.

"Hey, Ian," Luke says, bouncing on the balls of his feet, "Chase is gonna teach me how to ride a horse."

Ian's grin spreads wide. "That's what I've heard at least a dozen times."

Chase chuckles, and I catch a hint of pride in his expression. Like Luke's excitement means a lot to him.

And I get it. Because it means the world to me.

"Chase is great with horses," I blurt. My kids, my friends, and Chase all turn to stare at me because...duh...hello, Captain Obvious.

He shrugs and...whoa...adorable blush on the cowboy. "I've had a bit of experience."

Sadie elbows me. "You're also good with flowers."

"Well, Chase has been a huge help with that too."

The kind of help I didn't know I needed and definitely didn't want, but I appreciate it more than I can say.

Laurel grabs mine and Sadie's hands, swinging our arms. "Can Piper come to Sadie's for manicures?"

I smile. "I'm sure Piper has plans."

"She doesn't," Sadie replies, wrinkling her nose. "Since she's been back, she's barely left the house. Besides her hospital shifts and walking Max, she's gone full hermit. It's like she..."

My friend trails off, something flickering behind her eyes that I can't quite name. She lets it pass with a slight shake of her head. "I'm sure she'd be thrilled with a pizza and spa night."

I glance down at my hands, dirt caked beneath my fingernails from this morning's market prep. "I could probably use a manicure myself."

"We could pick you up for dinner," Sadie offers. "A little nail polish and some pizza could be exactly what the doctor ordered."

"Tempting," I say with a grin. "But I've got paperwork."

"Paperwork," she repeats, drawing out the word like it's code for something scandalous. "Right. Your *very important paperwork.*"

"I *do* run a business, you know." I try to keep my tone serious but feel my cheeks heat. "This ankle's slowed me down way too much already."

"Uh-huh." She gives me a look like she can see right through me. "I'm sure you'll enjoy all that paperwork."

I narrow my eyes at her. "Depends on who's helping me file it."

She lets out a laugh, nudging me with her elbow. "You're terrible."

"I'm aware."

"Grownups are weird," Laurel says, eyeing us suspiciously. "Who wants to do paperwork on a Saturday night?"

"Your mom, apparently." Sadie's eyes are downright twinkling now. "I bet she's going to have a paperwork adventure."

My cheeks are flaming. "Something like that." I shoot her a warning look.

Her grin widens. "Do you need help taking this stuff back to the truck?"

I start to tell her that Chase and I can handle it, but remember what he said about accepting help.

"Yes, please," I say instead. "If we all grab something, we can probably get it done in one trip."

"Luke, we're packing up," Laurel calls to her brother. "You gotta help."

Luke is busy flying his stuffed animal around the booth like it

164

has wings, but at his sister's command, he moves to stand next to Chase, watching him stack the empty flower buckets. Normally, he clings to Ian's side whenever the ex-quarterback is around, so the shift catches my attention.

"What are you naming him?" Chase asks, crouching down to Luke's level to admire the puppy.

My son takes stuffed animal naming seriously, so there's a long pause before he answers. Chase waits, his attention fully focused on the boy like he's got all day and there's nowhere in the world he'd rather be.

"Wow," Sadie murmurs at my side. "That's quite a connection."

"Yeah," I agree, my skin tingling like I've brushed up against something electric. At the same time, my stomach seems to be tying itself in knots, because I can feel the kids falling for Chase just as fast and hard as I am.

"Barkley," Luke says softly, cradling his new stuffed dog like it's fragile. He looks up at Chase, almost as if he's bracing for a laugh or a joke at his expense.

"That's a cool name," Chase says without hesitation. "Nice to meet you, Barkley." He gives the stuffed dog a gentle pat on the head, then stands and flashes me a smile as sweet as the first lick of an ice cream cone on a hot summer day.

"Mommy, his name is Barkley!" Luke shouts proudly.

"Barkley's a great name," I agree, then mouth a silent "thank you" to Chase.

Despite the casual cruelty Laurel described, I know my late husband loved our son. But the way Chase shows up in the quiet moments is a version of caring Luke needed more than I realized.

We finish packing up and head to the truck, stopping to talk with a few other vendors along the way. When it's time to say goodbye, I lean down to kiss and hug both kids, but what surprises me most is when *they* each turn to hug Chase, too.

Laurel wraps her arms around him like it's normal. Luke holds up the stuffed dog and insists Chase kiss it goodbye, which he does without hesitation.

Sadie gives me a quick hug, whispering, "That was firefighter-with-a-kitten-calendar hot."

She's right. Is there anything sexier to a single mom than watching a man show your kids kindness, especially when he doesn't owe them a thing? I glance over and catch the flush in Chase's cheeks, the pink at the tips of his ears.

I'm basically a breathing pile of goo right now. A giant mix of lust, longing, and something far deeper that I'm not ready to name.

I try to calm my nerves *and* my hormones as I wave goodbye and watch the kids walk off with Sadie and Ian.

"I guess it's just you and me," I say, turning back to Chase.

Only, it's not just the two of us.

He's staring at a man standing a few feet away, and all the excitement and good feelings of the farmers market vanish in an instant.

The air is so cold and crackling with tension, it's like a blizzard and an electrical storm had a baby. The result is a terrifying mix of absolutely nothing good.

20

MOLLY

"Is everything okay?" I ask, starting to scoot forward, but Chase holds up a hand with his palm flat like a shield, as if he's protecting me from a threat I don't recognize.

"It's fine. Get in the truck, Molly. I'll be there in a minute."

"Nothing about my son turning pussy is fine with me," the man growls, and I feel the words like a slap to the face.

Shock ripples through me, not just from the word, but the venom behind it.

This is Malcolm Calhoun? Chase's father?

Now that I'm really looking, I can see the resemblance. They have the same strong jaw and broad shoulders. But while Chase's features capture his rugged beauty, his father's are weathered and cruel. His eyes are bloodshot and glassy, with ruddy skin and spider veins around his nose and cheeks.

He carries himself like a man who's been bitter for so long, he doesn't remember what it feels like not to be.

Chase's hand curls into a fist at his side. I swear I can hear his knuckles crack from the tension.

Is this some kind of twisted father-son dynamic I should stay out of? I can't just turn away like none of this is happening.

"I don't think that language is necessary," I say, my voice steadier than I expect.

Chase's father's eyes drag slowly up to meet mine, his glare as sharp as broken glass. "Who the hell are you?"

Before I can answer, Chase steps forward like a human shield, full-on protector mode. "She's none of your business, old man. Go home."

His father snorts, arms crossing over his chest. "Last time I checked, you don't tell me what to do, boy."

Chase doesn't move as his dad inches closer, but I can tell he's wound as tight as a wire stretched to the point where it could snap at any moment.

I'm frozen, gripping the scooter's handlebars so hard my knuckles have gone white. The tension between them feels charged and unpredictable. Whatever this is, it's been building for a long time.

Chase glances over his shoulder at me, his eyes as wild as the sea in the middle of a storm, his voice low and grave. "Molly, please get in the truck."

"I think I'll wait here," I say quietly, refusing to leave him alone.

"Molly." Malcolm Calhoun repeats my name, his tone foul like stale smoke. "You're Teddy's widow." His gaze returns to Chase. "Hiding behind the skirt of your best friend's wife?"

"Dad, go away. I'm not doing this with you here."

"You fucking her, too? Getting back at Teddy for—"

"Teddy's dead," Chase says, his voice flat, but I can hear the heat in his words. "And my life is none of your business."

"What he and Mariah did to you..." Malcolm spits on the ground.

I blink as my mind spins back to those awkward moments between Chase, his high school girlfriend, and her mother who clearly wants them to rekindle what they had before. The comment about how they were supposed to ride off into the post-high school graduation sunset together. But that didn't happen. And now I know why.

"Chase is doing a favor for my mother-in-law," I offer, as if anything can diffuse the tension pulsing between them.

"Oh yeah, Linda always was a big fan of my son." Malcolm sneers. "Like she had the damn market cornered on being a good parent. When Teddy didn't even know his father because it could've been one of a dozen different—"

"Shut the fuck up," Chase snaps as his arm draws back.

"Don't," I whisper, and he turns to meet my gaze again. There's so much emotion swirling in his eyes. Mostly rage and resentment, but also fear—not of his dad, but for me. He thinks he needs to protect me.

I want to tell him I'm not afraid of Malcolm Calhoun, but I also understand that Chase isn't going to let his father disrespect me. Not now or ever.

"Please get in the truck, Molly."

"Okay," I agree. Only because I'm afraid of what will happen if this continues to escalate.

"You think you're better than me?" Malcolm snarls as I slowly maneuver around the side of the truck. "I can see that woman is afraid of you."

"You don't know anything about her *or* me," Chase seethes. "Get out of here, Dad."

"There's nothing wrong with that, son. It's the way I raised you. Some women need a firm hand. Your mother—"

"Keep her name out of your mouth."

I place the scooter in the back seat and climb into the passenger side, but don't let the door shut completely. I won't leave Chase alone, not with his father standing there spewing verbal poison.

"Your sister put me on the restricted list for visiting. She's my goddamn wife."

"Your *ex*-wife."

"I never agreed to a divorce."

169

"Not much of a choice from jail."

"I want to see her, and you need to help me."

"I don't need to do a goddamn thing for you." Chase's voice drops to a dangerous growl, low and gravelly with barely contained fury. "There's nothing for you in Skylark anymore."

"You think *you've* got a chance at a life here? If you can't get back on a bull—"

"You don't need to worry about me." Chase huffs out a humorless laugh.

"I *know* what's going on, Chase."

"Goodbye, Dad. Don't try to contact me or Mom or Ada."

"It's not your fucking leg or too many concussions," Malcolm continues. "You're scared."

In the rearview mirror, I watch Chase go completely rigid, his jaw clenching so hard I can see the muscle tic beneath his skin. "Shut. Up."

His father ignores the command. "I know weakness when I see it. It's your mother's fault, you know. She coddled you and your sister. If it were up to me—"

"If it had been up to you," Chase cuts in, "I'm not sure I would have survived childhood."

"Let me tune my tiny violin," Malcolm mutters. "You need to man up, Chase. Get back in the damn ring. Like I said, I didn't raise you to be a pussy."

Tension rolls off Chase in waves as he squares off with his father. "Stop using that word."

"You going to stop me, boy? Let's see what you got. I learned some tricks in the joint, and you're not as tough and angry as you used to be."

"I wouldn't be too sure."

Chase says something else under his breath that I can't hear then shakes his head. Malcolm answers with an angry cackle that sends shivers through me.

"That's right, run away. You can't even find your own woman. Had to poach off a dead man."

There's a scuffling noise, and I turn to see Chase dragging his dad away from the truck by the collar of his shirt. I cringe as he shoves Malcolm back, the old man stumbling and then landing on his ass in the gravel parking lot.

"Stay down where you belong." Chase's tone is as searing as the blue flame at the center of a fire.

Then he's heading back to the truck.

I close the passenger door and quickly fasten my seatbelt. He gets in, breathing hard like he's just run five miles at full speed. He turns the key in the ignition and backs out of the parking space. Gravel spins up from the tires as he peels out, and in the side mirror, I see Malcolm waving his fist and still shouting insults as we pull away.

The air in the truck is thick and heavy with the weight of what just happened.

"You are nothing like your father," I tell him after a moment.

"You don't know me well enough to say that." His voice is so hollow, it's like there's a canyon between us.

I want to reach out to him. To put my hand on his arm and offer him whatever comfort I can. But I know that's not what he wants, even if it might be what he needs.

Instead, I stay quiet. I don't know where I stand or what we are to each other, but I do know he means more to me than I'll admit to either of us. Still, I let that silent chasm widen. By the time we pull down the long driveway to the house that I want to be mine—the house that might be his if I can't make it work—we might as well be in different time zones.

"Do you want to come in?" I ask quietly.

"I'm not good company right now."

"I don't need good company," I say with a smile that feels forced. "But maybe you need—"

"No."

The word feels like a slap.

"I'm sorry," he adds quickly. "I just..."

"I get it," I say, even though I don't. I mean, I do. He's upset, and I'm not the person he wants to go to for solace. It's stupid to let my feelings get hurt by that. To think that it has something to do with some sort of lack in me.

"I can get the scooter," he says, unfastening his seatbelt.

"I'll grab it. If you can just leave the containers next to the greenhouse, I'll put them away in a bit."

"I can—"

The late afternoon sun casts long shadows across the flower fields, and my chest aches watching him struggle with whatever's churning inside him.

"I'm okay, Chase. Do whatever you need to do to get yourself right again. But know that you're not wrong for what you're feeling."

"I feel like it would be easier if my father were dead," he says, like he's trying to shock me.

"Plenty of people—both kids and adults—have had that thought about a parent on more than one occasion."

"Do you ever *not* see the good in someone?" he asks softly.

"I can't find much good in your father."

"You aren't wrong." He's quiet for a moment, his hands tight on the steering wheel. "I never told you why I owe Linda."

I wait, heart hammering in my chest. I've been wanting him to tell me, but not like this, when he's so raw and hurting.

"It was the summer after high school graduation. I was partying my ass off every night, trying to forget that a few weeks earlier I'd found my best friend and my girlfriend fucking in the back of his pickup. I was a mess, and I walked into the house to discover Dad beating on my mom—again. Things had gotten better between them, or so my sister and I thought. Turns out, Mom had just gotten better at hiding it. Something in me snapped. Too many years of living in fear or maybe I needed an outlet for the anger and hurt I wouldn't let myself feel over Teddy and Mariah. Either way, I nearly put my father in the hospital."

His voice is flat, like he's reading from a police report. "The cops arrested me, and while I was sitting in that cell, he sold my horse. Orion was the only thing I had that mattered and my shot at a future bigger than my past."

My throat tightens. "Chase—"

"Linda bailed me out. She and Teddy bought Orion back and kept him hidden at the farm until I could get my rodeo permit. They helped me buy a trailer and gave me enough money to leave town. I started with roping events before I moved to bull riding, and I couldn't have done any of it without them." He finally turns to look at me. "That's the debt I owe. That's why I'm here."

The weight of it settles between us as all the pieces finally click into place.

"I'm glad they helped you." I have to look away before the ache in my chest shows on my face. I want to reach for him, to tell him I understand why he made the choices he did. That he isn't alone. But understanding doesn't change anything between us. "Thanks for your help today. And for telling me."

He nods but keeps his gaze on the steering wheel like it's a Magic 8 Ball. I wish it could give me some answers.

I climb out of the truck, shut the passenger door, and take out the scooter. I can't wait until I get this stupid boot off my foot, so I can get rid of the ramp and every reminder of Chase Calhoun's kindness. I'll earn the money to buy this farm outright and move on—for me and my kids.

Then maybe I'll stop aching for things I can't have.

Because Chase is a man tied to a past that won't let him go, and I need to stay focused on the future. Sure, he makes me feel seen and safe and alive in ways I never expected. But he also makes me hope, and hope is dangerous when the man you're falling for is only here because he owes your dead husband.

I can't afford more heartbreak, and Chase isn't the man for me, no matter how much I want him to be.

21

CHASE

I<small>T TAKES</small> a two-hour trail ride in the national forest surrounding the farm before I come close to working through the feelings churning in my gut.

I should have gone to see my father once I decided to retire. I should have known he wouldn't let the past rest without saying his piece, no matter how much I didn't want to hear it.

I spend more time than usual brushing down Fancy after the ride. She gives me some wicked side-eye over her shoulder as I run the slicker down her flank, then huffs a soft breath like she's calling me out on my bullshit. Maybe she knows I'm thinking about Molly and the shock in her gentle eyes when Dad and I did our usual thing.

"It's better that I'm giving her space," I tell the animal. "I don't want to be like him, but he's part of me, and I can't ever take the chance of repeating his mistakes with a woman. Especially not Molly."

I have a feeling my horse knows how much I want to go to Molly. To make sure she understands that the version of me she saw today isn't who I want to be. But the problem is, it might be exactly who I am deep down.

"Did anyone ever tell you that you make a good therapist?" I ask, scratching Fancy between the ears just the way she likes. She leans into my touch, and for a moment, I wish things could always be this easy. But nothing is simple or straightforward when my father is involved.

I give the horse some hay and then head to my trailer. I'm sweaty and sore and need a hot shower like my next breath, but I can't imagine Molly will want me turning up on her doorstep after how I shut her out. There's a good chance somebody saw me squaring off with Dad in town, and both Ray and my sister have heard about it by now, which also makes me not want to reach out to either of them.

"Hey, Princess," I say as I lower myself onto the sofa next to the sleeping cat.

She yawns, stretches, then gets up and moves toward me like she's going to climb into my lap. I reach out to stroke her patchy fur, and she rewards me by swiping my hand.

"Ow. What the hell, girl?" I glance down at the scratch mark across my knuckle. "That was downright mean."

She hops off the couch and heads toward the bedroom.

First Fancy and now Princess? I rub a hand over my jaw, wondering if I'm losing it to believe they're giving me the not-so-subtle message to pull my head out of my ass.

I might be a slow learner, but I'm not a complete idiot. Usually, anyway. And I owe Molly an apology and an explanation.

I'll go to the house to apologize and possibly shower, I tell myself as I gather clean clothes. That's all, though. As much as I want to forget this day by spending the whole night with her in my arms, it's better for both of us if I pull back. Say what I need to say and get out before I do something we'll both regret.

Besides, I don't think I'm strong enough to stay away. God knows I've never been good at denying myself what I want, and I want Molly with every fiber of my being.

Maybe I can keep myself from reaching for her—that's a

boundary I can honor. But just being in the same room as her calms me down, and I need that right now.

I'm not used to needing people.

The setting sun casts the farm in that golden hour glow that makes everything look soft around the edges as I walk from the trailer to her front door. The world feels still and quiet, like it's holding its breath and waiting to see what happens next.

Join the club.

The door opens before I can knock, with Molly standing on the other side looking like the answer to every prayer I never knew I was sending up.

"It's about time," she says as she takes me in from head to toe. She's wearing loose sweatpants and an oversized T-shirt with a deep V that gives me a tantalizing glimpse of the top of her breasts. Her hair is damp at the ends, falling around her shoulders in fiery waves. "You're a mess."

"In more ways than one." I notice her flushed cheeks along with a slightly glassy look to her eyes. "Are you drinking?"

"On my second glass." She hops backwards, keeping the orthopedic boot off the floor. "It's five o'clock somewhere."

"It's five o'clock here."

She smiles, and as usual, it completely undoes me. "I might have uncorked a few minutes early."

"I'm sorry, Molly," I say before I lose my nerve. "If you don't want me here, I—"

"What are you sorry for?" she asks, hopping toward the kitchen. I follow because, let's face it, I'd follow her anywhere. The kitchen is easy.

"I'm sorry for that scene with my father. I should have known he wasn't going to let me ignore him forever."

She points a finger at me, then grabs a glass of rosé from the counter and takes a sip. "You're sorry for the wrong thing."

"Okay, then." I massage a hand along the back of my neck. "I'm sorry for whatever else you need me to apologize for."

"Not good enough." Her delicate brows draw down over those green eyes as she glares at me.

I want to smile, because she's so damn cute when she's angry. And while she might look like she embodies the ferocity of a butterfly on its first day out of the cocoon, I know there's more to her. More than most people give her credit for.

"You should be sorry for shutting me out," she says over the rim of her wine glass. "For thinking you need to apologize for your father's behavior when you have no control over it. Trust me, I'm an expert at wishing I could have controlled the behavior of other people."

"I'm sorry for that, too." I don't close the distance between us even though I want to. But letting me in more than she already has might make her sorriest of all.

"Do you know what I'm sorry about?" she asks as she finishes the wine and places the glass on the counter.

I blink. "You don't have a thing to be sorry about."

She rolls her eyes. "I'm sorry you believe you deserve how your father talked to you. Those things he said..." She shakes her head. "I'm sorry you're so busy caring for everybody around you that you won't let anybody close enough to return the favor."

I bite down on my inner cheek when pain slices through me at her words. "I don't need--"

"I know what you don't *think* you need," she counters. "But everybody needs something, Chase. Even you."

Oh, I need something, all right. I look away because her words are knocking down the walls I've built around myself one soft syllable at a time. And if I truly let her in, it might drag us both under.

"I need a shower," I say instead of answering her.

Her lips twist. "You know where it is."

"Thank you." I pause, watching her, then add, "Molly, you have to know—"

"Do *not* give me another lame-ass apology," she interrupts.

"Did you just call me lame?" I clap a hand to my chest like she's wounded me.

"I called you a lame-*ass*," she says with a smirk. "I think that's worse than lame."

I nod. "I've been called plenty of awful things in my life, most of them by my father at one time or another. Lame is a new one." I offer a mock bow. "Well done, and I'll be out of your way in a bit."

She nods, but I don't miss the disappointment that flashes in her eyes. I hate that for her. I hate that I've done that to her.

"You're not like him," she says as I walk away.

The words rumble through me like the sound of distant thunder. It doesn't matter how many times she tells me, they aren't words I can believe.

"He wasn't always that way." I turn back to her. "The awfulness was always inside him, but my parents had moments of happiness. Dancing in the kitchen or laughing and making jokes. He loved her. Probably still does. Or at least what he considers love in that fucked-up mind of his."

"Sometimes that makes it harder," she says softly.

The tension gripping me unfurls the tiniest bit because she's cut right to the heart of the matter.

"Yeah," I agree. "The good times gave me false hope that it could be different, that he would be different. It's easier when you don't hope for something better."

She scrunches up her nose. "At least the bad stuff and hard times are consistent. You can create a little shell that protects you. But those good times, they break through and..."

"It hurts more," I finish, and we both know I'm not talking about physical pain.

"I'm sorry that you understand what I'm talking about, Molly." I don't bother to hide the emotion in my voice. "That the people who should have been kind to you and kept you safe didn't."

She dashes a hand over the tears that run down her cheeks. It takes every ounce of willpower inside me—and some I didn't even know I had—not to cross the room and gather her into my arms. But I don't.

Because I don't trust myself to be able to let go when she needs me to.

I still feel dirty and dusty, and not just because of the work and the ride. The poison that spewed from my father is still on me, and I don't want it anywhere near Molly. So I turn away and make my way up the stairs.

I'm almost done showering when the curtain flutters, and the air in the steamy room shifts. It goes hotter and thicker and I hold my breath, waiting for her to join me. Only nothing happens, and I think maybe I imagined it. Maybe it's just me wishing and hoping for a chance I was never meant to take.

22

CHASE

I TURN off the water and open the curtain to find Molly standing with one hip against the bathroom sink.

Neither of us speaks, but she hands me a towel and her gaze follows my movements as I dry off. I don't try to hide the fact that my dick is hard as a rock. Her eyes widen slightly when she takes in that part of me, and I swallow back a frustrated groan.

"What are you doing?"

"What if..." she begins quietly. "We could be easy with each other?"

I finish drying my body and wrap the towel around my waist. "Is easy what you want from me?"

"I guess that depends on what part of you we're talking about, because I definitely want you hard, too." She bites down on her lower lip, and my heart flings itself against my ribcage. "Mainly, I don't want to think about the things that happened to us in the past, or the way people made us feel. I want to feel good."

"I can make you feel so fucking good." I cup her face in my hands.

"I know," she whispers just before I kiss her. It isn't gentle or soft. I ravage her mouth, plunging my tongue into her sweet heat like I'm going to steal every bit of her light to chase away the shadows lurking in the corners of my mind and heart.

She wraps her arms around my neck and gives as good as she takes. I lift her, her legs circling my hips, and walk the two of us to her bedroom, careful not to smack the boot into the wall or doorframe.

It's impossible to go slow as I undress her. I reach around and unfasten her bra, then lean in and suck one stiff peak into my mouth while I cup the other breast in my hand.

She grabs onto my shoulders like she needs to balance herself, and I fucking love the thought of making her lose control. Easy, hard—I'll do it any way she wants it. Her nails dig into my skin, and my dick twitches in response.

The sound that escapes my lips is more growl than groan, and she immediately loosens her grip. I cup her face again and look deep into her eyes.

"Don't hold back," I command, my voice rough and hoarse. "Mark me, claim me, whatever you want or need, Molly. I'm here for it."

There's a beat of silence when she searches my face like she's trying to figure out if I really mean it. Then her mouth lifts at one corner.

"I think what I need most of all is the bed."

"Done," I say, and lift her onto the mattress.

Once again, I take care removing her boot, and she pushes her pants and panties down over her hips. I peel them off the rest of the way, then pause.

"We have a tiny problem," I say. "My wallet is back in the trailer so unless you have a condom..."

She flashes a proud grin. "I got them in the grocery order this week."

I laugh at that. "Granola bars and condoms in the same shopping trip—you are efficient."

Her gaze skates to the nightstand. "They're in the box in the nightstand. The key for it is in the top drawer of the dresser, back right corner."

"Hell, yeah." I give a fist pump. "Does this mean I'm going to get a look at your famous toy collection?"

She barks out a laugh. "It's not famous, and no. You will be closing your eyes while I unlock the box."

"But now I know where the key is so..." I waggle my brows.

She smiles. "You won't use it without me."

"No doubt," I say with a laugh. "But I wouldn't mind taking a look."

When I turn back after retrieving the key, she's sitting on the side of the bed, hand out, palm up. Something about how demure she's acting despite being naked makes me grin like an idiot. She's so damn adorable.

"Seriously, no on the toy box," she says in a perfect imitation of a teacher scolding a student. It's kind of hot.

I return to the bed, the towel still wrapped around my waist, and place the key in her hand.

"At least show me your favorite," I tell her. "I won't look at the rest."

"Are you trying to get out of doing the work?" she says with an arched brow.

"I want to see how you touch yourself when I'm not around."

She draws in a shaky breath. "I don't know if I can do that."

"I think you can, Molly. You can do anything."

She takes out a compact storage box, unlocks it, and pulls out a box of condoms. I think she's going to close it after that, but she surprises me—and possibly herself—by pulling out a hot pink vibrator.

"Why is that your favorite?" I ask.

"I like how it feels." She swallows, then whispers, "On my clit."

"Show me."

Her cheeks are flaming, but she lies back on the bed, clicks a button, and then moves the device between her legs.

"Wider." I yank off the towel and take my dick in my hand, almost instantly losing it. Because Molly spread out before me, her red hair across the pillow and pale skin flushed with need and desire, is the hottest fucking thing I've ever seen.

She does what I ask, bringing one knee up, and I can see her folds glistening as she moves the head of the wand back and forth across her clit. I rub a finger over the moist tip of my cock, then begin to slowly pump my hand back and forth along the rock-hard shaft.

I take a step closer to her. "Open your eyes," I command. "I want you to look at me."

Her gaze is hazy, and she uses her free hand to pinch one nipple between her fingers.

"You like how that feels?"

"Yes," she says, voice trembling.

Her legs fall farther open, and she circles the vibrator around her center—fast and then slow—like she's trying to make the moment last. I climb on the bed and run my hand up her leg until I reach the junction of her thighs, then push two fingers inside her.

She cries out and starts to move the device away, but I put my hand over hers.

"Keep going," I say.

"I'm so close, Chase."

"I know, baby. Keep going."

Her hips are moving now in time with my fingers pushing in and out of her. She's so fucking wet, and her breathing is ragged—or maybe that's my breathing—but I feel it when she starts to lose control. I feel her muscles tighten around me, and she presses the vibrator more firmly against her clit. Then her whole body shudders as she cries out.

"Yes," I say. "You did so good, sweetheart. That's such a good girl."

I grab the box of condoms, rip one open, and sheath myself.

She's still holding the vibrator loosely in one hand, so I take the device from her, turn it off, and toss it to the other side of the bed.

"But I need you to come for me again." I lean down and kiss her, and she wraps her legs around my hips as I drive forward. She feels so fucking good. This feels like where I was meant to be.

"I don't know if I can," she says, breath hitching again.

I continue to pump into her, but reach a hand between us, gently tracing that sensitive, swollen nub.

"You can, Molly. There's no one else here. Just the two of us. And right now, we're all that matters. *You* are all that matters. This is easy, remember."

Then I press the pad of my thumb more firmly against her and feel her break all over again. A moment later, I follow, burying my face in the crook of her neck as I whisper her name.

This right here is everything to me—and more. This woman saw me at my lowest and believed more for me than I could believe for myself.

And somehow, she made me believe in more, too.

We lie together after, her head on my chest, our breathing slowly evening out. I run my fingers through her hair, memorizing the feel of her body against mine.

"Stay," she whispers against my skin, so soft I almost miss it.

The word hits me like a punch to the gut. Because I want to stay more than I want my next breath. But we've already crossed too many lines. And I can hear in her voice that she's already halfway to falling for me—another man who doesn't deserve her.

23

MOLLY

WHEN I BLINK awake Sunday morning, light is streaming in through the edges of the thick curtains. Next to me, the bed is cold and empty, like Chase was never there.

But I know it was real. My body holds traces of our night together in both sore muscles and a bone-deep sense of satisfaction. I can still almost feel his stubble on my skin in the most delicious way.

I roll over and press my nose into the pillow. There it is—the clean, woodsy scent of him. An unexpected rush of shivers courses down my spine.

Maybe he's gone downstairs for coffee, or out to the barn to feed Fancy. He wouldn't just leave. Whatever this situationship is, we're long past hookup behavior. Right?

I pick up my phone from the nightstand. No messages. But... wow. It's almost nine.

I haven't slept this late since before Luke and Laurel were born. I didn't even know my body could stay in bed so long. To be fair, Chase and I mostly dozed between rounds of lovemaking.

I climb out of bed and pull on pajama shorts and a tank, throwing an old fleece over the top before lacing up the boot over my injured ankle. Sleeping naked is another thing I don't do, but being pressed up against Chase's warm body, skin to skin, was too irresistible to let modesty get the best of me.

The main floor of the house is also empty, but the coffee maker is filled with water and fresh grounds, ready to brew. I flip the switch, then look out the window.

My heart does a funny lurch when I notice his truck's gone.

Not a big deal, I remind myself. Maybe he had something to take care of on a Sunday morning. He doesn't owe me a note, or an explanation.

After coffee and a granola bar, I head out to the greenhouse, only to find that Chase has done all my chores. What time did he get up? And, seriously, how did I manage to sleep away the morning?

When I stop at the pasture behind the barn on my way back to the house, Fancy greets me at the fence. I reach out to scratch her between the eyes and manage not to flinch—much, anyway—when she nuzzles my arm.

"Did he tell you where he was going?" She gives a soft snuffle. "I take that as a yes. You'll always be number one in his heart, huh, girl?"

I start to pull my hand away, then freeze as Fancy nips lightly at my wrist, telling me she wants some more love. I give her another few pats, then slowly make my way over the uneven ground, feeling more unsettled by the second.

Why would I think I hold any place in Chase Calhoun's heart? That way lies madness and goes against everything I've been trying to do with my life.

Love makes me weak. Too willing to put aside my needs and wants for the sake of someone else. Hell, before the bucket list challenge, I was unwilling to admit I even *had* my own desires. There's no way I can let some casual connection and a few rounds of great sex distract me from my path.

I shower, get dressed, and am baking a batch of muffins when the kids rush through the front door, followed by Piper.

"Mommy, Ian made chocolate chip pancakes," my daughter reports as she and Luke take turns hugging me.

"Piper made homemade whipped cream," my son reports. "It was delicioso."

"That sounds like an Ian Barlowe description," I say, ruffling his hair as I share a smile with Piper. "And you seem to be saving a bit of chip for later." I rub the chocolate smear from the corner of his mouth.

"Look at my nails, Mommy." Laurel holds out her hands for inspection. "Piper did nail art. I got flowers—you know, because we're flower farmers."

We're flower farmers. Be still my heart. "I love that, sweetie."

"Are you making muffins?" My daughter glances past me to the counter.

"Banana," I confirm.

"I love banana." Luke rubs his hands together. "We haven't had muffins in forever."

"It was like two weeks ago," I say with a laugh. Tough crowd, these two.

"Can we go see Fancy?" my son asks, unaware that his simple muffin comment has launched me into a torrent of full-on mom guilt. "Where's Chase?"

"He's not here right now," I tell the kids. "But Fancy's out in the pasture. You can say hi, but stay on this side of the fence."

"She's not going to hurt us." Laurel sounds affronted, like I've dissed the horse with my words of caution. "Fancy is nice."

My stomach dips, and I don't bother to tell them that nice things can hurt, too. It was nice spending the night in Chase's arms, but his absence this morning hurts like hell.

Since I'm fully back in mom mode, I only smile. "She's very nice and also huge. Stay on this side of the fence."

Laurel rolls her eyes.

"Hey." I touch a hand to her shoulder when she turns away. "You heard me, right?"

"I heard you," she confirms. "Let's go, Lukey."

"Did you thank Piper for bringing you home?"

"Thank you, Piper," they chorus as they rush past her out the front door.

"You're welcome," she calls to their retreating backs, then turns to me. "I need at least two cups of coffee to hit that energy level. Kind of jealous right now."

"My little Energizer bunnies." I gesture to the coffee pot. "Can I offer you a cup?"

"Raincheck," she tells me. "I ended up spending the night at Ian and Sadie's, so I need to get home." She makes a face. "Sometimes being in Mom's house, even with Max, is a little lonely. How was your night?" She inclines her head to study me. "Do single moms get lonely, too?"

I feel my eyes widen and my mouth drop open. I fix my expression, but it's not quick enough.

"Hold up. You weren't alone, were you? Was it Chase?" she asks with a delighted laugh. "Good on you, Molly."

"I don't know about that," I mutter and wipe a spot of flour off the front of my shirt.

"That cowboy looks at you like you're his favorite horse."

I laugh. "Then you haven't seen the way he looks at Fancy. It doesn't mean anything. Chase and I want different things in life. Or more accurately, we both want the same thing, but only one of us will get it."

"You," she reminds me. "You're going to get it."

"Yeah." I nod, wishing I felt so certain. "Thanks for being nice to my kids. Sometimes I'm so busy doing life that I forget having fun is just as important as the serious parts. It's important that they feel like kids, not just little adults helping me survive. Laurel loves having her nails done."

"I could do yours sometime," Piper offers.

"It would be a waste of time." I curl my hands into fists. "They'll just get chipped and dirty again."

Her smile turns a little bit wistful. "Who cares? Feeling pretty and taken care of has its place, even if it's only for a few minutes. It's part of that fun you mentioned."

"Then I might take you up on a manicure very soon. I'm hosting a wedding here in a couple of weeks. I'll be working the event, but it would be nice to feel pretty while I'm doing it."

"There you go. And if you decide the cowboy isn't your type, I have it on good authority that wedding hookups are legit."

"Good authority?" I ask, raising a brow. "Or personal experience? Pretty sure the last wedding you attended was your sister's, with Ian's very sexy brother as the best man."

She makes a choking sound. "Felix Barlowe is *not* my type."

"Adrenaline junkie cowboys aren't my type either, but—"

"Mommy, come quick!" I stop mid-sentence as Laurel's voice rings out. "You have to see this!"

"Quick!" Luke echoes.

Dashing is impossible with my booted foot, even now that I've been cleared to start reducing my time on the crutches, but I hurry outside as fast as I can. My heart is pounding in my chest. What could be so urgent? Did someone get hurt? Is there an emergency?

Chase and the twins are standing in the middle of the driveway. With a horse that is not Fancy. This animal is smaller and—

"It's so I can have riding lessons!" Laurel shouts.

"You, too, if you want them, buddy," Chase adds, patting my son's shoulder. Luke practically bounces on his toes, his eyes as wide as saucers. "This is Gumdrop," Chase announces to all of us. "He's a long-time trail horse who was ready for a new adventure."

"New adventures," Piper murmurs and elbows me. "A guy who brings your kids a horse isn't *at all* interested in something more than sex."

"He's just being nice." I press a hand to my chest like that can protect my heart from the onslaught of Chase's particular version of kindness, and everything that goes with it.

"I don't think guys like him are ever nice for no reason." We're standing on the porch, and the twins are peppering Chase with so many questions, I know they can't hear our conversation. "Chase Calhoun likes you, Molly. It might be time to start believing you're worth somebody making that effort."

I glance at her, and she squeezes my hand. "Trust me. I know it's not easy to admit you want more than what life has given you. But you're worth it. Sometimes happiness is like a nice manicure—you just have to enjoy it while it lasts."

"Mommy, I'm gonna ride Gumdrop! Come and watch!" Laurel calls.

I can feel the weight of Chase's gaze on me as Piper moves off the porch. But I don't follow.

She's right, of course. I can just let this moment be what it is. He didn't ditch me after our night, although this gesture hits me even harder than the idea of him not caring did.

"I need to put some shoes on, and then I'll be out," I say. My throat tightens as I watch him interact with the kids like he belongs here. Like we're already a family. The thought terrifies me. But somewhere deep in my heart, there's a glimmer of hope that Chase might be part of the happily-ever-after I never thought I'd get.

"Hurry, Mommy," Laurel shouts.

"We'll wait," Chase says. "We've got all day and night."

His voice—those casual words—sends heat flooding through me. Because I'll gladly take whatever time this man is willing to give me.

24

CHASE

WHEN MOLLY ENTERS the barn ten minutes later, I search her face for some sign that I've screwed things up as much as I'm afraid I have by bringing Gumdrop to the farm.

Although Laurel is riding the horse around the ring with an ear-to-ear grin, I'd bought the animal with Luke in mind.

Ray texted me about the outfitter looking for a new home for the animal, and I drove out early this morning. Once I saw the docile gelding, I knew he was my best shot at helping the boy feel comfortable enough to climb into the saddle.

And right now I need something to focus on besides my growing attachment to my best friend's widow. I've never been the kind of man to confuse sex with something more meaningful, but I've also never felt anything close to what I do for Molly.

I know she doesn't need me to take care of her, but that's not stopping me from wanting to protect her.

As much as that scene yesterday made me want to pull away, I couldn't do it. She took the dumpster fire of that confrontation with my dad in stride. Finding out I was made a fool of by my best friend and the girl my stupid, youthful heart thought was going to become my wife didn't change anything. She absorbed every ugly truth about my past and current failures without looking at me like I was suddenly less than the man she thought she knew.

Bailing is my go-to when things get real, but having Molly bear witness to my mess is somehow freeing. It also scares the shit out of me.

So yeah, buying a horse? That's a great way to take the attention off me.

Of course, I realized I made a huge tactical error when she walked out on that porch. Because in all my hurry to be the man I want Molly and her kids to need, I forgot to ask her permission.

Which is another thing I watched for years in my family. My dad made decisions and expected Mom to accept them without an iota of respect for her opinion or letting her have any voice in her own life.

From her childhood with her grandparents to Teddy and now Linda, Molly's had too much of other people stealing her power. She's finally working on finding her voice, and I did what everyone does—took the power away from her. I could kick myself for being such an idiot. I criticize every other person who's steamrolled over her choices, then turn around and do the exact same damn thing.

Laurel waves from the center of the ring. "Mommy, I'm like a real cowgirl."

"You're a natural, honey," Molly calls as she comes to stand next to Luke and me at the edge of the indoor ring. She isn't using the crutches at the moment, but still walks slowly with the orthopedic boot.

"I should have asked you first," I tell her immediately. "He doesn't have to stay. My friend Ray is willing to—"

"Gumdrop can stay," she says simply.

My heart settles, and then skips a beat when she reaches out and touches her pinky finger to the edge of my palm. Oh hell, I must be down bad when that kind of feather-light touch makes me want to rush out and buy her a whole stable full of barn animals.

Llamas, sheep, baby goats—pick your pleasure. I'm here for anything that keeps that smile on her beautiful face.

Instead of leaning into her touch, I shove my hands in the pockets of my jeans, earning a slight frown. She'd get it if she knew where my heart and mind were at, which is so far beyond how this thing between us started.

"You want a turn, bud?" I ask Luke as if my heart isn't free-falling off a cliff with no parachute.

His brows draw together in an exact imitation of his mother, and I'd like to reach out and soothe both of them, but I don't.

"No pressure," I say quickly. "You just let me know."

"I do want to," he says on a rush of breath, then grabs Molly's hand. "Is that okay, Mommy?"

"Of course, sweetheart. Chase says Gumdrop is a nice horse for learning to ride, and we can trust Chase." She glances up at me from beneath her lashes.

Right hook straight to the feels.

I *want* to be a man this woman and her kids can trust. I want to be the exact opposite of the type of man my father is, even though I'm not sure that's possible.

"We'll take it at your pace," I tell him as I wave Laurel over. "You call the shots. If you want to stop or get off at any point, you just say the word and it's all good."

Luke crosses his arms over his chest and studies my face like he's trying to gauge whether I mean it, and I nod.

"It's all good," I repeat, keeping in mind what Molly told me about how Teddy parented his sweet and sensitive son.

I step into the ring and help Laurel dismount. She undoes the helmet strap and hands it to Luke, who has followed me out.

"You're going to do great, Lukey."

I see Molly brush a finger across the outside corner of each eye, obviously moved by her daughter's words of encouragement.

Luke and Laurel are good kids because she raised them that way. Sure, they spend plenty of time at each other's throats. My sister and I did our share of arguing growing up. But the sibling bond is no joke. And with the twin connection, it's even stronger.

For better or worse, these kids have been through a lot together. Different challenges from what my sister and I faced when we were younger but still rough. Despite all his flaws, I don't doubt that Teddy loved them. Losing a parent is no small thing. It changes how you see the world and leaves holes in your heart that never quite heal.

I would never try to step into the role of father, but I'm grateful for anything I can give them and their mother.

Luke puts on the helmet and then stands next to me at the horse's side.

"Why don't you take the reins and let's walk with him a couple of laps?" I suggest.

"Laurel didn't have to do that," he answers, but wraps his hand around the leather.

"Everybody has their own journey." I don't bother to mention that Gumdrop is docile enough to follow us without Luke even holding the reins.

"I've watched you over the past couple of weeks and can't help but notice how easy it is for you to put together Lego sets." I pitch my voice low enough that Molly and Laurel can't hear our conversation from where they're standing at the edge of the ring.

"Legos *are* easy," he says, like *duh*.

"I'm not sure your sister would agree. She has to follow the instruction booklet when she starts to build something, and usually gets frustrated at some point in the process."

"She doesn't like Legos the way I do."

"She's also not a natural at them like you are. She sure can't build her own starfleet in one afternoon."

"I guess," he agrees. I can tell he's trying to sound casual, but there's a hint of pride in his voice.

Luke needs the reminder that there are things he's good at, even if they aren't the things his dad thought were important.

"There's also nothing wrong with figuring things out your own way, Luke. Or being afraid and doing the thing anyway."

We make one lap around the ring before he stops and hands the reins back to me.

"I'm done," he announces.

"Okay." I rub a hand over the back of my neck. "That's fine, buddy. If you want to try again later—"

"I'm done walking." He keeps his gaze on Gumdrop. "I'm ready to ride."

"Alright then. Let's do this." I glance over my shoulder and give Molly a small nod. She offers a thumbs-up in return, as if she really does trust me.

I have to tell you, I've witnessed a lot of Hallmark movie moments with horses over the years, and experienced a few of them myself. Animals don't care about your reputation or your bank account or what happened yesterday. When a horse decides you're worth their trust, and you find the courage to trust them back, it's pure magic.

But the look on Luke's face as he settles into the saddle and rides Gumdrop around the ring hits me square in the chest.

I tell myself it's because this is my childhood best friend's son, and I'm helping him overcome his fear. But a deep-down, secret part of me knows this is more than paying back my debt to Teddy. This is about my feelings for Luke *and* my feelings for Molly.

Laurel has returned to the house, but Molly remains at the edge of the arena. She's looking at me like I invented the internet, and damn if that isn't its own kind of adrenaline rush. One that's quickly becoming my favorite addiction.

"Keep your heels down, and your hands loose," I call out as Luke makes another lap. "The horse can feel everything. Think of it like having a conversation instead of giving orders."

"Can I take him out on a trail ride?" Luke asks when he climbs off the horse's back twenty minutes later.

"Eventually, and with your mother's permission," I tell him.

"Mommy, it's okay with you, right?"

"Let's do a few more lessons in the ring first." She opens her arms wide as Luke runs toward her. "Then you can explore the trails. There's a whole network that borders the farm. Your dad loved to talk about his epic rides through the mountains."

She meets my gaze. "I assume you were with him?"

"Always," I answer with a nod.

"We could go on a trail ride together?" Luke's expression is wary, like he's still not sure of what my response will be. I hate that for him and for Molly, whose eyes close for a moment as if her son's uncertainty causes her physical pain.

"Or maybe you could bring more horses here for Laurel and Mommy to ride." Luke tugs on Molly's hand. "We could have a flower horse farm."

"Now you're pushing it, buddy," she tells him with a laugh and another hug. Once again, I appreciate the kind of mom Molly is with her kids—fully present and willing to let them say whatever's on their mind because they know they're safe in her unconditional love.

Normal is an underrated way of being in life. People like me or Teddy, with our flash and bigger-than-life adventures, get all the attention. But it's people like Molly who make the world a better, more beautiful place. In her case, one bright bloom at a time.

"I'm going to tell Laurel that I can ride just as good as her," Luke says, squaring his shoulders.

"Not everything between you two has to be a competition," Molly reminds him. "You can both be good riders."

"We are," he clarifies, then grins. "Only I'm better."

He runs out of the barn, and I open the gate to the arena to lead Gumdrop back to his stall.

I tip my hat toward Molly. "You have a standing offer for riding lessons."

"I think you've given me plenty of lessons," she says, deadpan.

I throw back my head and laugh. "You give as good as you get in that area, sweetheart." After glancing past her to ensure the coast is clear, I lean in and kiss her.

She sighs and sways closer to me, and immediately my body shifts into high gear.

"Last night was amazing," I say against her mouth.

She pulls back and searches my gaze. "I was worried when I woke up and you were gone."

Gumdrop nudges my back, but I keep my focus on the woman in front of me. "Worried about what?"

"Just...you were gone."

"But I came back." I smile. "With a horse. I got the coffee ready and watered everything in the greenhouse so you wouldn't have to."

Her mouth lifts at one corner. "But you didn't leave me a note."

I shake my head. "I figured you knew I'd be back."

"Sure, because your horse and your trailer are here, and you owe—"

"No, Molly. I'd be back because of you. Sure, I left to get the horse, but also because I thought you could use some sleep after I kept you up half the night." The real truth is that I forced myself to leave. To prove that I could when everything inside me wanted to stay.

"I didn't mind," she says, and I kiss her again.

"You're the reason I came back. Not a debt. You."

She draws in a slow breath. "Next time, leave a note."

"Next time I'm going to wake you up kissing my way down your body so there's no question in your mind of where I want to be."

"That would be okay," she says, like we're discussing the weather.

I lead Gumdrop into his stall, give him a scoop of oats, plus one for Fancy because I can't ignore my girl.

"I'm not going anywhere," I tell Molly as I reach out and link our fingers together. "And I've got to tell you, it fucking kills me not to be able to touch you whenever I want. I was never good at keeping secrets."

I feel the change in her immediately, the tightness that grips her.

"I'm not ready for my kids to know."

I press a finger to her lips. "I understand."

And I do, even though I hate it, because it's a reminder she isn't mine. This is just some la-la-land fantasy we're playing at, but it's bound to end, and I'm afraid it's going to end with my heart in a thousand torn and tattered pieces in the dirt.

25

MOLLY

OVER THE NEXT WEEK, we fall into a rhythm that feels as natural as breathing. I'm still frustrated by my lack of mobility, but I'm much more comfortable with the walking boot. Chase seems in no hurry to pull back on the amount he's helping with the flowers, the driving, and overall being an integral part of our lives.

I feel like I should remind him that the better my business does, the more likely he is to lose his chance to buy the farm. Linda texted me a few photos from her trip to share with the kids, but she hasn't asked how things are going with the nanny she sent to my doorstep.

And I haven't given any updates.

It's going to be difficult for her to accept that we're not moving to Albuquerque, so I don't want to put a damper on her time away. Plus, there's no need to mention anything until I know I have the money to buy the property.

My friends think I should lean into the idea that Teddy would want his kids to be raised in his family's home, but my mother-in-law isn't a sentimental woman. I might be working on losing my fear of living life on my terms, but it's not a dragon I can slay on the first try.

If I've learned anything from watching my friends succeed at their bucket list challenges, the important part is doing the work, making the changes, and accepting that fear might come along for the ride.

The kids are excited to help with a wedding in the barn. They also seem happier and more relaxed recently, and I'm quickly realizing how much living with Linda affected them. Maybe even more than it did me. She made it clear to us that we needed her because we couldn't survive on our own.

But now? We're doing more than surviving—we're thriving.

Laurel is less snappish, and Luke is becoming more confident. He even asked to join one of the local T-ball teams so he could hang out with some of his new friends from school.

I won't lie. The first time I watched Chase take my son out to the backyard to practice tossing the ball, I had to blink back tears. In that simple moment, I understood with startling clarity how much Teddy's constant criticism fed our son's anxiety. While Luke's worries haven't vanished completely, there's been something transformational in the way Chase accepts him exactly as he is. It's the same gift he's given me with his genuine interest in my work and respect for what I'm creating here.

The morning of the wedding, the book club arrives like a small army to help transform my utilitarian barn into something that might pass for romantic. They've volunteered their decorating expertise to help me create magic from what is, let's face it, still a building where livestock lives. Not that the bride minds. She's too thrilled with the steep discount in exchange for letting me feature her photos on my website.

The one silver lining to my messed-up ankle is that it slowed me down enough that I've been able to devote time to making the flower farm's online presence look more professional. It's good that my mother-in-law only uses Facebook, and I've blocked her from seeing anything I post.

Luke begs Chase, who has also been helping all day, to let him show my book club friends how much he's progressed riding Gumdrop. And because they're the best kind of friends, they ooh and aah as they watch him ride around the outdoor ring. My heart pinches once again at the pride and excitement on my son's face. Chase coaxes out the best in Luke with his genuine encouragement and belief in what the boy can accomplish.

"You look good on that horse," I hear Eric Anderson tell him when Luke climbs out of the saddle. Eric, Taylor's fiancé, moved to Skylark with his teenage nephew a few months ago and retired from nearly a decade playing professional hockey in Germany after he and Taylor fell in love.

"I'm playing T-ball now, too," Luke reports. "I scored at our first game last weekend."

"That's fantastic, bud," Eric says. He squeezes Luke's thin arm and nods approvingly. "Oh yeah—I feel the muscles. Maybe you want to try hockey?"

"I can't skate," Luke says with a frown.

"I can teach you to skate," Eric replies.

"Or you could give football a try." Ian moves to stand next to Eric. "I work with the local youth league. Your sister might like it too. Flag football is getting real popular with girls."

"Girls can play hockey, too," Eric says.

Chase meets my gaze over Gumdrop's head and flashes a grin. "You got yourself some pretty awesome coaches ready to work with you," he tells Luke.

Luke glances between the trio of men.

"I'm about to choke out on the testosterone," Piper says as she comes to stand next to me.

"Is that a bad thing?" I ask.

She grins. "Not at all."

"Thank you very much," Luke says when Eric and Ian continue to stare at him. "Those are nice offers."

"Nice," Piper repeats, amusement lacing her tone.

"I'm going to be a cowboy. A bull rider like Chase."

"Good for you, kid," Eric says, patting my son on the shoulder.

"Just know the offer stands," Ian adds, and the two of them saunter off toward the nearby stack of folding chairs that need arranging.

Piper gently elbows me. "Someone's made quite an impression."

I know exactly what she means, and she's not wrong.

"It's complicated," I murmur. But even as I say the words, I wonder if maybe it doesn't have to be.

"Not if you don't want it to be," she tells me before turning away.

"Do you think I can do it?" Luke asks Chase when the other men are out of earshot. "Ride bulls, I mean. I might not be as good as you, but—"

"You can do anything you want." Chase crouches down so he's eye level with Luke. "But I don't know how your mom would feel about bull riding. Mine didn't love watching me climb on the back of an animal that wanted to send me flying through the air."

"You can get hurt playing hockey or football," Luke argues. "And you could teach me to be safe."

"It would be my honor," Chase says solemnly. "There's a lot of runway between first grade and being in the rodeo, buddy. If your mom says it's okay, we can sign you up for mutton busting when the rodeo comes to town this summer. That's how I got my start."

"Nana showed me pictures of Dad mutton busting," Luke says excitedly.

"Your dad and I did everything together back then," Chase answers.

"Maybe I'll make a best friend at the rodeo," Luke offers.

"Sometimes it takes a minute to find your person," Chase tells him.

My heart flutters as his gaze shifts to me before returning to my son.

"But I can tell you're going to be a great best friend."

"Hey, Lukey," I call as I walk forward. "Find your sister. It's time for the two of you to get cleaned up. I'll be back to the house in a bit for my turn. We all need to be in tip-top shape."

"I hate cleaning up," Luke says with an exaggerated eye roll.

"Do it anyway," I answer with my own eye roll.

"Don't forget to wash behind your ears," Chase adds.

Luke gives him a funny look. "Why would behind my ears be dirty?"

"To be honest, I don't know." Chase chuckles, and the low rumble sets sparks cascading across my skin. "That's something my grandpa used to tell me. All I know is he was a wise man."

"I'll wash all my parts," Luke promises, like that explanation makes perfect sense, before he takes off for the house.

"Mutton busting," I repeat, turning back to Chase.

"Obviously, only if you agree." Chase frowns. "Sorry if I didn't make that part clear."

"I'm glad he wants to try something new." I make a face. "Although I wouldn't be sad if his rodeo career ended there."

"He's a smart kid," Chase assures me. "He'll figure out he's meant for more than cowboying."

I only wish the man in front of me would realize the same thing applies to him. "You're really helping him."

His steel-gray eyes darken to a shade that reminds me of the sky when a storm is gathering over the mountains. I know Chase well enough at this point to know he isn't one for accepting compliments, but he's going to have to deal with it.

"He hasn't had much of a..." I want to say father figure, but that feels both disloyal to Teddy and too much pressure to put on Chase. "A male role model in his life. At least not one who appreciates him for who he is."

"The kid just had two professional athletes ready to throw hands over who gets to teach him their sport," Chase reminds me with a shake of his head.

"Ian and Eric and Iris's fiancé, Jake, are all nice, but it isn't the same as how you are with him."

"It's not hard to be nice to you and your kids."

At the reminder of how little I expect from everyone in my life, I once again feel foolish. It isn't hard to be nice, but it's also easy to let people walk all over you when you feel you don't deserve anything more.

"We're almost finished, and I need to get cleaned up before the guests arrive."

He grabs my hand for a moment before releasing it. Almost reluctantly, like he wants to keep holding on. Lord help me, I want him to.

"I *like* being nice to you and Luke and Laurel," he says, moving his hand to Gumdrop's soft neck. "And *not* because I'm paying off a debt. You understand this is..."

It's what, I want to ask when he trails off. I want to ask if it's the same for him as it is for me. This connection is something more than temporary or convenient. It feels real. It feels special.

But before he finds the words, Sadie calls for me from across the barn.

"Molly, can you make sure we've got the tables at the entrance set up the way you want them?"

"You bet," I answer over my shoulder, then turn back to Chase. "Thanks again." I hope he knows how much more I want to say.

"I'll be here if you need anything," he answers quietly.

Because it's my default programming, I shake my head. "You don't have to—"

He holds up a hand. "I'll be here, Molly."

Emotion clogs my throat. "Thank you," I whisper.

My friends and the guys are finishing up stringing lights along the edge of the white tent the rental company set up behind the barn. The flower fields are a sea of color on either side, with early wildflowers blooming in shades of pink, purple and orange. We arranged the tables in a crescent shape that follows the natural curve of the hills beyond the farm, covering them with white tablecloths and setting up folding chairs. Mason jars with the bouquets I carefully arranged sit at the center of each table. It looks elegant without being too fancy, and is everything I imagined.

"Is there more you need?" Taylor asks as the book club members gather around me.

I'm overwhelmed by how they've rallied around me today, transforming my anxiety into something that feels almost manageable.

"I think things are under control, and Chase will be here if I need anything. The catering company should arrive shortly, so I'll have plenty of hands on deck."

"Chase is different than I thought he'd be," Sloane says. "Gentler than I expected from a bull rider. Maybe falling for Molly—"

"No." I hold up a hand. "We're not talking like that."

Avah snorts. "You can't deny how he looks at you."

"I don't want to talk about that either."

"Honey, part of living life on your terms is also living your love life on your terms," Sloane says.

"I know, but it's different for me. I have kids I need to think about."

"I just watched him with your son," Piper says, then makes a show of fanning herself. "It was disturbingly hot. I didn't even know that maternal kink was a thing."

I know she's teasing, but the moment between Chase and Luke feels too precious to be turned into something casual. "It wasn't any kind of kink," I answer.

"You know what I mean."

"We *all* know what you mean." Sadie wraps an arm around Piper's shoulders.

"We love you, Piper," Avah adds, "but have you ever heard of the phrase 'say less'?"

All of us grin at that, then Taylor reaches for my hand. "Don't rule out a future because it didn't start the way you thought it should," she says. "Not all happy endings are straightforward, but a curved path can get you there just the same."

"And if a guy can give you a happy ending—" Piper starts, until Sadie pinches her arm "Owww."

"Is this what it's like talking to me?" Avah asks no one in particular.

"Yes," we all answer.

"Good to know."

"Are you sure you don't want the kids to spend the night with us?" Sadie asks.

"Or they're welcome at my mom's house," Piper offers.

"It's your house now," Sadie reminds her.

The tall blonde nods but doesn't look convinced. I get that. I might be working hard to make the farm mine, but I wonder if it will ever truly feel that way.

"The twins are excited about the wedding," I say with a smile. "The bride said they're welcome, so I think I'll let them stay. When I buy the farm and expand what I'm doing, we're going to have lots of events. I need to make sure they're on board with what this will mean. It's going to be a big change for all of us."

"You're investing in yourself," Sloane says, her eyes bright with excitement. "The bucket list strikes again."

I hold up a hand. "I'm not there yet, so don't jinx me."

"Cheering you on," she counters, "is not the same as jinxing. I'm proud of you, Mols."

The rest of my friends echo that sentiment with warm hugs and reminders that they want to hear all about how tonight goes. As I watch their cars pull away, I'm struck by how different this feels from the isolation I carried through my marriage. These women have shown up for me in ways I never expected.

When the dust settles and silence returns to the property, I realize Chase must have slipped away while we were saying our goodbyes. Butterflies flutter across my middle as I think about the potential of what this night could mean. In a few hours, I'll find out if my leap of faith could pay off.

Luke and Laurel are on the couch watching a show when I come in.

"Hey, what's the rule about TV on the weekends?"

My daughter grins. "We're in our nice clothes, so we figured today could be an exception. We didn't want to get dirty before the wedding. Right, Lukey?"

"Right," he says, his voice not quite as sure. He shifts closer to his sister in a quiet show of solidarity.

Solidarity and love. Their bond is strong, and I love that for them. I love knowing they'll always have somebody in their corner.

"That's a good point," I say.

Laurel's eyes widen as Luke breathes out a sigh of relief.

I check the time. The bridal party and guests will be arriving soon. "I'm going to shower and get dressed. When I'm done, I need to talk to the caterers. Then I could use your help placing the ceremony programs on the benches."

"I've never been to a wedding," Laurel says.

"Me neither," Luke echoes.

"If this one goes well, we'll hopefully be holding more of them here. Maybe we'll fix up the old office in the barn so the bridal party can use it to get ready."

I grab the remote and mute the television before turning to my kids. "I want you both to pay attention to how you feel tonight, and if you think it will be okay to host these sorts of events in the future. Some areas of the farm will be private for us, but if we're going to stay here, this is going to be part of it. We all need to be okay with it."

Luke sits up straighter. "Is Chase going to be our neighbor once your ankle is better?"

"He's not going to stay in that Airstream forever," I say with a laugh that they hopefully don't notice sounds tight.

"But he grew up next door," Luke reminds me.

"His childhood home burned down a few years ago. You know that."

"He can build another house," Laurel offers. "And keep Fancy and Gumdrop in our barn."

My heart trips over itself at their hopeful faces. They don't know about the financial tightrope we're walking--that if I can't scrape together enough money to buy this place outright, Chase might end up purchasing it from their nana instead. The irony isn't lost on me. The man my children are already counting on as a permanent fixture could end up owning the ground beneath our feet.

I can't bring myself to crush their dreams with those harsh realities, especially when part of me shares their longing for him to stay. Taylor's words about curved paths echo in my mind, but right now I can't see around the bend to imagine how any of this works out.

"Let's just focus on tonight," I say finally, hitting the button to turn on the sound again. "One step at a time."

26

CHASE

I'M STANDING NEXT to Laura Lovejoy, who I've known since I was in diapers and who runs the catering company providing food for the reception, when I see Molly and her kids walk out of the house.

I've been to a few weddings over the years, all of them happier in tone than Molly and Teddy's, and one thing I never understood is why the groom typically looks shell-shocked when his bride appears at the end of the aisle.

Let's get real. Maybe he's in a tux for the first time in his life and she's wearing a white dress and a veil, but they aren't complete strangers. We're not talking about one of those married-at-first-sight reality shows. So why do the guys get so choked up?

I figured it must be a combination of fear and adrenaline. I've experienced enough of both of those when climbing onto the backs of bulls, but I usually had more of an inclination to shit my pants than cry.

But as Molly and her kids approach us, I'm blinking like a sandstorm blew up in my face. She's breathtaking in a long dress in a shade of soft sage that makes her eyes pop. Her creamy skin appears almost translucent, and her hair falls around her shoulders in soft waves. I swear it looks like she stepped out of an enchanted fairy tale forest, and I'm completely under her spell.

The kids are adorable. Luke's typically tousled hair is combed to one side and Laurel is wearing a yellow sundress with her long hair neatly braided. The whole picture is what I imagine a happy family looks like in my mind. In my heart, if I'm being honest. And I want to be part of it.

"Close your mouth, Chase," Laura tells me with a laugh. "Either you're trying to catch flies or you've got it bad for Molly McAllister."

"I'm helping her until her ankle heals," I answer, my voice hoarse. "There's nothing between us." Not because I don't want it to be. I'm just not sure I believe I deserve it yet.

I suck in a breath when that realization lands with the force of a swift kick to the family jewels. Then Molly offers me one of her sweet smiles, and my heart scrambles for purchase.

"You keep telling yourself that." Laura laughs again and walks forward to greet them.

I'm still wearing my work clothes, so I wave at the trio then head to the Airstream to grab a change of clothes before going to the house to shower. I'm not going to be interacting much with guests, but the way Molly looks tonight makes me want to wear some version of my Sunday best. Maybe I need to remind both of us that I'm more than a dusty, washed-up cowboy.

The upstairs bathroom still smells like her shampoo, and I imagine fanning her glossy hair out across the pillowcase in the morning.

I haven't spent the night in her bed since the confrontation with my father. She's visited the RV several evenings this week after putting the kids to bed, but doesn't stay long. I figure beggars can't be choosers, and I'll take whatever she's willing to give me—of both her time and her body.

As I come downstairs again, I can't help but wonder what

would happen if we weren't competing for this property, but working together on it?

I don't have any real passion for becoming a cattle rancher. It's just something I know I can do with the land that came from my mom combined with the McAllister property. But maybe I could do something more. Maybe I could be a part of Molly's dream. A real part of her life.

As I look around the main floor of this house I spent so much time in as a kid, I realize it feels more like home to me now than any place ever has. Not because of my agreement with Linda or the thought of owning it, but because being with Molly and her kids makes me feel like I belong. Like I've found my place in this world when I didn't even realize belonging was important to me.

I comb a hand through my hair, which is mostly dry now. It feels a little weird not to have my hat on, but today I'm not Chase Calhoun, soon-to-be-retired bull rider. I'm just a man who's helping the woman he cares about to make her dream a reality.

The guests are beginning to arrive, and Molly and Laura appear deep in conversation in front of the greenhouse. The twins are nowhere to be seen, but doesn't take me long to find them in the barn.

"You guys clean up pretty well," I say.

"I hate wearing dresses," Laurel tells me with an eye roll that would make a surly teen proud. "Mommy said I have to tonight."

"I'm not big on formal clothes either," I admit. "But we're here to do whatever your mom needs."

The girl sighs. "She had us put tissues on all the benches out back. She said people cry at weddings." Laurel pulls on the end of her braid. "People should be happy at a wedding. Seems like a dumb time to cry."

"People cry for lots of reasons," I tell the girl. "Sometimes the emotions just get too big, and you have to let them out, both good and bad."

Luke tugs at the collar of his button-up shirt like it's suddenly too tight. I know the feeling.

"Crying isn't a bad thing," I continue, because I want to clarify that point. Luke's been doing less of it recently, which seems like a win, but still. I don't want him growing up like I did, believing that showing emotion—anger notwithstanding—makes a man weak.

I broke my arm when I was nine years old, falling off the roof of the barn I'd climbed when my frisbee landed up there. It hurt like hell, and you can bet I bawled my eyes out. It wasn't until I got home from the hospital, arm in a cast, that my dad hauled me out back to tell me tears were for girls and pussies, then demanded to know if I was either of those.

Christ, at that point, I thought he was talking about a cat. But I didn't want to be a girl or a pussy. His tone made his opinion on both clear, and told me everything I needed to know about expressing emotions.

Tears weren't something Calhoun men did.

Linda wasn't as harsh as my dad, but Teddy spent his childhood under his mother's thumb, an only child raised by a single mom who indulged his every whim while never letting him forget her sacrifice. Sometimes it felt like I got the better deal with a run-of-the-mill asshole dad we could never make happy. At least he was consistent.

Teddy's childhood was like walking through a live minefield, not knowing when he was going to set something off. He was the golden boy who could both do no wrong and never live up to Linda's exacting expectations.

But I want Luke to know emotions–and expressing them–are okay. It's what real men do.

His shoulders, which had inched their way up to his ears, relax at my words.

"I don't think I'm going to cry," Laurel says, stabbing the toe of her boot into the dusty ground.

"You don't have to. But know it's okay if you do."

"Do you three want to watch the ceremony with me?" Molly asks.

I glance up, and my heart kicks into high gear once again at the sight of her in the doorway at the far end of the barn. I wonder how long she's been standing there, and how much of this conversation she overheard.

"I do," Luke calls and runs forward.

"How about you, sweetie?" she asks, inclining her head toward Laurel.

"Yeah," Laurel agrees, then glances up at me. "You're coming too, right?"

"I sure am."

Then she puts her little hand in mine like it's the most natural thing in the world. And hell, I might need those tissue packets because damn if I don't feel the backs of my eyes burning.

We gather at the edge of the field where the ceremony takes place. Just as I expected, the groom looks bowled over when his bride appears at the end of the aisle. She joins him under the arch that I built and Molly decorated with flowers and greenery. With the mountains in the background, I can't imagine a more picturesque setting for two people to begin their lives together.

"It's gorgeous, Mols," I say softly. "You've created something special here."

Her eyes are a little misty when she looks at me. "I couldn't have done it without you."

And just like that, I know what I need to do. I see my future as clear as if I'm the groom watching my bride walk toward me.

Sure, being trampled by a bull is terrifying, but thinking about opening myself up to love takes it to a whole other level. And yet, there's also the thrill that comes from the possibility of finally feeling like I belong. Maybe Molly isn't the only one who has something in common with the mermaid princess.

I choke back a laugh at the thought. Dad would have

backhanded little kid Chase for expressing that type of emotion. But he's not my problem anymore, and I've let his screwed-up values and expectations rule my life for way too long.

When the ceremony ends, we watch the guests move under the tent. The dinner, a down-home buffet of barbecue and all the fixings, goes off without a hitch. The kids snag giant platefuls of meat and macaroni and cheese, and I see several of the guests approach Molly to compliment her on the centerpieces and the whole flower farm aesthetic.

She's in her element, and I thank God that she's still dealing with that walking boot and unable to drive, because this version of her is so different from the exhausted, uncertain woman in her wet T-shirt that first morning. This Molly can handle anything. She doesn't need some half-broken former bull rider, but I'm not giving her up without a fight.

Luke and Laurel join some other kids on the dance floor as the DJ starts spinning wedding reception classics.

I shake my head when Molly gestures me out for "YMCA."

I might be stupid head over heels for the woman, but I have some dignity. I do make my way toward her when the first strains of a slow song begin and several couples take the floor.

She arches a brow when I hold out my hand. "I thought love songs were for saps," she says.

I shrug. "A sap isn't the worst thing I can think of being called."

Her grin softens as she places her hand in mine and steps closer.

"I'm not exactly graceful with this boot on," she whispers, placing her other hand on my shoulder.

"I got you," I promise, pulling her body against mine.

It shouldn't feel new and different. Hell, I've memorized every inch of her these past couple of weeks. But this isn't the same. I'm holding her as if I have some right to claim her. Like we're a real couple. My heart and body have zero doubt that this woman belongs to me.

We don't speak as we sway together, and I keep my hands at a respectful place on her back even though I want more. I want everything. Hell, for all I know, she's going to kick me to the curb as soon as I'm not of use to her. But even the idea of rejection doesn't tamp down my need.

The song ends, and she pulls away. "I should go check on..." She waves her hand between us. "Other things."

"You do that, Molly. I'll be here when you're done with the *other things*."

I pitch my voice low because I want her to understand what I'm saying. When her eyes darken, I think she might, but it could also be purely physical for her. Normally, that's all I'd want, but damn, I really am a sap because my heart tightens as I watch her walk away.

I turn to do the same thing, but Laurel and Luke grab onto me from either side.

"It's a line dance, Chase," Luke says. "All cowboys know how to line dance, right?"

I swallow back a groan. "Knowing how and wanting to are two different things."

"But you *want* to teach us, right?" Laurel asks, and it doesn't sound like I have much choice. "That's what a nanny does. We watched *Mary Poppins* during inside recess last week when it was raining."

I rub a hand over my face to hide my grimace at the comparison. We're surrounded by wedding guests, and the three of us have ended up in the front line.

"Shit," I mutter, realizing there isn't much hope for escape at the moment.

"You're not supposed to say shit," Laurel reminds me.

"You're not supposed to say shit either," Luke tells her.

"Start moving," I tell the kids as I muster a smile for the people on either side of us.

I give them instructions that match up with the steps of the dance, because they weren't wrong about line dancing. Most people who spend any time on the circuit know the classics. There's always a barn dance or a party at a dive bar at the end of each evening. For the life of me, I don't know why the hell people like line dancing so much, but they do.

I'm pretty good, if I do say so myself.

"You're terrible at this," Laurel tells me with a giggle toward the end of the song, cutting me off at the knees when I was so impressed by my own skill. "Are you sure you're a cowboy?"

"I'm a bull rider," I clarify. "Not a dancer."

She grins up at me. She lost a tooth last week and shoves her tongue into the gap. I have to admit, it's cute as hell.

When the song ends, I step off the parquet tiles laid to form the dance floor. I'm not getting sucked into another dance. "The reception is going to be winding down soon. Let's find your mom and see if she needs help with cleanup."

They each grab one of my hands, and we weave through the tables and out of the tent until we find Molly standing with the bride and groom under the light of the stars.

"This was perfect," the woman says, practically glowing with newlywed bliss. "I'll have our photographer send everything over, and you're welcome to use whatever photos you want on your website."

"We'd be happy to give you a testimonial or be a reference for other clients, too," the groom adds.

"I'm not to that point yet," Molly says, but I can hear the excitement in her voice.

"She'll definitely reach out." I give Molly a pointed look, and she nods to the couple, her eyes sparkling. She needs to remember that she kicked ass tonight. She's been kicking ass, and there's no doubt in my mind that's going to continue.

The bride hugs her, then turns her attention to Luke and Laurel.

"Thank you both for your help and for getting the party started on the dance floor. A good reception needs that."

The groom reaches into the back pocket of his tux and pulls out a wallet, holding out two crisp fifty-dollar bills.

"Oh, no," Molly says. "You don't need to do that."

"Your mom said you helped with the setup too," he says to the twins, whose eyes have gone wide. "I'm guessing she couldn't have done it without you."

"That part is true," Molly agrees. I meet her gaze and wink. "If you're sure..."

"Oh, my gosh," Laurel says. "This is the most money I've ever seen."

Molly arches a brow. "What do you say?"

"Thank you," the kids shout in unison.

Molly laughs. "Yes, thank you. I'm glad everything came together the way you pictured it."

"It was better than we imagined," the man tells her. He looks at me, then at his wallet.

"I'm all good," I say, holding up my hands.

"Right," he agrees. "We're going to have one last dance before things wrap up."

"Thank you again for trusting me with your big day," Molly tells them. "It's been so much fun."

The bride's eyes get a little misty. "You know, I felt like my dad was here today. There's something about this place." She squeezes Molly's hand. "He would have loved seeing me get married here."

"That means a lot to me," Molly whispers.

As the couple walks away, the twins dance around us.

"We're rich! We're rich!"

Molly laughs and draws them close. "Okay, we're going to talk about how much you want to spend and how much you want to save tomorrow."

"Spend it all," Luke says in a demonic voice.

"I want to save it," Laurel tells her mother. "You can add it to the money we need to buy the farm from Nana."

"Oh, sweetie." Molly presses two fingers to her chest. "This is your money. As much as I appreciate that, I've got things under control with your grandma."

"Does that mean we for sure get to stay?"

Molly's gaze shutters. "We'll talk about that tomorrow." She tugs on Laurel's braid the same way the girl did earlier. "But right now, I do need to finish wrapping up this party. Do you guys think you can put yourselves to bed tonight?"

"Chase can do it," Luke says. "He's good at reading stories."

Am I, I want to ask. I've done it a few times over the past couple of weeks, but I figured I was about as good at that as I am at line dancing. I'm going to take the kids' word for it and ignore how much their confidence means to me.

An emotion I can't name flickers in Molly's green eyes. "I think Chase—"

"Would love to tuck you guys in," I finish before she can say anything more.

"Okay then." Molly's smile is a little wobbly at the corners. "I'll be in later. Give me a goodnight kiss."

Both kids do and then turn to me. "You have to read two stories," Laurel tells me. "We each get to pick one."

Luke nods. "Eeny meeny miny moe for who gets to go first."

"Eeny meeny miny moe it is," I agree.

I walk back to the house with the kids, a small hand in each of mine. There's a knot in my chest I can't explain. It doesn't exactly hurt, but feels full in a way I'm not used to. Is it possible for a heart to expand as much as mine feels like it has since becoming a part of Molly's life? More importantly, what am I going to do if it ends up broken?

27

MOLLY

I'M STILL WALKING on a cloud the next morning, as much from another night spent in Chase's arms as the success of the event.

I know my happiness shouldn't be tied to a man, but I can't help how Chase makes me feel. I don't want to. It's more than just sex, although how am I supposed to go back to a nightstand drawer of toys after becoming spoiled by the way he insists on drawing every bit of pleasure from me before taking his own?

He makes me feel like I'm the only woman in the world when he looks at me. Like every little thing I do matters.

I know I should pull back. I have an appointment with the doctor on Monday. If all goes well, I'll have the boot removed, which means I won't need Chase.

Except I can't imagine our lives without him.

But I have to stay grounded. There are bills to pay and kids to raise, and I won't let myself get so caught up in this feeling that I forget my goals—my bucket list challenge.

"How'd things go?" Frank, the older man in charge of the rental company crew, asks me.

"It was perfect."

"It's a nice setup you've got here." I follow his gaze around the property, which has never looked better. Even the barn looks like it got a fresh coat of paint. "Will you host other sorts of events? The flowers make it something special."

"I hope so," I say, then shake my head. "I mean, definitely."

"I'd be happy to share your business cards with our customers."

"And I'd love to return the favor by recommending you to my future customers," I say as if I'm a businesswoman with future customers. It feels good to speak as though I'm already the person I'm working to become.

He nods. "Appreciate that."

I start to turn away, then hear him suck in an audible breath.

"Everything okay?"

"Is that Chase Calhoun?" He gestures to where Chase is securing hail cloth to the posts around the far field.

"Yes. He's a...um...friend of the family and has been helping me with the farm since my accident."

"A hometown favorite," Frank adds. "It's hard to believe he's retiring. I hoped I'd see his name on the entries for the spring exhibition."

"The what?" I ask, trying not to sound like I have no idea what he's talking about.

Chase hasn't talked in detail about his career or his life before the accident. Or even after it. I've been so focused on my own problems that I haven't asked enough questions, and that needs to change.

"It's a charity rodeo they hold every year before the season gets going. It's not a sanctioned event, but a lot of big names participate because it's for a good cause."

"I'm not sure about his future plans," I say, and realize how true that is, especially if I manage to convince Linda to sell me the farm. Where does that leave Chase?

One of us is bound to lose. As much as I don't want it to be me, I want him to win as well.

"I'm sure another rider will take his place on the leaderboard. But some people are unforgettable, you know?"

I breathe out a small laugh. "Yeah. I know."

A gust of wind whips up, and Frank turns to the two teenagers working with him.

"Get everything strapped down, boys. We have a couple of other stops to make before the storm rolls in." He points to the dark cloud forming above a far peak. "They're forecasting a doozy."

"I heard that. We're counting on the hail cloth to protect the flowers from the worst of it." My throat feels suddenly dry, and not from thoughts of the impending storm. There's an unsettled feeling in my chest, like I'm missing something important about the man I've been sharing my bed with.

My kids are lounging on the sofa watching a movie when I stop in at the house to check on them before doing what I can to finish getting the property storm ready. They look content and comfortable, like this is exactly where they belong.

"I'm going to designate this as an official slow Sunday," I tell them.

"Does that mean we can watch all the TV we want?" Laurel asks hopefully. "All the shows and no chores?"

"Maybe not all the shows," I answer, wrinkling my nose. "But definitely no chores. Let's ask Chase if he'll drive us into town for pizza after the rain passes."

"And ice cream," Laurel adds quickly.

I smile at that. Someone inherited my sweet tooth. "As many scoops as you want."

"I want twelve," my daughter announces. "Or maybe two," she amends when I raise a brow.

"Mommy, are you going to have a slow Sunday?" Luke asks.

The hope in his voice makes my chest feel tight. I don't regret working so hard, but sometimes I just want to be their mom, not the woman always rushing to get everything done. "I need to make sure everything's buttoned with the weather heading our way, but then I will."

"You used to like bubble baths before we moved in with Nana," my daughter reminds me.

"You're right, sweetheart. My Sunday night treat after *one* scoop..." I hold up a finger. "Will be a bubble bath."

"I really want to stay here." Laurel flashes her new gap-toothed smile.

Luke sits up a little straighter. "Me too."

"Me three," I make my voice light, as if the thought of our future hasn't been weighing on me. "I'm meeting with someone from the bank next week to discuss—"

The blare a several sharp horn honks in a row cuts through my words. Even before I look out the front window to the man climbing out of the beat-up pickup, I know the visitor isn't someone I want here.

"Get your ass out here, Chase!" Malcolm Calhoun shouts, looking between the Airstream and the house. "You think you can ignore me? Is that how I raised you?"

"Mommy, what's going on?"

"Stay here," I tell my kids as I walk out the front door.

Chase is already jogging toward his father. "Go away, old man," he says, his voice so cold it's like a glacier just slid across the property.

"Not until you explain what the hell you think you're doing."

"What I'm doing is no business of yours."

"It's okay, Molly," Chase says, meeting my gaze over his father's shoulder. "He's leaving."

"The fuck I am," his dad snaps, then turns to me. "Does your mother-in-law know you're shacking up with my son?"

Normally, the kind of rage radiating from Malcolm would send me into a fit of stuttering and stammering to explain myself. Even though I'm still working on being an advocate for myself, I have no problem using my voice to defend Chase.

"Actually, she arranged it, and you aren't welcome here, Mr. Calhoun."

He blinks a few times, as if he expected me to cower in the face of his bluster.

"I won't be long," he tells me, then turns back to his son. "Why aren't you signed up for the rodeo? It's your chance to prove to everyone you've still got it."

"I'm not interested, and I've got nothing to prove," Chase says. His voice is calm, but I hear the edge of temper—and something more—lacing his tone.

"I wasn't making a request," his father says. "I'm telling you. Get your ass on that entry sheet."

Chase shakes his head, running a hand across his neck. "No."

"You aren't letting one damn bull end your career," his dad insists.

Chase steps back as if his father landed a physical blow. The wind whips dust across the driveway, and angry clouds swirl in the sky like they're gathering for their own fight.

Malcolm jabs a gnarled finger at Chase. "I didn't raise you to be a pu--."

"I don't give a fuck how you think you did or didn't raise me," Chase answers. "This is not about you."

"It's about you being soft and giving up when things get hard." His dad steps forward until the two men are standing boot to boot. "I'm fucking telling you to man up."

He shoves Chase hard, but Chase holds his ground like he was expecting it.

"You need to leave."

"Maybe I'll find a way to talk to your mother about this. See if she can—"

"Don't you fucking go near her."

"You think some banned visitor list can stop me?" His dad pushes him again. "Not going to fight back this time, huh? Because you know I can still kick your ass."

"I'm not going to fight back because you aren't worth it," Chase says through gritted teeth.

I let out a little shriek as Malcolm's fist lands with an ugly thwack on Chase's jaw.

He staggers back but then rights himself. "Is that the best you've got, Dad? Felt like being punched by a toddler."

I can already see a pink welt beginning to form on his cheek, so I know that isn't true.

"You want more? I'll give it to you. You know how much I can give."

I take an automatic step forward, waiting to see what Chase will do, unsure of what I'm going to do. But before either of those things becomes clear, Luke rushes past me.

"Don't touch him!" he shouts. "Leave him alone!"

He barrels into Chase's father, knocking the man off balance. Before I can move, or Chase can stop it, Malcolm backhands my son, sending him to the ground in a crumpled heap.

"Luke!" Laurel and I scream at the same time.

"Gotta have a kid do your—"

Whatever Malcolm was about to say is cut off as Chase slams a fist into his father's face.

Once, twice, then a third time.

The old man falls to his knees.

I gather Luke in my arms, tears streaming down his face. Laurel runs to join us, and I pull her close, too.

"If you ever—" Chase growls, "lay a hand on that boy—or *any* child—again, I will end you."

His father's face is a bloody mess. He flicks a gaze toward me and my kids.

"Fucking tears," he mutters. "Weak."

Chase grabs his father's collar, lifts him off the ground, then punches him again with a swift uppercut to the stomach. Malcolm grunts and doubles forward.

"Chase." I say his name softly, hoping he hears my voice. Rage rolls off him in waves, and I know what it means when that kind of anger is unleashed.

He pauses for a second, like he's trying to rein in his temper, then yanks his father toward the truck. "Leave and don't fucking come back." He opens the door and shoves Malcolm inside.

His cowboy hat on the ground in front of us, Chase drags his hands through his hair and grips the side of his head. Luke, my sweet, sobbing son, crawls forward and grabs the hat as I lift Laurel to her feet.

"Back to the house," I say.

His father is still parked, unmoving, and I don't know what happens next. But I do know my kids don't need to see it.

As I get to the top porch step, I hear the truck peel out, gravel spraying. The kids are already in the house, moving much faster than me.

I turn to see Chase standing there, a cloud of dust swirling around his legs, watching his father drive away. As if he can feel my eyes on him, he glances over his shoulder.

Although it's nowhere near as bad as how his father looks, the mark on his face hurts my heart. For him and all of us. For what that man did today, and the violence I imagine he inflicted on his family for years. Does the violence end here?

Chase must be able to read the question in my eyes because he gives a slight shake of his head, then stalks toward the barn.

I don't follow, of course. My kids need me, and I have to know they're okay. There will be time later for Chase and me. I have to believe we still have time.

28

MOLLY

"Is he back yet?" Laurel asks as I move away from the front window later that night.

"Not yet," I say, shaking my head. "He'll be back soon, though. He just needed some time to clear his head."

I hope that's true. Chase left in his truck several hours ago, and I have no idea where he went or when he's planning to return. It's been raining for hours, and the wind is howling outside. The house seems to tremble at each deep rumble of thunder, and the walls feel like they're shaking with emotion. Which is relatable. I've been doing the same thing off and on since the confrontation this afternoon.

I couldn't hold back my tears as I put ice on Luke's cheek, the skin angry and swollen where Chase's father hit him. He's been in his room most of the night, skipping our dinner of frozen pizza. I placed a plate with a couple of slices on his bedside table even when he told me he wasn't hungry.

It's the first time my kids have experienced physical violence firsthand. Teddy wasn't a great father, but he never would have hurt one of our kids. Linda can cut me down with a well-placed barb, but she's always kind to her grandchildren.

"That man was bad," Luke had said in a small voice as he held the ice pack to his face.

"Yes," I agreed without hesitation. "We won't let him come back here."

"Chase won't let him," Laurel clarified.

I chose not to address the fact that we witnessed Chase beat the shit out of his dad in front of us. I don't condone violence, but I wanted to do the same thing after that man struck my son. I figure there'll be time to sift through things once we're settled.

Once Chase comes home.

Because this *is* his home.

"Should we watch a movie before we paint our nails?" I ask my daughter as I step away from the window. "Or paint our nails and then watch a movie?"

"Nails first," Laurel says. "And Luke should pick the movie. Can we make caramel popcorn? It's his favorite."

I cup my daughter's cheek. "You're a good sister. You know that, right?"

"Not always." She bites down on her lower lip then whispers, "Today was scary, Mommy."

"Do you want to talk about it?"

She shakes her head. "Kind of. Did you know Chase could get that mad?" Laurel looks at me with solemn eyes that make her seem older than her years.

I wonder if she's asking if I still trust the cowboy we've let into our lives and our hearts.

"I didn't, but he was defending Luke and you and me," I tell her. "I'm not saying that excuses what happened, but he's still the Chase we know." And love, I add silently.

"I think so, too," she answers.

I should tell her violence isn't the way to handle problems. But I'm still too upset at the memory of seeing my child knocked to the ground by a grown man to make that particular point.

"Let's get this mini spa night going." I make my tone bright, both for my daughter's sake and to remind me that I won't let other people's ugliness steal our happiness.

Laurel climbs off the couch. "If Chase is back when we start watching the movie, can we invite him or are you mad?"

"I'm not mad at him." I tuck a strand of hair behind her ear. "I wish today didn't happen, and I have a feeling he's plenty angry with himself. But people aren't perfect, and I know Chase is a good man."

"Daddy was a good man," she says softly, but there's a question in the statement.

"Yes, he was," I assure her. "He loved you and your brother." I take a deep breath and continue, "He loved all of us."

"I miss him."

"Of course you do."

"Sometimes I forget what he looked like." Her honey-colored eyes fill with tears. "I know we have pictures, but I can't remember him in my mind. Does that make me a bad daughter? Am I going to forget him?"

"Sweetie, no." I pull her into a hug. "You'll always remember him in your heart. But it's okay for us to be happy without him. He'd want that, Laurel."

"I feel happy. Not right now because of Luke, but mostly I feel happy."

"Your brother's upset, but he'll be okay. Without the times we feel sad or angry, it would be hard to appreciate the happy feelings. A full life has both. That's what I want for you, and your father would want that, too."

She runs a hand across each of her cheeks. "Let's go tell Luke he can pick the movie. He's probably gonna choose something babyish."

I shrug. "Well, I'm in the mood for babyish."

She rolls her eyes but takes my hand as we walk up the stairs, still slow with the boot, but I'm so close to being free of it that I barely even mind.

Luke is lying on his bed, staring at the ceiling when we walk in.

"Hey, buddy," I say. "We're going to paint nails. You want to join us?"

"No."

"You want to talk about anything yet?"

"No."

"We're watching a movie tonight," Laurel tells him. "And making caramel popcorn because it's your favorite." I squeeze my daughter's hand, then let go so she can take a step closer to Luke's bed. "We can be sad sometimes, Lukey," she continues. "And we can be happy. Because they're both okay."

He shifts on the bed, looking at his sister like she has a unicorn horn growing out of her forehead.

"Just think about what movie you want to watch," I say softly.

I gather my small stock of nail supplies from the bathroom, and Laurel and I spend the next twenty minutes on the floor next to my bed painting each other's nails. She's better at it than I am, which thrills her to no end.

"Piper gave me all her tips," she reports as she smooths a final coat of gloss over my nail beds. "She's got like a million colors."

"I'm pretty partial to this one," I tell her, holding up my right hand to examine my nails. The color a deep shimmering red called *Not a Waitress*, and I think it fits my current vibe.

"I'm going to ask for a gel machine for my birthday," my daughter tells me.

"Aren't you a little young for gel nails?"

"Miranda and Lola get theirs done at the salon with their grandmas every month."

"Wow." I smile. "Somehow, I can't see Nana at the nail salon."

She giggles then asks, "Did your mom get her nails done?"

I try to remember back that far.

"I don't think so." I take Laurel's hand in mine. "But her hands were delicate, just like yours."

"You remember her hands?"

"Yep." I smile because I don't think about my mom often. Mostly when I do, thoughts of her are conflated with vague feelings of being hungry or cold or hiding in the closet when her rowdy friends came over.

But I remember her hands smoothing over my hair when she'd brush it. My mother loved the bright color so much that until I went to live with my grandparents and somebody made fun of redheads at my new school, I thought having red hair made me pretty.

We both startle as a deafening crack of thunder pierces the air. The storm has been gaining steam, and as if on cue, the lights in the room flicker on and off.

"Let's get your brother. I'll put this stuff away later, but I want us all together and to pull out the flashlights in case we lose power."

I follow Laurel out of the room.

"What movie did you pick?" she asks as she pushes open his door.

Only his room is empty.

"Luke, what movie?" she shouts, turning for the stairs.

There's no reply.

"I know you hear me."

She thunders down the steps as I take a moment to grab the untouched plate of pizza from the nightstand. My kids shared a room up until Linda left for her trip. Luke is now in his father's old room with mementos from Teddy's childhood—sports trophies and adventure posters—surrounding him on the walls and dressers. But there isn't much that represents my son besides a bookshelf filled with his completed Lego sets.

When I buy the farm, the first thing I'm going to do is let both kids pick new paint colors and themes so the bedrooms feel like they belong to them.

"Mom!"

The panic in Laurel's voice makes my breath catch.

"Luke's gone!"

I hurry down the stairs as fast as I can with the blasted boot. "Luke," I call. "This isn't funny."

The lights flicker again. "Buddy, come out now. I know today was rough, but—"

I head toward the laundry room, continuing to yell for him, and grab two flashlights from the cabinet across from the washing machine.

Laurel follows me. "He's not here."

"It's pouring rain, plus he hates thunder. Why would he leave?"

"I don't know, but his boots are gone."

"What?" My heart is pounding so loud I can feel it in my throat. "What do you mean his boots are gone?"

"His cowboy boots. The ones he wears when he rides Gumdrop. They're not by the front door. Neither is his rain jacket." She stares at me, her eyes wide. "Mommy, I'm scared."

"Get your shoes on. Let's go to the barn," I tell her without hesitation.

Even without the missing boots and rain jacket, I know enough to trust the twin bond. If Laurel says her brother isn't in the house, I believe her.

I don't bother with the waterproof cover that goes over the orthopedic boot, but as I open the door, the lights go out. The property is so dark I can't even see through the torrents of rain.

"Take my hand, honey. I'm sure he's in the stall with Gumdrop."

"When is Chase coming back?" Laurel yells, as if his return will make everything better.

"I don't know. Hopefully soon. Right now, we need to find your brother. He probably wanted to make sure the horses were safe and dry."

I'm not sure she hears my words or if they're swallowed by the wind howling around us.

We're wearing rain jackets but are still soaked to the bone by the time we enter the barn.

"Luke," I call, shining the flashlight toward the end of the wide aisle.

A horse's whinny is my only answer.

"Luke, you're scaring your sister." I pitch my voice low, soothing. "I need you to come out."

Laurel squeezes my hand more tightly as I stalk down the aisle. "Seriously, Luke—"

My voice cuts off, and my heart drops to my toes as I peer into Gumdrop's empty stall.

Fancy lets out an agitated snuffle, like she's telling us to get our asses in gear because this isn't good.

As far as I'm concerned, that could be the understatement of the century. My son is out in a violent storm on the back of a horse.

A horse he has very little experience riding.

"Mommy, where did he go?"

"I don't know, but we're going to find him." Yet my mind races as it catalogs all the terrible ways this night could end.

We both jump and grab each other as thunder booms around us so loud it rattles my teeth. A moment later, the hairs on the back of my neck stand up at the sharp crack of lightning that's too close. There's a horrible sound of glass breaking, and I run to the end of the barn and pull open the door to see that a giant branch from one of the old cottonwoods has landed on the greenhouse roof.

"Your flowers," Laurel sobs.

"They aren't important now. We need to find your brother."

I shoved my phone in my jacket pocket when we left the house, and I pull it out, ready to call emergency services. I'm sure they're inundated, but I don't know what else to do.

No service. Damn.

I turn the phone off and on again, hoping for a signal. Nothing.

"Laurel, I need you to go back to the house while I search for your brother."

"I want to stay with you."

"It's too dangerous, and—"

Just then, headlights sweep across the far window of the barn, casting shadows along the wall.

"Chase is back," Laurel says.

God, I hope so.

"Take the flashlight while I—"

"I'm staying with you," she insists, her voice trembling.

"Okay. Fancy, you're good here, right?"

The horse's eyes are wide, and she's pawing at the ground.

"I know the feeling, girl," I say, then grab Laurel's hand and head out of the barn.

It doesn't feel like my flashlight makes a dent in the sheets of rain, but a moment later, I see a brighter light moving toward us.

"You need to go back to the house," Chase says, all business. "I'll take care of the horses."

"Luke is gone." I try to keep the fear out of my voice for Laurel's sake. "So is Gumdrop. We didn't realize he'd left the house."

He goes perfectly still, like he's the eye at the center of the squall. I don't know what I expected of this man—for him to freak out or curse or lecture me on my son's recklessness—but he reaches out and takes my hand, the warmth of his touch giving me the hope I desperately need.

"Get in the house," he repeats. "I'll take Fancy to find him. Call the authorities."

"I have no service."

He reaches into his jacket and pulls out his phone. When the screen illuminates, I can see the mark on his cheek left by his father. Raindrops drip from the brim of his hat, but his eyes are steady when they meet mine again.

"Keep checking," he shouts over the wind. "As soon as you

have service, tell them I'm heading southwest toward Miner's Peak. Then call Ray. Gumdrop is a creature of habit, so he'll stick to the trails he knows."

"You'll be able to find them?" My throat burns as I force out the question over the roaring storm around us.

Chase hears, or maybe he's just guessing the question, but he squeezes my fingers and nods.

"I'm going to bring your son home."

"And Gumdrop!" Laurel adds in a trembly voice.

He bends down and slicks the wet hair off my daughter's face. "And Gumdrop, baby. I promise."

Another round of thunder booms, a little further off this time, and I lift Laurel into my arms and run as best I can to the house.

"Your ankle—"

"It's fine," I tell her. I don't think I could feel pain in my body right now if someone took a mallet to my foot.

When the door closes behind us, I sink to the floor.

Laurel keeps her thin arms wrapped around my neck. "I'm scared."

"Me too. But Chase will find him. We have to be brave."

"That's what you said when Daddy had his accident."

I suck in a sharp breath, refusing to believe this is anything like that awful night.

"Chase is going to bring him home, sweetie."

"He promised," she whispers.

I nod. "I believe him."

I have to believe.

29

CHASE

THE HOUR it takes me to find Luke is the longest sixty minutes of my fucking life.

Sometimes an eight-second ride felt like it dragged on forever, but I'd rather have Black Tornado trample me a thousand times over than the bone-deep terror of thinking about Molly's son out in the storm.

When I finally spot Gumdrop's tail through the deluge, they're huddled under a tree. Thank God he kept hold of the horse's reins instead of letting the animal go. Gumdrop could have found his way back to the barn, but I'm not sure I would have spotted Luke on his own or shouted loud enough for him to hear me over the roar of the wind. I dismount and drop Fancy's reins, knowing she's not going anywhere without me.

"Luke. Buddy."

His head is down, thin arms wrapped around his legs. He's wearing a raincoat and cowboy boots, but looks drenched to the skin, which I am, too. I don't let myself think about how long he's been here, the possibility of lightning strikes, or how long it would take hypothermia to set in at this temperature.

"Luke."

I put a hand on his shoulder and he startles. I can't tell if his cheeks are wet from raindrops or tears.

"Chase," he sobs and scrambles into my arms, throwing his arms around my neck. "I'm sorry. I know I shouldn't have taken Gumdrop without—"

"Hey."

I cup a hand on either side of his face, and it takes a second to get him to lean back enough that I can look him in the eye.

"You're safe, and that's all that matters. Your mom is scared out of her mind, so we need to get you home, okay?"

"Okay." He nods. "I think I can still ride and—"

"You'll ride with me, and Gumdrop will follow Fancy. I've got you, buddy."

His chin trembles. "You've got me."

"Yeah."

We climb out from under the tree and I lift him into the saddle. I tie Gumdrop's lead to Fancy's saddle and swing myself up behind the boy, then take off my jacket and wrap it around him like a blanket.

"You need that," he says, looking over his shoulder at me.

"I'm fine," I say. My heart is beating with so much relief, I'm not sure I could feel anything right now.

As the rain beats down on us, my horse—the best fucking animal that ever walked the planet—is steady and sure-footed as she makes her way back to the barn. Thank God for Fancy because I can still barely see three feet in front of us.

Luke begins to tremble, and I pull him tighter against my chest, wrapping an arm around the front of him and hoping that some of the warmth from my body seeps into his. The house and barn are still dark as we approach, and I waste no time putting both horses in their stalls, Luke at my side. I lift him into my arms, and once again, he wraps his arms around my neck. His heartbeat thunders through the layers of clothes he's wearing, and I run to the house through the darkness.

Molly opens the door just as I reach the top porch step. As long as I live, I'll never forget the look on her face when she realizes I'm holding her son. If I never do another thing right in my life, I can die a goddamn happy man because I did this thing for her. I kept my promise to bring her boy home.

I start to back away through the open door as Laurel throws her arms around Molly's waist, and the three of them hug. But with faster reflexes than I've seen before, Molly reaches out, grabs my wrist, and tugs me forward.

My heart is in my throat as Laurel clamps a hand around my thigh, and I'm drawn into their group hug as if I'm part of the family.

Like I belong.

And as much as I want to, I still don't know if I can let myself believe that. Luke would have never ridden into that storm if it weren't for what he witnessed from me earlier, plus the riding lessons that made him comfortable enough to take Gumdrop out on his own.

I'd like to blame my father, but Malcolm fucking Calhoun wouldn't have entered their lives if it wasn't for me.

Yeah, he started the fight and pushed me past my breaking point when he slapped Molly's son. I let that rage consume me, just like I did back when I was eighteen and ended up in jail for beating the shit out of my dad when he went after my mom one too many times. Just thinking about the horrible cycle of violence makes me want to cry the way the three of them are.

When Molly meets my gaze and glides a thumb across my cheek, I realize it's not raindrops she's wiping.

She's brushing away tears.

That thought has me pulling back even though my body screams at me to stay.

I clear my throat. "I need to take care of the horses. We'll talk tomorrow."

"I'm coming with you," Luke says, even though I can see him shivering.

"Sweetie, you need to get warm," Molly tells him.

I nod. "It's okay, Luke. You—"

"I want to take care of Gumdrop."

It's funny, because if you'd asked me before this moment, I would have said Laurel was the spitting image of her father and Luke took after Molly. But there's a stubborn set to his jaw that is all Teddy.

I lift my gaze to hers, and she gives me a slight nod.

"Put on some dry clothes," I tell the boy. "You're not going to be any good to Gumdrop if you can't ride because you catch your death of cold."

Molly swipes a hand across her face, but an almost smile curves her lips. "My grandpa used to use that saying," she tells me.

"Mine too."

"We'll bring him out in a few minutes."

I take another step away. "I'll be in the barn."

I have to break this connection. It might be invisible, but it's as strong as any chain binding me to her. Which is not smart for either of us. I just don't know how to stop it from getting stronger.

The rain is still coming down in sheets, but the wind has died down and there's no more thunder or lightning, indicating the worst of the storm has passed. I gather dry towels and fresh hay, then start rubbing down Fancy with long, steady strokes to get the rain and sweat off her coat. Her breathing has settled, but she's still damp and needs attention. It means something to me that Luke wants to be responsible for Gumdrop after everything he's been through today and tonight.

The three of them enter the barn a few minutes later, and Luke dries and brushes Gumdrop the way I taught him. Molly stays at his side, but Laurel comes into Fancy's stall with me. When we're finished, the twins help me put the supplies away. They work quietly, like they understand this is part of releasing the trauma hold this day has on all of us.

"Okay." I nod. "I'll see you—"

"Will you read us a bedtime story?" Laurel asks.

I feel my jaw go slack.

"Honey, Chase has to be exhausted," Molly says with a smile that trembles at the corners.

"Please," Laurel says, with those big brown eyes.

"*Charlotte's Web*," Luke says.

And there you have it. I'm a fucking goner.

"You guys go to the house and get your jammies on, brush your teeth, whatever else your mom tells you to do. I'll change into dry clothes and be over in a few minutes."

They nod like there was never any doubt I'd say yes.

Molly mouths, "*thank you*," before taking their hands.

I give Fancy and Gumdrop another half scoop of oats each because they've more than earned it, and then head to the Airstream. Princess is on the bed in her usual spot, clearly not bothered by thunder, lightning, or the fact that her owner has fallen head over heels in love with a woman who might never belong to him.

"Tell me it's going to be alright, Princess."

She scratches an ear then heads for the litter box.

Great. I ask my cat for advice, and she goes to take a shit. That sends a clear message.

I change into a pair of loose-fitting athletic pants and a sweatshirt, grab a different rain jacket than the one I wrapped Luke in and shove my arms into it, then push my feet into my Muck boots.

The rain is finally starting to ease up when I walk into Molly's house, and I place my boots on the mat next to the front door, hang my wet jacket in the laundry room, then head up the stairs.

The kids are together in the bed in Laurel's room, the sheets and quilt tucked under their chins.

"Luke," Molly says as I enter, her voice soft but stern. "What do you want to say to Chase?"

The boy scoots up to a sitting position. "I'm real sorry I broke the rules and took Gumdrop for a ride without you. I wanted to clear my head like you do sometimes, but I promise I won't do it again."

This kid is killing me, one sweet sentiment at a time. "Trust me," I tell him, my voice hoarse with emotion. "You're looking at somebody who spent his life learning lessons the hard way. I also owe you an apology." I rub a hand across the back of my neck. "All of you. What happened today... Luke, no one should ever lay a hand on you the way my father did, and I hate that he was here because of me."

Molly, who's sitting on the side of the bed, reaches for my hand, but I shift away. I'm afraid I won't be able to get the words I need to say out with her touching me.

"I'm sorrier than you'll ever know that I reacted the way I did. My father was wrong, but I was also wrong to hit him. Physical violence doesn't solve problems. I want you to know you're safe with me. You don't have anything—"

"We know," Laurel says matter-of-factly. "You saved Luke from the storm."

"You were defending me," Luke agrees then adds in a softer tone, "I don't like your dad."

"Me neither," Laurel says.

"That makes three of us." Molly's eyes are gentle when I meet her gaze. "Thank you for the apology, Chase, and for rescuing Luke."

"And Gumdrop," Luke adds, then lets out a wide yawn. Laurel follows suit.

Molly stands and hands me a book, careful not to touch me this time. And even though it's what I needed a few seconds ago, now I want to howl in protest. Instead, I sit down, flip the book open, and start reading.

Molly slips out of the room and returns a few minutes later in pink polka-dot pajama pants and a faded flannel shirt.

"Okay, lights out," she says, and neither of the kids protests. "Are you going to sleep in here, Lukey?"

"Yeah, he is," Laurel answers as he nods.

"Okay, but I want you asleep, not talking all night."

"Alright, Mommy," Laurel answers. "Love you."

Luke snuggles closer to his sister. "Love you, Mommy,"

"Love you, babies."

I follow her out of the room, and we don't speak until we're downstairs.

"Your kids are too forgiving," I say with a shake of my head. "But you shouldn't be. What you saw in me today isn't the man I want to be. I haven't been that angry for a long time. But my dad..."

She reaches for my hand, and this time I don't pull away.

"I wanted you to hurt him because he hurt Luke. I'm not proud of that, but one moment doesn't define either of us."

I don't know that I agree. Because every single moment with her has molded me into someone new. A person I desperately want to be, even though I'm not sure how to go about it.

I kiss the top of her head. "How are you real?" I ask against her hair. "You're too good. Like I dreamed you up just to feel like a better man than I know myself to be."

"Then be the man I believe you are," she says.

I don't mean to kiss her. I don't plan on kissing her. We both have too many emotions swirling inside us to work them out physically. Then she sways closer, I lean down, and our lips meet, soft and desperate.

She tastes like sunshine and rainbows after a storm, and I catch her soft moan in my mouth, wanting to hold on to it. Wanting to be the only man who ever pulls that sound from her.

Molly makes me want in a way I never have.

Nothing has ever mattered like this. Not a championship or a buckle. Not the ride of my fucking life. I've gone after a lot of things, but none of them compares to her.

I force myself to end the kiss. "I need to go before—"

"Stay."

Her hand grips mine more tightly. I feel the calluses on her palm. They mean more to me now than they did the first time I noticed them.

She isn't the fragile thing I once believed. She's the steady ground beneath my feet. The center that holds everything together, solid and true. But also as rare in her goodness as a prize orchid.

"You know I can't. The kids will—"

"Just for a little bit," she says, her voice shaky. "They've got each other, Chase. But I don't want to be alone right now."

"Molly—"

"I don't want to be alone," she repeats.

Those words undo me.

I lift her into my arms, walking up the steps slowly. She buries her face in the crook of my neck, and her sweet scent winds around me like fog rolling in from the sea. Until all I can see is her. All I know is the feel of her body in my arms.

I enter her bedroom, pull back the covers, and lay her on the sheets.

"Close the door and lock it," she tells me quietly.

I feel my eyes widen a fraction. "I can just hold you. We don't have to—"

"Please, Chase. They never wake up when they sleep together."

I should hold my ground. I have no business in this house after everything that happened today. But that cord that binds us tightens like a noose around my heart. I don't even try to fight it.

I lock the door, already pulling the sweatshirt over my head as I turn back to her. She unbuttons the flannel, and my breath catches as inch after inch of creamy skin is revealed.

We don't speak as we undress the rest of the way. But I don't need words right now. Nothing needs to be said that I can't tell her with my body.

I join her on the bed, careful of her ankle once again because I don't want to cause her even a second of pain. If I'm being honest, I don't know how I'm going to prevent that, but it's a worry for another time.

After grabbing the key from the dresser, I unlock the box in the nightstand, take out a condom and roll it onto my hard length. She wraps her legs around my hips when I fit my cock at her entrance, and I enter her slowly, pressing kisses along the underside of her jaw until she grabs my face in her hands and fuses her mouth to mine.

We move together, and although this joining lacks any of the creativity or—hell—the foreplay of the previous times we've been together, I'm ready to explode inside her almost immediately.

Afterward, we lie tangled together in the quiet darkness, our breathing slowly returning to normal. The storm outside has settled, but I can feel the tremor in Molly's hands as she traces patterns on my chest.

"I saw something in you today," she says softly. "When you were fighting with your father. It scared me."

My stomach drops. "Molly—"

"It scared me because I understood the pain you've been carrying and how much you've been holding back." She pauses. "But it didn't scare me away."

I don't know what to say to that. How do you respond when someone sees the worst parts of you and chooses you anyway?

"I care about you." Her voice is steady in the darkness. "More than I probably should. Even the parts you think are too damaged to care about."

The tightness in my chest goes slack at her words. I've spent so long thinking I was too broken to find happiness. But holding her close while her children sleep safely across the hall, I almost believe we have a chance. One I deserve.

30

MOLLY

I WALK OUT of the exam room of the orthopedic surgeon's office the following morning without crutches, a boot, a scooter, or anything aiding my gait for the first time since the accident.

Piper, who volunteered to drive me to my follow-up appointment, is waiting in the lobby. She's here instead of Chase because he's been out since first light repairing the damage to the greenhouse.

"Look at you," she says, tossing her magazine on one of the nearby tables as she stands. "Walking on sunshine and all that."

I smile because the waiting room is filled with patients, most of them now staring at me, and I'm blinking away tears.

"Oh, Molly." Piper hugs me tight. "It's going to be okay."

"Can we get out of here so I can have a breakdown in your car instead of with an audience?"

"Of course." She takes my hand and leads me out of the office.

Her Jeep is parked on the far end of the lot, and as we walk toward it, I think about exiting this same office so many weeks ago with my mother-in-law at my side, wondering how I was going to manage my life.

This should be the moment I feel like I *am* walking on sunshine. Instead, it feels like a dark cloud of challenges is following me, and right now, the emotions are overwhelming.

No more boot means I don't need Chase's help anymore. But I'm not ready for him to leave. Not when the future feels uncertain and the farm still stands between us.

We woke up this morning to a mess of leaves and broken glass. By some miracle, the two fields Chase helped me plant survived the worst of the storm. But it will take time and money to fix the greenhouse—the space that has become more than my happy place over the past couple of years. It's filled with my hopes and dreams for the future. Seeing the destruction hurt my heart even though it could've been so much worse, and I know having Luke safe is the only thing that truly matters.

I put in a call to the insurance company this morning, but I'm not sure Linda will be willing to file a claim. And the loss of income from the starter plants and seedlings is going to hit my bottom line hard.

To his credit, Chase didn't say a word, even though he has to know the loss of inventory puts my plan in jeopardy. I'm afraid it could impact my chances of securing the loan I need to buy the property. The setback is also a reminder that I'm still competing with him. He's done so much to make me feel like we're on the same page. The same team. But I don't dare allow myself to wonder what it might be like if that were true. What we could accomplish if we worked together toward our dreams.

I haven't even told him that I love him, but he has to know. I want to believe he feels the same way. Even more, that it means he'll stay.

"I'm sorry," I say to Piper after a few minutes of ugly crying in her car. I wipe a sleeve over my wet cheeks. "Yesterday was a lot, and I'm tired. But I'm also so happy my ankle is healed."

"You need a latte," she says instead of directly addressing my mini-meltdown. To be honest, I appreciate the tactic. "We're stopping at The Roasted Sky on the way home."

"I made a pot of coffee this morning and should—"

"Also an apple fritter," she says.

I have so much to do, but a fancy coffee and one of Sally's homemade pastries is exactly what I need.

I wasn't sure how I felt about Sadie's little sister when she returned to town. Sadie had given up so much to raise Piper after their mother died, and it didn't feel like Piper appreciated it. Plus, based on her engagement to Sadie's former high school crush—who, by all accounts, is a complete tool—she has horrible taste in men.

But Piper is even younger than me, and I tried to give her the benefit of the doubt. Lots of people make stupid choices when they're young. I also understand what it's like to grow up as a motherless daughter. Turns out we have more in common than you'd think, and I've grown close to her these past few months.

When we walk into The Roasted Sky, Sally stands behind the counter at the coffee shop she bought a few years ago. She was Sadie's best friend growing up, which made her like a big sister to Piper. And while everyone who works there is fantastic, I suspect Sally has a secret stash of unicorn tears she adds to make her concoctions particularly magical.

"Hey, ladies," she says as we approach. It's mid-morning and the start of the work week, but the crowd is a testament to the cheery shop's popularity. "How about that storm last night?"

Piper grimaces as she glances over at me and makes a slashing motion across her neck.

"Oh, no." Sally's gaze follows Piper's. "Was there damage at the farm?"

I nod, my stomach clenching automatically. "Lightning struck one of the cottonwoods, and a branch fell on the corner of the greenhouse."

"I'm so sorry." Sally shakes her head. "Did the flowers survive?"

"For the most part." I offer a tight smile. "The main crops this time of year are in the fields and the hail netting protected them. But there are some losses, and the repairs aren't going to be cheap."

"Then I think an on-the-house emotional support coffee is just what you need."

"We'll take an apple fritter, too, please," Piper tells her. "But this is also a celebration. As of a few minutes ago, Molly's leg is boot-free."

"Fantastic. I'll make something special that will fit both." Sally winks. "Off my secret menu."

That pulls an actual smile from me. "I didn't know you had a secret menu."

"We all have secrets," she says. "Mine are of the delicious variety. How are the twins?"

"They're good." At least I can say that with some certainty, but I need to change the subject. It's not that Luke getting lost in the storm is a secret. I just haven't told anyone why he went out in the first place. The emotions are still too raw and too close to the surface. And despite my close call with tears in the doctor's office, I prefer not to lose my shit in public on the regular.

"Is Trina enjoying pregnancy?" Sally and her wife are expecting their first baby in a few months.

"He kicked for the first time the other day." Sally grins as she steams the milk. "It scared the crap out of us, to be honest. But it was also pretty amazing."

"You two are going to be the best parents," Piper says.

"You're going to be a heck of an auntie. I can't tell you how many times my wife has reassured herself and me that we can get through anything having a nurse in the family."

Piper's smile goes a little tight around the edges. "I can't wait to be an auntie."

I know she means it, but there's something she's not saying. As the coffee maker whirs, I think about Sally's comment that everybody has secrets. It seems like Piper is holding hers close.

Sally places our drinks and a plated apple fritter on the counter and refuses to let us pay.

"Celebratory coffee and an emotional support pastry," she explains, and I blow her a kiss.

It's not as if caffeine and sugar can take away all my troubles, but somehow they do make life seem more manageable. Piper and I turn toward one of the tables that's just been vacated.

"Hey, Molly," an older man says as he enters the shop, the bells above the door ringing cheerfully.

"Hey, George. Did you get my message about the greenhouse? Like I said, I don't know that it's worth a call to Linda. It might be easier to wait until she's back, but I'd love to have you come out and take a look if you have time."

He frowns and adjusts the belt that is barely visible underneath his round belly. "The decision to file a claim or pay for repairs needs to be made by the new owner."

Coffee sloshes over the side of my cup. Piper, who has already placed hers on the table, takes the mug from me.

"What do you mean, new owner?" I'm unsure which is racing faster—my mind or my heartbeat—as I watch George process the question. "She has a tentative agreement to sell the farm to Chase, but nothing has been finalized."

He shakes his head. "They signed the contract last week. It's all e-signatures these days. The closing is set for a few days after she returns." He offers a sympathetic smile. "I'm sorry. I figured they would have told you. I guess it doesn't matter."

Which sounds a whole lot like I don't matter, if you ask me.

He glances down at the floor, then back up at me. "You're missing the boot. Congrats on being done gimping around."

"You can't say gimping around," Piper tells the man with a sharp glare.

George looks as if he wishes he'd skipped the trip to the coffee shop. "It's just an expression. You're Sadie Hart's little sister, right? Your sister is real sweet."

Piper bares her teeth. "I'm not sweet, and don't use that word. It's derogatory and offensive. You know the McAllister property should stay in the family."

"Okay, well...I won't say it again. But as far as the sale, I had nothing to do with that." He holds up his meaty hands. "I'm the insurance guy, Molly. I'm sorry this is upsetting you, but it's business. That's all."

The business of me losing the future I've been working so hard to earn. My vision goes hazy at the edges, and even though I'm standing on two good feet, I feel like I'm about to lose my balance.

I shake my head. "I don't want to shoot the messenger, George." I try to sound normal, as if my insides aren't shattering into a million pieces. "I knew they were in talks, but I didn't realize things had gotten that far."

"I'm sorry about the damage to your greenhouse. I'm sure Chase and Linda will take care of things."

The smile I give him feels like it could crack my face. "I'm sure." And here I am once again, relegated to the children's table while the adults work things out.

Piper takes my hand and leads me to the table. "You doing okay?"

"I'm trying not to have another meltdown in the middle of the coffee shop."

She grabs the keys to the Jeep from her purse and hands them to me. "You go out to the car. I'll have Sally put our drinks in to-go cups and meet you out there. You can scream or cry or whatever you need to do. Do you want me to call Sadie or Avah?"

I shake my head, the pain in my heart at Chase's betrayal making it difficult to breathe. "I think I might kill him." My voice sounds thready. God, I feel so weak and so stupid. I assume Piper knows I'm joking about murder, but she nods.

"I've got a shovel in the back of the Jeep, and I'm strong."

Piper sounds completely sincere. "I can bury a body with the best of them."

I can barely manage a smile, but it's exactly what I needed to hear. All joking aside, Piper's support is a reminder that there are people who have my back, even if the man I've fallen in love with isn't one of them.

31

CHASE

"SHE'S HERE," Luke shouts from his lookout point at the front window of the farmhouse.

I glance around the farmhouse's kitchen and give him a thumbs-up. "I think we're ready."

Sure, the cupcakes we made are from a box mix and definitely not decorated to Molly McAllister standards, but we sampled one and they're tasty. It's the thought that counts, right?

"I'm almost finished with my card," Laurel says from the table, her tongue sticking out at one corner in concentration.

I'd planned to work on the greenhouse the whole time Molly was at her appointment, but the twins are off school today thanks to some electrical issues in the building after the storm. When they suggested putting together an impromptu celebration for her boot removal, I couldn't resist.

I managed to get most of the glass and wrecked pots cleaned up and a tarp over the shattered corner to protect it from the elements. The weather forecast is clear for the next few days, with bright sun and blue skies expected to stretch wide over the foothills. I've already ordered glass from the local hardware store that we can use to replace the panels.

After the chaos and emotion of last night, we need this. A moment to celebrate and the reminder that healing is possible, even when things still feel messy. Being with Molly and her kids has given me a taste of an emotion I have very little experience with—hope.

I haven't told her about signing the contract with Linda yet or my plan for subdividing the property. I wanted to make sure I had all the details worked out, and I have to believe she'll share my vision for the future. The real estate attorney I spoke with assured me that what I want to do is actually doable.

"I'm done." Laurel hands me the bucket of markers and crayons and adds her card to the stack in the middle of the table.

I even made a 'congratulations on giving the boot the boot' card. My footwear drawing looks more like a wet noodle, but hey, once more on the thought counting.

"She's coming up the stairs," the kids whisper-shout, bouncing on their toes.

There's a strange flutter in my chest, like nerves before a ride. Something loosened in me last night. Maybe it was simple relief or the realization of just how much these three have come to mean to me. The way they looked at me with trust instead of fear absolutely destroyed all the walls I've spent so long building.

The three of us crouch down behind the sofa as the door opens.

"Now," I whisper, and they pop up, throwing the streamers I found in a bin in the laundry room into the air.

"Surprise!" we yell.

I'm grinning ear to ear as I stand, but my smile falters as I take in Molly's expression. Something's not right. I don't know what it is, but something's for sure not right.

"What's this about?" she asks as Luke and Laurel run toward her.

"It's a bye-bye-boot party, Mommy," the boy tells her. "We made cupcakes."

"You know I love cupcakes," she says as she hugs them both. Her gaze snaps to mine, then quickly away. I don't know what's going on behind those green eyes, but my stomach knots. She's pulling back. I can feel it like a door closing between us.

"Are you all better?" Laurel asks.

"One hundred percent," she says, "but there's no need for a party. We knew this was going to happen."

"The cupcakes were Chase's idea," Laurel tells her mother.

"That's very nice." But she doesn't look like she thinks it's nice. She looks pissed as hell as color rises on her cheeks, and not the good kind.

"Congratulations," I say as I move forward, then stop when she stiffens.

I feel like I did that day at the assisted living facility when my mother reacted so aggressively after mistaking me for my dad. Molly's not screaming at me not to touch her, but the message is coming through loud and clear.

"Come on, Mommy." Luke tugs her forward. "Let's have cupcakes."

"That sounds great." But her voice is hollow.

"Hey, guys..." I make a show of glancing at my watch. "I forgot I told Ray I'd help him with something at his ranch this afternoon. Can I take my cupcake to go?"

"Does he have more kittens yet?" Luke asks.

"Not right now, but I'll be sure to ask when the next litter of fosters is coming."

The kids have moved away from Molly and into the kitchen to start loading their plates. I peeled some oranges and took out a couple of packages of string cheese, too, because protein balances the sugar. At least I think it does.

"What's going on?"

"Thank you for your help, Chase." Her gaze doesn't quite meet mine. Something is very wrong, but how can I knock down the wall between us when I don't know why it's there? "You've more than paid off that debt you think you owe."

"What is—?"

"I don't need your help anymore."

"Mommy, do you want one or two cupcakes?"

"Just one."

She turns and opens the door, staring at a place just over my shoulder.

"Molly, talk to me."

"What should we discuss?" She makes a little humming sound in the back of her throat and taps a finger against her chin. "How about me running into George from the insurance company. And him telling me you went under contract on the farm last week."

My stomach drops like a rock off a sheer mountain face, plummeting with no way to stop and nothing to catch my fall.

"I can explain—"

"What's under contract mean, Mommy?" Laurel licks a bit of icing off her finger as she glances between us. "Is Chase going to keep working here after you buy the farm from Nana?"

Molly crosses her arms tight across her chest as if she's trying to hold herself together. "Now that I'm better, we'll have to figure out our plans going forward."

"We want to stay here," the girl insists.

"Forever," Luke adds.

"I know," Molly whispers, her voice breaking.

"Let me explain," I say again. I'm trying to stay calm, but the words come out rougher than I intend.

"We'll talk later." Her tone manages to be light and menacing at the same time. "Right now, you've got to get to Ray's, and I've got a cupcake celebration to enjoy."

"I want to keep taking riding lessons," Luke says, "because I'm going to be a cowboy."

Molly smiles at her son, but she's blinking rapidly. Like she's blinking away tears I caused. "We'll work that out, too, sweetie," she says. "Goodbye, Chase."

The unspoken message—don't let the door hit you in the ass—lands hard.

"You have to let me—"

She gives me a little shove forward then turns to her kids. "I'm going to walk Chase out to his truck real quick."

I start to turn when the front door shuts behind her, but she points forward.

"Not so close to the house. I don't them want to hear this."

Despite the slight breeze cutting through my chambray shirt, my palms and pits are sweaty. "This isn't what you think," I say when we get to the bottom of the steps. "I'm not kicking you out."

"You signed the contract without giving me a chance to talk to Linda first."

I rub a hand over my jaw and look up at the cobalt blue sky, trying to figure out how the good deed I wanted to do went so bad. A few fluffy clouds drift over the mountain peaks, but it feels like we're right back in a storm again.

"I saw Bryson in town last week. He said there's a developer from the East Coast looking for available land in the area for a master planned community. They were going to approach Linda as soon as she got back with an offer bigger than anything you or I could make."

Molly narrows her eyes. "Why would he tell you that?"

"He thinks keeping the land around Skylark locally owned is better for the town." I shrug. "I'm the hometown boy people want to see win. I had Bryson contact Linda to expedite the sale."

"You didn't think to talk to me first?"

"You were so excited about the wedding reception, and I didn't want you to feel discouraged before your big event." I wince at how weak my reasoning sounds now. Fucking hindsight. "Then everything happened with my dad and the storm..."

I shake my head. "I talked to a real estate attorney about

256

subdividing the property so you can buy the acreage you need. We'll split the land, and you keep the house. I'll sell it to you for a fair price." I offer her what I hope is a convincing smile. "You kind of have an in with the owner, you know."

Molly goes perfectly still, her lips pressing into a thin line. "Because I'm having sex with you."

"What? No. That doesn't have anything to do with—"

"You should have told me."

"You said you might not have the money until the end of the season. I didn't want you to worry about whether or not you'd be able to swing it or if Linda would wait. I was trying to take care of you."

"Right. Like everybody in my life tries to take care of me. And make my decisions without me. Because nobody seems to think I can handle it."

Her words land like a slap, and I visibly flinch. But I don't know how to fix it. How do I make her see this came from love, even if I haven't said those three words out loud?

"I didn't do this to control anything. I did it because—"

"No." She holds up a hand, and her voice cuts like broken glass. "I can't talk to you right now. I'll say something I'll regret."

"Molly—"

"Please leave."

She's looking at me like she doesn't even recognize the man in front of her. I need to make her see that I wanted to protect what we were building. That I thought I was doing the right thing. But the way she refuses to meet my eyes, holding herself closed off and still, tells me I've broken something that might not be fixable.

So I do the only thing I can. I walk away for now, hoping like hell I haven't just ruined the best thing that's ever happened to me.

32

MOLLY

CHASE MOVED the two horses and his Airstream back to Ray's ranch the morning after I asked him to leave.

Neither of my children was happy to find him and the animals gone when they got off the bus that afternoon, but I reminded them that the deal with Chase had always been him helping until my ankle healed. And with Linda due to arrive home next week, there's no point in him staying here any longer.

I didn't bother mentioning the small fact that he's about to own our home.

"Have you talked to her about us staying in Skylark?" Laurel asked as we shared an after-school snack of apples and peanut butter. "She can't stop us, right?"

Luke hugged Barkley the stuffed dog close to his chest. "She's not the boss of us." His tone was one-hundred-percent quiet defiance.

"Your Nana doesn't want us to move to New Mexico to prove she's the boss," I assured them, although I'm not certain that's true.

"We're going to stay here, right?" I felt the weight of Laurel's scrutiny as she asked the question, at once amazed and terrified at how insightful my daughter can be.

"Laurel and me can help with weddings and stuff," Luke offered. "You don't even need to pay us like that guy did."

"Such a sweet offer," I told my son, then tried to sell my kids on how moving to a brand-new city might be fun. Neither of them bought it, just like my friends aren't now.

I'm sitting in Sloane's office in the back of the bookstore while the kids are at the library for Taylor's popular Saturday morning story hour. It's been five days since my fight with Chase, and my heart hasn't stopped aching for a moment.

The death of my dream is devastating, but I also can't deny how much I miss him. How much I miss us.

Avah points her fork at me, then stabs at another bite of the cinnamon roll we're sharing. "You can't let this one thing change your course."

"I've heard Albuquerque's nice." I smile over the rim of my vanilla latte, but who am I fooling?

"It's not your home," Sloane says, like she's dropping a big fat mic on my head.

The ache inside me intensifies until it's an excruciating pulse that feels like it could eat me alive. "That's the thing," I say quietly. "I don't have a home."

Linda texted this morning to let me know she's selling the farm to Chase. She said we could take all the time we need to move out, but she also wants to pack everything up and leave as soon as the school year ends in a few short weeks. Mixed messages much?

"Molly, come on." Avah looks at me like I'm missing something obvious. "You have to tell her you aren't moving."

I bite down on the inside of my cheek as tears threaten to spill over. If I start crying now, I'm not sure I'll be able to stop. "Why would I stay?"

"Because Chase is willing to subdivide the land. Even with the cost of repairs to the greenhouse, you should be able to afford it given the success of the season so far." Avah pitches her voice low in the quiet of Sloane's office. "You know he'll work with you on terms and a timeline."

"Which puts me in the same spot as always—relying on somebody else to take care of me. How can I accept that when I've fallen in love with him?"

Oh, yeah. I finally admitted to my friends—and myself—that I'm completely, hopelessly, head-over-garden-clogs in love with Chase, making this situation ten times worse. Loving him means I want to stand on my own even more, not be someone he has to rescue.

"I'm no expert," Sloane says slowly, twisting the thick silver cuff on her wrist, "but isn't that the point of loving someone? You want to take care of them. Did you ever consider that Chase might have feelings for you? The kind he's just as scared to say out loud?"

Avah points her fork in my direction. "Exactly. This could be his grand gesture."

I breathe out a shaky laugh. "I highly doubt that. In my experience, needing someone to take care of you means being a burden. You can't love someone who's a burden. Not really."

Love isn't supposed to come with strings attached, but my heart always ends up a tangled mess.

My friends stare at me like they suddenly don't know what to say. Because they understand where my hang-ups about being loved come from, and it's not an easy fix.

"Then give up the farm but stay anyway," Avah says, like it's easy peasy.

I don't see how that's possible. Not only because it would break my heart not to be Molly the flower farmer. It would also break my heart to watch Chase go on with his life and not be a part of it.

"Can I be honest with you?" Avah asks as she slugs another gulp of coffee.

"Have you ever not been?"

"You're screwing this up, Mol. I'm not going to judge you for it, because I've screwed up plenty of things in my life, but I will say you're going to regret it."

"Think about the bucket list," Sloane adds in a gentler tone.

"I *am* thinking about the bucket list," I insist. "The whole point of the challenge was to make my own way in the world. To take control of my life and my future. I can't do that if he hands me my dream on a silver platter."

"The horror." Avah gives a mock shudder. "I hate it when a man checks all the boxes. He's hot and kind and good with your kids..." She leans forward. "And even though you haven't spilled the beans, which I find highly annoying, I know by your ridiculous smile every time you talk about him that he's good in bed. Heaven forbid he cares about you so much he bends over backwards to make your dreams come true."

"He cares about my late husband. He feels *sorry* for me." At least that's the explanation I went with after all my doubts and fears came rushing back like they'd never left in the first place.

Avah snorts. "The fuck he does. I'd bet my last nickel that man is head over heels for you. I don't know why you can't see it when it's clear as a newly washed window to the rest of us."

"You don't understand."

"Sweetie, *you're* the one who doesn't understand." Sloane takes my hand. "You've been chewed up and spit out by so many people who were supposed to care about you, you don't know how to let yourself be loved. Don't you see? You haven't truly been loved before now, at least not in the way you deserve. Not in the way that makes you feel special and cherished."

"Chase makes me feel like that," I say around the tears clogging my throat.

Avah smacks her palm against her forehead. "And there's no doubt you make him feel the same. Because that's your superpower, Mol."

"One of many," Sloane adds.

I let out the breath I didn't realize I was holding. Was I too harsh with Chase? So desperate to protect myself and prove that I'm worthy of the life I want, I didn't see how hard he was trying. Not just for me, but with me.

"I think I ruined everything," I whisper. The truth sits heavy in my chest. "But you're right. I don't want to walk away. I want to stay and fight for a future here. For me and the kids...and with Chase."

Sloane holds up a hand, palm facing toward me, for a high five. "Hells to the yeah."

Avah nudges our sweet, cancer-warrior friend. "Sloane, I love you but don't ever use that phrase again."

"Is yay acceptable?" Sloane asks with an amused eye roll. I swear she looks stronger every time I see her.

"Yay," Avah drawls. "That works."

"Yay," Sloane echoes and comes around the table to hug me.

For the first time in a long time, it doesn't feel like I'm balancing on a steep rock face that could crumble beneath my feet at any moment. It feels like I might actually be standing at the beginning of something amazing.

33

CHASE

THE DOOR to my mother's room is open, and I hear my sister's voice as I approach.

I knock softly, then walk in, unsure of the welcome I'll receive. I haven't been to visit my mother since the morning I scared her so badly. While I know that wasn't her, just like Molly told me, the memory of her shrinking back from me still slices deep.

Understanding it's the disease doesn't stop the mountain of guilt crushing my shoulders. Guilt for being too much of a coward to return and face her. Guilt because I look like my dad. Most of all, guilt that I'm similar enough to a man who hurt us both that she'd mistake me for him.

"Chase is here," Ada says brightly. "Your sweet son brought you flowers."

"And chocolate." I hold up the bar.

Mom offers me a rare wide smile. "Daffodils are my favorite."

They aren't as pretty as Molly's, but those feel as far out of reach as she does. "I'll put the vase on your dresser so you can see it from both the bed and your chair."

My sister raises a brow. "You know her favorite flower?"

"It's not a big deal." Shit, am I blushing?

Ada inclines her head to study me. "Are you sure you're my brother?"

"You're so funny I forgot to laugh," I answer, rolling my eyes.

I place the flowers on the dresser and approach the bed, hesitating a second longer than I mean. Last time I stood here, Mom begged me not to hurt her.

Ada watches me carefully. "What are you doing here?"

I glance between them, unable to tell if my mom is following our conversation. "I wanted to talk to her about our family land."

"You're not going to build on it," Ada says like she knows exactly what I'm thinking.

I shake my head. "Holding onto the past isn't going to give me the future I want."

I'm not sure anything will when everything I want is tied to Molly, and I've solidly screwed that up.

"But you're staying in Skylark?" Ada demands. "I thought you and Molly—"

"You thought wrong."

"Did you mess it up?"

While I'm not surprised my sister makes that assumption, it still stings.

I sit down in the chair facing my mom's recliner and cross my arms over my chest. "Everything I touch is bound to go to shit. I'm a chip off the old block, you know?"

Ada narrows her eyes. "You aren't like him."

I switch my attention to my mother. "Mom, I want to sell the land. Are you okay with that?"

Her eyes have drifted closed, and when she doesn't answer, I realize she's fallen asleep. I came here for her blessing, but I want my sister to understand my decision just as much.

"I'm going to the exhibition rodeo tomorrow to work with a team out of Wyoming. Ray told me they're looking for another coach, and he has a friend in that area who could use some help with his operation. It's about three hours north, so I can come down on the weekends or whenever you need an extra set of hands." I look up and meet my sister's eyes. "You won't have to take care of everything on your own."

Her smile is sad. Or maybe disappointed is a better word.

"Did you ever think I want you to stay in Skylark because I like you, not because I need your help or you owe me some phantom debt?"

I take off my hat and scrub a hand through my hair. "To be honest, that never crossed my mind."

"You're an idiot," she says, like it's a fact. "I saw how you were with Molly. You were lighter, Chase. You were different—happy."

"I can't be different than who I am on the inside," I insist.

"No."

We both startle as Mom leans forward, wide awake now. For a terrifying heartbeat, I think she's mistaken me for my father again and is about to flip out like she did the last time. I don't know if I can take seeing that fear in her eyes again.

But she holds out her hand, palm side up, and when I place my fingers in hers, she squeezes tight.

"I know what you did," she accuses. Talk about some loaded words.

I shoot a help-me glance at my sister.

"Mom," she says in her best kid-wrangling teacher voice. "This is—"

"Chase," my mother whispers and I sigh, but the relief flooding through me turns to ice when she continues. "You acted out when he got mad."

Blood roars in my head.

"I got in trouble because I was made for it." I force a chuckle. "We all know that."

She shakes her head, her lips rolling together in concentration, like she's searching for a memory that's just out of reach.

"Mom, it's okay," I tell her. "You don't have to—"

"When he came home angry or had too much to drink, I knew

265

what was coming." Her features pinch as her hold on my hand loosens. "You'd spill a glass of milk or knock something off the shelf. You drew his attention to get it away from me."

I hear my sister gasp.

"His moods made me nervous," I say, and try to slip my hand from my mother's grasp, but she tightens her hold again. "I got clumsy when I was nervous."

"You were never clumsy." Her lips curve up on one side, the barest wisp of a smile, but her gaze reflects decades of sadness as it meets mine. "You tried to save me."

Shit. The giant ball of emotion lodged in my throat is suffocating. I can't move or breathe. That has to be why my eyes are stinging with tears.

She releases my hand and pats my cheek, her paper-thin skin soft against mine. "You're a good boy."

"I love you, Mom," I whisper as her praise washes over me.

Her smile turns gentle, then she yawns and sits back in the chair, her eyes closing once again.

When I finally glance at Ada, tears are streaming down her cheeks.

"It's okay," I say softly. "It wasn't exactly like that."

"Hallway. Now," she says, jerking her thumb toward the door. With a sigh, I stand and follow her out of the room.

"Ada, I swear I'm not going to leave you alone."

"Do you love her?" she demands.

"You just heard me tell her I love her. I know Mom wasn't perfect, but she did the best she could."

"I don't mean Mom, dummy. I'm talking about Molly."

I force myself not to react, but Ada's delivered a hit I didn't see coming. "What does that have to do with anything?"

"It has *everything* to do with why you can't leave."

"She wants the McAllister property and thinks I bought it because I didn't believe she could do it on her own."

Surprise flashes in my sister's gray eyes. "You bought it because you take care of people."

Damn. It feels like that bull is on top of me again. Only this time it's not the pain from the beast crushing me. The weight of the truth is draining the breath from my lungs.

"Molly wants to take care of herself."

"Then honor that, but don't walk away or give up on her. You heard Mom. You shouldn't need either of us to convince you, but you aren't like Dad."

"I..." I want to deny it, but my throat locks around the words.

Ada grips my arm like I need her to ground me in this moment, and maybe I do. "You look like him, and I know you've got a temper. But the darkness that's inside him." She shakes her head. "It isn't part of you."

"How do you know?"

"You tried to save us." She swipes the hand not holding mine across her cheeks. "Mom isn't the only one who remembers."

I wrap my arms around my sister and pull her into me. "I hate him for what he did to us."

"Me, too," she whispers and pulls back enough to look into my eyes. "Don't give that kind of power anymore. You have to take your life back. Fight for Molly. Sell the property or keep it. That doesn't matter. What matters is being happy. You deserve to be happy."

I close my eyes as her words take hold deep inside me. I can't imagine being happy without Molly or those kids or the damn flower farm that smells like sunshine and hope. And I want all of it.

Yeah, I've been thrown and ended up bruised and broken. But that didn't stop me from climbing back on, and it won't this time either. I'm done letting fear rule the day. Molly is worth every fight, and I'm going to hold tight and not let go.

34

MOLLY

LATER THAT NIGHT, while the kids are upstairs rearranging the bedroom they're once again sharing now that Linda is back, I sit at the kitchen table with my mother-in-law, who surprised us by returning several days earlier than scheduled. Did she call to let me know about her change in plans? Of course not. Instead, the kids and I got home to find her unpacking in the bedroom.

Luckily, I had most of the house cleaned, which is how I've been dealing with my mood and missing Chase.

While Linda told the kids about her trip, I quickly changed the sheets, packed up the clothes I had in her room—plus anything else that belonged to me—and moved it into Laurel's bedroom. I waited until they went downstairs to move the locked box from the nightstand. The last thing I need is to have to explain the box to my mother-in-law. Talk about mortified.

She didn't seem too interested in hearing about what's been going on here, but the kids regaled her with stories of Fancy, Gumdrop, and Princess anyway. I don't think I misinterpreted the look of surprise on Linda's face when she realized how close my kids have become to their late father's friend.

"Was it necessary for Chase to park his Airstream on the

268

property? The kids take the bus to and from school, and I know you set up grocery deliveries, so there couldn't have been that much for him to do."

"He was helping us," I remind her. "You arranged for him to be here."

"Not full-time," she counters. "You were supposed to be winding down your flower operation during my trip. From everything I saw in the fields and the greenhouse, you're ramping things up."

"I *did* ramp it up," I tell her, not bothering to hide the pride in my voice. "In fact, I hosted a wedding reception here."

"Excuse me?" Linda looks stunned. "Why in the world—?"

"I wanted to make enough money for a down payment on the farm by the end of the summer."

"Part of the agreement was if Chase helped you, I'd sell him the farm."

I exhale a slow breath. "I know that now, but I didn't at first. Even after I found out, I thought that if I could make it work, you'd sell the property to me rather than Chase or some stranger."

"Why would I do that when you and the kids are moving to Albuquerque?"

"We're not, Linda," I say quietly.

Her eyes narrow and her nostrils flare. "You promised..." she begins.

I shake my head. "I didn't promise anything. You told me how it would be, and I went along even though it wasn't best for us. That's on me. I'm sorry I didn't speak up sooner."

"After everything I did for you—"

"Skylark is my home." I sit up straighter and hold her gaze, no longer willing to be the mouse people expect. "It's where my kids feel at home."

After all this time and worry over how to talk to my mother-in-law about this decision, the nerves I once felt are completely gone.

Because I know I'm doing the right thing. It's as if the hold she had over me has faded away these past few weeks.

"Chase has offered to subdivide the property so we can stay," I inform her. In case he didn't mention it to her. I want all the cards on the table now. "And I'm going to take him up on it." If he's still willing after how I reacted.

"What if I don't sell it to him? The closing isn't until next week." She shakes her head, clearly frustrated by my change of heart. "There's a developer willing to pay enough that I could recoup my losses from breaking the deal with Chase."

"I heard about the East Coast developer," I tell her, hoping I'm right that she's bluffing. "But you made a promise, and Chase lived up to his end of the bargain."

"But if I did, you won't have a reason to stay."

"This town is my home," I repeat. "That's the only reason I need. It's not about Chase or the land. Of course I want it. I've invested in it, and the kids love it here. And I'd like to have your blessing. But no matter what happens, we're staying."

She drums her fingernails on the table as she studies me, then reaches across the table.

For a moment, I think she might actually slap me, which tells you how well I can read my mother-in-law. Because instead, she pats my hand. Not exactly a gentle touch, but it's a big gesture for Linda.

"It's about time," she says, looking both resigned and a little relieved.

I blink. "Time for what?"

"Time that you stand on your own two feet. I wondered if you were ever going to manage it."

Maybe I should be offended, but I'm not. "That makes two of us. To be honest, I didn't think you were interested in me standing on my own two feet because of what it would mean for you."

"I wanted you to move with me to keep my grandkids close,

but I also understand why you want to stay. I'm ready for a change, but Skylark will always have a place in my heart."

"I need to do what's best for the kids." It's still easier to be strong for them than for myself.

Linda bites down on her lower lip then whispers, "My son was a good man."

I'm not sure where that comment came from, but it's clear she needed to say it. "He was. I loved Teddy."

"He was my whole world." She exhales what appears to be a painful breath. "He was also reckless and selfish. I blame myself. I know what it's like to be a single mom. The stigma and pressure and loneliness. I thought if I indulged every wish and whim Teddy had as a boy, it would make up for him not having a father. But I couldn't fill that gaping hole. Instead..." She clasps her hands tightly together. "Teddy never knew his father, but he turned out a lot like him, which is not a compliment."

It's my turn to reach across the table and squeeze her hands. "I know how much you loved him."

"And I see how much you love your kids. Being happy is the best thing you can do for them. I didn't support this flower farming business at the start, but I've seen the changes in you. They're important."

Emotion clogs my throat, and I have to look away for a moment. I didn't expect any sort of validation from my typically fault-finding mother-in-law, but her words resonate deep in my soul. "They feel important."

"Do you want me to back out of the contract with Chase?"

I pull my hand back, closing my fingers into a fist. "And sell to the developer?"

She shakes her head. "I don't want somebody to bulldoze this house and subdivide the land into postage-stamp-sized properties. I would have waited for the right buyer, and I'm confident in Chase's commitment to stewarding our family's legacy."

I open my mouth to agree, but she holds up a finger to silence me. "I'm also confident in your commitment to building a life in this town for you and the twins. If you want me to break the contract, I will. We'll come up with terms that work for you to buy the farm. Even if it takes a couple of years or you do a lease-to-own or..." She waves a hand like the details aren't important right now. "We'll figure out something."

"Why would you do that now? To be honest, Linda, I didn't think you liked me, let alone believed in me."

"You were an easy scapegoat for my frustration over Teddy's unwillingness to—let's call it what it is—grow up, and then for my grief. My son knew better than to take a raft out on the river when it was running so high and fast. He should have been wearing a helmet and a life vest. He was always impulsive, and he and Chase got into plenty of trouble together. But Chase also tempered him. Just like you did. And I *do* mean that in a good way."

I think about what I want for the future, my feelings for Chase that have been a big part of me changing, and my friends' advice about letting someone love and take care of me.

"I'm in love with Chase," I say quietly, done hiding or feeling guilty for my feelings. I want to show up for him the way he's been showing up for me.

She laughs softly. "I should have thought about that as a possibility when I wrangled him into helping."

I guess there are worse ways she could have reacted. "I don't know if he feels the same, but—"

"What does your gut tell you?"

I can't help my smile. "That we have a chance at something really special. I don't want to own this land *instead* of Chase. I want it to be part of our future." I make a face. "Although I'm still not sure how I feel about Luke's goal of becoming a cowboy."

"One way or another, adventure is in his blood."

"Maybe the greatest adventure is being brave enough to live a full life," I say, more to myself than her.

"I wish Teddy could see you now."

Linda's words hit me right in the chest, but in the best possible way.

"He'd probably tell me to stop overthinking and go do something," I say with a watery laugh.

"Sounds like Teddy."

"I need to talk to Chase." The certainty I feel finally knowing what I want almost catches me off guard, but I'm not backing down now. "He's staying at Ray's. Would you mind if I went over there? I don't want to wait another minute."

Linda's expression shifts, a shadow dimming the light in her brown eyes. "Chase is at the rodeo exhibition."

My stomach drops. "What?"

"My friend Sarah gave me a ride from the airport, and she said it's the talk of the town. The rumor is Chase Calhoun will be making his comeback tonight. I thought you knew."

I feel the blood drain from my face. Chase's words about what the doctor told him play in my mind. *I can't handle another concussion.* My heart starts racing as the pieces click into place. He'd been so certain about retiring, at least until his dad started goading him into getting back in the ring. And then our argument...

"This can't happen again," I whisper, more to myself than Linda.

"What is going on? You look like you've seen a ghost."

"I have to go." I'm already moving toward the door, panic clawing at my throat. "He's being reckless, just like..."

The words stick in my throat, but I know Linda understands. She knows Teddy went out on the river that day after a fight with me. History can't repeat itself. Not with Chase.

35

CHASE

MOST FAIRGROUNDS SOUND and smell the same during an event. The scent of popcorn, funnel cake, and leather mix with the dusty aroma of animals in a way that's both unique and as familiar to me as the smell of a mountain forest after a spring rain.

I remember the first time my dad brought me to a rodeo. I thought the lights, the crowd, and the cowboys with their buttoned-up shirts, tight jeans, and Stetsons were the coolest thing I'd ever seen. I still feel that way.

Unlike the little boy I was back then, the grown-up version of me no longer yearns to be a part of the spectacle. Telling myself—and other people—about my retirement...well, they were easy enough words to say. Still, I wasn't sure how I really felt about them.

As soon as I stepped out of my truck tonight, I knew I made the right decision. I don't need or want the adrenaline rush that climbing onto the back of a bull gave me for so long. The shadows that were chasing me, the darkness I was so sure would rise up from deep inside my soul and swallow me whole—those demons have no hold on me. Not when the future I want is so filled with light.

SOMEONE TO HOLD

It's filled with Molly and the twins and what I want us to build together. Risking my heart is almost as scary as how I've risked my body all these years. But the reward on the other end is going to be worth it. I believe that with every ounce of my being.

If she'll have me.

The young rider standing next to me fidgets and glances around the arena like he can't believe this moment is real.

"Take a breath. You've got this. Trust your instincts and your training. You know what to do out there." I incline my head toward the giant bull being loaded into the chute as memories come back to me in neon color. "Marvin knows what he's doing, too. He comes out fluid about four seconds into the ride, then he's going to switch things up on you. Anticipate it."

"Yes, sir." The kid, Christopher, swallows and nods. He's nineteen years old, and this is his first year as a pro.

"You ready?" one of the handlers asks.

Christopher draws in a slow, steady breath. "Yeah, I'm ready."

I clap the kid on the back. "You got this."

He starts to move forward, then pauses and meets my gaze. "You think so?"

"Yep, but you're the one who has to believe it."

"I do," he tells me.

"Then go get 'em."

"Dropping those Chase Calhoun deep-thought dimes on the kid?" Ray asks as he slides in next to me.

"I told him to hold on."

"Good advice." My friend chuckles. "Especially when you know why you're holding on."

I glance at him out of the corner of my eye. "And when it's time to let go."

"I take it you're letting go of this part of your life for real?"

"One-hundred percent."

"No regrets?"

"I have a whole wagon full of regrets, but..." I pause. "I'm slowly unloading them."

"Does that lighter load have anything to do with a pretty redhead?"

I scoff and elbow the older man. "You're as nosy as a gaggle of grandmas sitting on the front porch watching the world go by."

He shrugs and grins wide. "Janice told me to report back. She's the boss."

The countdown clock is on, and we fall silent as we watch Christopher make his final adjustments on top of Marvin. There's a breath of stillness just before the gate opens. I remember those moments vividly. I loved the connection with the heaving beast beneath me.

Okay, that's some philosophical shit for a broken and battered cowboy, but I think that's why I was so good. I lost myself in those eight seconds, over and over.

Now I'm ready to find myself again, thanks to Molly.

There's a decent-sized crowd filling the bleachers for a preseason event. They clap and cheer as the bull thunders across the dirt.

"Be ready for it," I say out loud, even though there's no way the kid can hear me.

Just as I told him, old Marvin changes direction midair and gives one, two, three sharp bucks in rapid succession. Christopher manages to hold on through it, but I see the moment when he loses focus. I don't know whether he's thinking of the girl he left behind in whatever small town he came from, or how many seconds are still on the clock, or the fact that his teeth are rattling inside his head. But I'm not the only one who notices.

Marvin senses that sliver of weakness and spins again.

Christopher sails through the air and lands in the dirt, and you can feel the crowd lean in, waiting to see what happens next and how this ends. The cowboy scrambles to his feet as the bull turns toward him. The bullfighters—the guys who used to be called rodeo clowns—draw the animal's attention as Christopher jogs to the edge of the arena and climbs to safety.

"That was a good start," I say to Ray. "He's got potential."

"He could benefit from more of your coaching."

I shake my head. "I have other plans."

"Cattle," my friend says simply.

"Flowers," I answer.

"Good for you, son," Ray says as the next rider climbs the gate.

"I hope so. First, I need to convince her to take me on."

He throws back his head and laughs. "Maybe you should have started with that."

"Probably." I rub a hand over my jaw. "I'm going out there tomorrow and—"

"Or you could talk to her now." Ray hitches a thumb over his shoulder.

I look past him, and my breath catches in my throat.

Molly is standing in the center of the open area under the arena, her long braid coming loose with strands of hair framing her face. Her eyes are wild as she glances around. Then her gaze crashes into mine. For a second, I see exactly what I hoped for in those crystal green depths—love and yearning and the future I so desperately want.

As I take a step toward her, I wonder if I imagined all of that, because her gaze turns ferocious.

But that doesn't stop me. Or scare me. Well, it worries me a little. But I'm a fighter, always have been. And she's given me something to fight for.

"What in the heck do you think you're doing?" she asks as we stand toe to toe, then punctuates the question with a little shove.

I feel the people around us staring with avid interest. Looks like I might be putting on a better show than the bulls tonight.

"Right now, I'm wondering why you're here." I hold up a hand. "I mean, I'm glad to see you, but—"

"You can't get on a bull again," she says. "I know you're mad, but you can't risk..." Her voice trails off as her eyes fill with tears. "I can't lose you," she says, a sob wrenching from her throat. "I love you too much, Chase Calhoun."

And just like that, everything that mattered before Molly loved me vanishes. The doubt and fear and darkness—she's chased it away with her light.

"I'm not competing." I cup her face in my hands. "I'm done with bull riding, sweetheart. The only moments that matter to me are the ones I spend with you. Eight seconds, eight years, eight decades—I'm here for all of it. I love you, Molly."

Her eyes search my face. "They said you were making your comeback."

"Rumors are good for ticket sales." I wipe a lone tear from the corner of her eye. "I'm giving some pointers to a few of the new guys, but I have too much to live for now that I have you and the twins. The only thing I want to risk is my heart. It's yours to do with what you want."

She smiles, her eyes drifting closed before locking on mine again. "I shouldn't have reacted so harshly about you signing the contract. I know you were trying to take care of me."

"No." I shake my head, my thumbs stroking across her cheeks. "I should have talked to you before I made that deal. I was just so scared you'd say no because..." I swallow hard. "Because I don't deserve someone like you."

"Don't you dare." She grabs my arms, her grip fierce. "I said I loved you, and there are no take-backs. You hear me?"

A laugh rumbles from deep in my chest, and I feel something I haven't felt in years—pure, unfettered joy.

"No take-backs," I agree, grinning like a fool.

She wrinkles her nose. "So we can talk about subdividing the land?"

"No." Her face falls, and I rush to continue, "It's ours together. We're partners, Molly. In life and business, I hope. I don't want to run cattle. I want to grow flowers."

She gasps as shock and hope mix in her gaze. "Are you serious?'

The words feel strange coming out of my mouth, but so damn right. "As a two-thousand-pound bull. I want to support your dream and make it into something we can both hold onto. Mostly, I'm going to hold onto you because I love you so damn much."

She rises up on her toes just as I lean down, and our lips meet in a kiss that tastes like coming home. The crowd that has formed around us erupts into cheers and whistles, but all I can hear is the thundering of my own heart.

When we finally break apart, breathless and grinning like fools, Molly rests her forehead against mine. "So this is it? You're in it for good?"

"So good, sweetheart. That's all thanks to you. I came back to Skylark months ago, but right here with you in my arms is where I've found my home." I brush a strand of hair from her face. "You *are* my home. The way you challenge me and believe in me even when I don't believe in myself. The way you love those twins with everything you've got. It's this moment and every moment after that I get to spend loving you."

"I love you, Chase." The sweetness of her smile makes my heart beat double time. "Forever."

Whatever comes next, sunny days or stormy skies, Molly and I will face it together. And that's the only forever I'll ever need.

EPILOGUE

ONE MONTH LATER

MOLLY

I enter the barn and follow the sound of Luke's gentle voice as he talks to our newest four-legged family member in the stall across from Gumdrop. Late spring sunshine filters through the windows, casting golden light across the hay-covered floor.

"You're such a good boy, Kevin. Yes, you are. Don't listen to Laurel. You don't need your bangs cut."

"He'd look even cuter with a trim," Laurel calls from where she's perched on a hay bale, rolling her eyes at her brother's commentary. "And I bet his hair would get even curlier."

I can't help but smile as I watch them fuss over the Highland calf we adopted two weeks ago. When Ray called about a calf whose mother had rejected him and would need to be raised as a bottle baby, there was never any question about our answer. The kids named him Kevin within five minutes, and he's been the center of their universe ever since.

Chase emerges from the feed room carrying Kevin's bottle, and my heart does that little skip it does every time I see him. Don't get me started on my reaction when he gives me one of those slow smiles of his. It's too embarrassing.

He's traded his usual work shirt for a clean button-down with the sleeves rolled up to his elbows, and there's something different about his energy. Like he's vibrating with barely contained excitement. I guess we're all smitten with sweet Kevin.

"Feeding time," he announces, holding up the oversized bottle.

Luke starts jumping up and down as the calf wiggles. "Can I do it? Please? I've been practicing tipping up the bottle just like you showed me."

"Me too," Laurel adds, hopping down from the hay bale. "We should take turns."

"You can both help." Chase lets himself into the stall. "Luke, you hold the bottle, and Laurel, you can help keep him still enough to take it."

I watch as Kevin eagerly latches on. The rust-colored hair on the top of his head sticks out in all directions like he's been electrocuted and milk runs down his chin, but the expression in his big eyes is particularly endearing as he drinks.

"He's getting so much bigger already." I take a seat on the hay bale my daughter vacated. "Are you sure we're not overfeeding him?"

"This guy's appetite is perfectly normal." Chase's smile is warm as he helps Luke adjust his grip on the bottle. "Though I have a feeling he's going to be spoiled rotten with all the attention you three give him."

"He deserves to be spoiled," Luke says seriously. "His mama didn't want him, but we do."

"We'll love him even better because we chose him for our family," Laurel adds with the kind of insight that makes my chest tighten.

These kids have been through so much loss themselves, yet their capacity for love and empathy continues to amaze me.

Chase catches my eye over their heads, and something passes between us. We've both been through enough to appreciate the sweetness of this moment and how perfect our life has become.

"Mommy," Laurel says, pulling my attention back to the present. "When Kevin grows up, will he still want to live in the barn? Or will he want his own pasture like Fancy and Gumdrop?"

"Well, Highland cows are pretty social animals," I tell her. "He'll probably want to be with the horses once he's big enough. They can all keep each other company."

"Like a family," Luke adds, grinning as Kevin finishes his bottle and starts nosing around his hand for more.

"Maybe we should get more animals that need homes," Laurel suggests thoughtfully. "We could be a flower farm *and* an animal rescue."

Chase and I exchange looks. "That's not a terrible idea," he says. "There's plenty of room, and a way for the farm to become an even more meaningful part of the community."

Laurel's smile widens. "The animals would be part of our family."

"Exactly," Chase agrees.

Something in his voice makes me look at him more closely. That buzz of energy from earlier seems to be building, and he keeps glancing between me and the kids.

"Speaking of family." He holds out a hand and pulls me to my feet. "I wanted to talk to you about ours."

Luke and Laurel seem like they're about to explode, and the air is charged in a way I don't understand, even though I seem to be the only one not in on what's happening.

"What's going on with you three?" I shoot a wary glance between them. "Have you already committed to more animals?"

Chase squeezes my fingers before releasing me, laughing softly. "Right now I'm thinking of a different kind of commitment." He reaches into his pocket, and my heart seems to skip a beat as understanding dawns.

"Molly." His voice is soft but steady. Hearing my name spoken with such reverence already has me blinking back tears. "You are the best thing that ever happened to me. Spending every day with

282

you and the kids, building your dream and our life together is like my dream come true. A dream I never let myself have, and a future I want more than anything."

He pulls out a small velvet box, and Laurel claps her hands over her mouth to stifle a delighted squeal.

I glance between my children and the man I love. "Were you two in on this?"

"He asked our permission," Luke announces proudly.

"And we said yes," Laurel adds, bouncing on her toes then adding an eye roll for good measure. "Obviously."

Chase chuckles, his gaze never leaving mine as he opens the box to reveal a stunning vintage ring, the oval diamond surrounded by smaller stones that twinkle like tiny stars.

"I found it at an antique shop in Denver," he says. "The owner said it belonged to a woman who was married for sixty-three years. I liked the idea of you wearing something with that kind of love story already in it. I hope you do, too."

Tears blur my vision as I stare at the ring. It's absolutely perfect.

"Molly," Chase continues, "you taught me what home really means. Not just a place, but the people who make you feel like the best version of yourself. You and Luke and Laurel are my home. You're my whole world." He takes a shaky breath. "Will you marry me?"

"Yes," I whisper, taking another step toward him. "Of course, yes."

The kids cheer as Chase slips the ring onto my finger. It fits like it was made for me, and I love the history of it and the way this is the start of our future together. Then he's pulling me into his arms, kissing me softly while Luke and Laurel dance around us and Kevin moos his apparent approval.

"I love you," Chase murmurs against my lips. "All of you."

"I love you, too," I say, reaching out to pull the twins into our embrace. "We all do. Our family."

We stay in the barn for another hour, taking turns loving on our fuzzy baby and talking about wedding plans.

"I might have been more scared talking to you two than I ever was getting on a bull," Chase tells the twins. They love that, and regale me with stories of how hard it's been keeping the secret for three whole days.

Luke wants Chase to wear his cowboy hat during the ceremony, and Laurel thinks we should get married in the flower fields now that everything's in bloom.

"A wedding in the field sounds perfect." I can't stop looking at the engagement ring on my hand. It feels like my insides are made of champagne bubbles, all light and effervescent. "Maybe next month? I don't want to wait too long."

Chase kisses my temple. "I'd marry you tomorrow if you wanted."

"Tomorrow," the twins chorus.

"I need a little time to plan," I say firmly, smiling at all of them. "I want it to be perfect."

"You said yes." Chase claps a hand to his chest. "Everything else is gravy."

As we head back toward the house, the late afternoon air warm and scented with the fresh smell of my flower fields, I fall into step beside Chase. The kids race ahead, still buzzing with excitement, and although I've walked this path a thousand times, today it's different. It feels like a new beginning.

My phone buzzes, and I pull it out of the back pocket of my jeans to see notifications from the book club group chat.

> Piper: Anyone available for a short-notice get together? I need to talk to you all about something.

Taylor: How about Casa Rosa? I'm craving
loaded nachos something fierce.

Avah: I'm in.

Sloane: Me too.

Sadie: Sure.

Iris: Can't tonight, sorry. Date with my guy.
Netflix and not chill.

Sloane: No one likes a bragger.

Iris: Jake likes me just the way I am.

Piper: Can we meet at my house?

I PAUSE, frowning at my phone. That's odd. Piper usually loves going out.

Sadie: Everything okay, sis?

Piper: Yeah, I'd just rather talk in private.

A memory surfaces of Piper's face in the coffee shop when Sally mentioned secrets. At the time, I was too consumed with my own issues to really pay attention to hers, but now I wish I had.

Avah: Private usually means the talk is going to
be really good or really bad? Which are we
dealing with?

Piper: I honestly don't know yet.

My steps slow as I stare at the phone, my protective instincts kicking in. Sadie also mentioned that Piper has been withdrawn lately. I think we both figured it was her adjusting to being back in Skylark after her broken engagement, but maybe there's something else going on.

"Everything okay?" Chase asks quietly.

"I'm not entirely sure. Piper wants to have an emergency book club meeting at her house. She says she has something important to tell us."

"Sounds like she needs her friends."

"Yeah." I look up at him, this wonderful man who's just asked me to spend forever with him, and feel that familiar surge of gratitude for the way he understands me. "Are you okay if I go? I know we just got engaged and should be celebrating—"

"Go," he says, drawing me forward then brushing a kiss across my lips. "We have the rest of our lives to celebrate."

"The rest of our lives," I repeat, marveling at how natural those words sound. How right they feel.

"Sounds good, doesn't it?" Chase murmurs.

I lean in to kiss him again. "Yeah, it sure does." I quickly type a response to the group chat.

> Me: I'll be there. What time?

> Piper: Seven? And thank you. I don't know what I'd do without you bitches.

As I slip my phone back into my pocket, I find myself wondering about Piper's secret. Whatever it is, she won't have to face it alone.

Chase takes my left hand, with its beautiful new ring, and we walk toward the house together. For so long, I've been a single mother trying to build a life on her own. Tonight, I'll go to sleep as an engaged woman, surrounded by love and possibility and the family I created.

And tomorrow? Tomorrow and all the days after, we'll keep building our forever.

But first, we need to find out what's going on with Piper. Something tells me that bucket list challenge or no, this meeting is going to change everything. Again.

That's how life works in Skylark. One unexpected surprise after another.

MORE SURPRISES ARE DEFINITELY on the way for Piper & Felix! Someone To Stay is releasing January 20, 2026. Keep reading for a sneak peek!

AND IF YOU'D like a little glimpse into Molly & Chase's future (including the adorable Highland calf, Kevin), head to my website (www.michellemajor.com) and click on the Bonus Content tab at the top.

SOMEONE TO STAY
SNEAK PEEK

PIPER

I came to the cabin in the Colorado wilderness outside Vail because I needed an escape from life. The kind that only a private, way-too-big-for-one-person mountain retreat can provide. My brother-in-law, Ian, bought the thirty-acre property when he moved to Skylark after retiring from the NFL. I guess being quarterback royalty means you need a six-thousand-square-foot log-and-stone "getaway" for when you need a break from small-town Colorado life.

I'm not complaining.

I also came alone because I didn't want any witnesses to my spectacular life implosion. While my plan involved wallowing in the—well, I wouldn't call it misery, more like the terrifying uncertainty of my current situation—I did *not* come to be murdered in the middle of the night by a high-country killer.

Yet, here we are.

I'm not ready to die. Not even at my lowest did I feel that desperate.

Not when I saw my ex-fiancé Bradley at the hospital yesterday, smugly cozying up to his new bride. The one he'd started dating approximately five seconds after I called off our wedding last summer. The one I walked away from the night before it was supposed to happen because I finally realized he's a condescending douche canoe who treated me like an accessory rather than a person.

I didn't get the memo that he'd returned to our shared hometown of Skylark, Colorado. And I sure as shit didn't know that he and the new Mrs. Bradley Carlson, a nurse like me, would be working at our small-ish community hospital where I couldn't avoid them if I tried.

I can't blame my entire meltdown on Bradley. That would be giving him too much power over me, and I vowed never again to let a man take my power that way. But it's been a rough month— longer if I'm being honest. And seeing them together in the break room with her wearing a diamond the size of a small planet was the last straw. I'd quit on the spot, packed a bag, and fled to Ian and Sadie's cabin before the Skylark rumor mill could start churning.

Which is why, as I creep down the darkened staircase, my bare feet silent on the hardwood steps and my would-be killer rattling the front doorknob, I'm wielding a tennis shoe in one hand and my e-reader in the other.

One to use as a weapon, the other as a potential shield. Because —once more for the bitches in the back—I don't want to die tonight.

I'd also hate to lose my new Kindle, the fancy one with the warm light setting. I highly doubt whether it could stop either a bullet or a knife swipe, but it seemed like a better option than the feather pillow from the guest bedroom where I'm sleeping. Though to be fair, the pillows are those fancy European ones that probably cost more than my monthly student loan payment, so who knows what they could do in a pinch.

If I make it through this night, I swear on all that is holy that I'll go back to leaving my phone on the nightstand when I sleep. I've been reading too much about blue light and beta waves, or whatever the hell it is that a phone emits, and while I'm not going to don a tinfoil hat any time soon, I figured keeping the phone in the kitchen would be a smart choice.

Being able to call 911 would have been preferable at the moment, but it is what it is.

I hear the soft snick of the door opening, and a deep voice muttering something about fucking light switches.

"Don't move," I shout, pitching my voice low like I'm the threat, which is ridiculous because I'm currently scared out of my mind *and* pants-less.

"The fuck?"

The intruder doesn't sound particularly cowed or predatory. More like...annoyed?

My Jeep is parked in the attached garage, so if I can get to it, maybe I'll have a chance at escape. The keys are on the hook by the mudroom, because I'm organized like that. There's a sliver of light coming in the front window—the June moon is nowhere near full —and all I can see is the hulking outline of a giant of a man.

Adrenaline spikes, and I think about how much I have to live for. Like the fact that I'm right now growing a tiny human inside me who deserves better than to have their mom taken out by a home invader.

"Yippee-ki-yay, motherfucker!" I shout as I hurl the tennis shoe in the man's direction. Apparently, when faced with death, I channel Bruce Willis.

I was a volleyball player in high school—not exactly All-State material, but I made varsity all four years and have decent aim. The shoe connects with a satisfying thwack, followed by a string of curses that would make a sailor blush.

This is my chance. I bound down the rest of the stairs just as the lights flip on. The sudden brightness is blinding, and I blink rapidly, trying to adjust.

"What the fuck, Piper?"

I'm nearly to the kitchen and stop mid-stride, whirling around, which knocks me off balance. I windmill my arms to keep from face-planting. That would be bad given the potential for general humiliation plus the pesky detail of me not wearing pants.

And suddenly I'm facing the last man—potential murderer, notwithstanding—I want to see right now. Relief washes over me, my body not quite on the same page as my brain, and my knees give out as Felix Barlowe, my brother-in-law's huge, handsome, currently-playing-in-the-NFL brother, stalks toward me.

All six-foot-five inches of him, with his stupid perfect jawline and his stupid dark hair that looks like he just rolled out of bed. The same hair I ran my fingers through that night in Denver when we'd...nope. Not going there. That was tequila and temporary insanity and a mistake we agreed to forget.

"Are you trying to give me a fucking heart attack?" I demand through raspy breaths. My heart is doing this weird galloping thing that I'm attributing entirely to adrenaline and not to how his gray t-shirt stretches across his chest. The same chest I...stop it, Piper. This is *not* the time.

"Your shoe nearly took my eye out." *His* eyes do a slow perusal of my current state, and I swear the temperature in the room jumps ten degrees. Just like it had in that bar in Denver when my friend's bachelorette party collided with his celebration for signing with the Denver Grizzlies franchise. When we'd had too many shots and ended up pressed against each other on the dance floor and then in the elevator and then in his hotel room and then... focus, Piper.

"I thought you were here to kill me."

"Only in my dream," he mumbles, and there's that smirk, the one that makes smart women do stupid things. The one that made *me* do stupid things when hours of trading insults somehow turned into foreplay. "Why did you throw a shoe at me?"

"Um, I thought you were a whack job coming to kill me. Maybe you should knock next time? Or, I don't know, text? Call?

Send a carrier pigeon? Literally anything other than breaking and entering?"

"Ian gave me a key." He rubs his forehead where my shoe made contact. "Nice arm, by the way."

"High school volleyball. Not that you'd remember anything about me that doesn't involve shit talk."

The look he levels at me shoots sparks up my spine. "I remember plenty that doesn't involve talking," His voice drops a fraction, and oh God, he's thinking about it too. April. Denver. The hotel room. The way we agreed the next morning that it was a terrible lapse in judgment, that we hated each other, and it would never happen again. And that no one, especially not Ian and Sadie, would ever know.

"Forget whatever you're remembering." I resist the urge to place a protective hand on my stomach, which is stupid because I'm not showing yet. It's only been two months. Not nearly long enough to figure out what the hell I'm going to do about my baby's father being a man who can't stand me and who told me to my face he doesn't want kids.

"Put some fucking clothes on," he says through gritted teeth, as if I'm the one being unreasonable.

I glance down at my faded T-shirt with "Night Shift Nurse: We Can't Fix Stupid But We Can Sedate It" printed across the front. It hits at mid-thigh, well below the danger zone, and I'm wearing my comfiest cotton bikini briefs, not even a thong.

I cross my arms, which—oops—makes the shirt ride up higher. "It's not like you haven't seen it all before," I tell him, and then immediately want to die because that's not going to help either of us forget that night.

His eyes go wide, and I suck in a breath that has nothing to do with the adrenaline comedown and everything to do with the way he's looking at me like he's remembering exactly what's under this shirt.

"I'm referencing legs in general, you asshat. You've seen plenty of female body parts." With plenty of women who aren't his brother's sister-in-law or carrying his secret baby. Women he actually likes.

"I'm not here to murder you, Piper," he says, his cadence painfully slow. "And I'm trying to be respectful." He pauses, his jaw working like he's physically forcing himself to keep his eyes on my face. His gaze drops for just a second before snapping back up.

"Put on a bra, while you're at it," he commands. Like he has a right to command anything where I'm concerned.

I clutch the Kindle closer to my chest. The device might not protect me from bullets, but it's definitely shielding me from Felix's opinion of my braless state. "How about I go back to bed and you turn around and go back to whatever whore hole you crawled out of?"

The murderer accusation clearly bothered him, but the man-whore comment makes his lips twitch. Interesting. Either way, I've gotten under his skin, which pleases me to no end. He's been under mine since April. Literally and figuratively.

"I'm not going anywhere." He glances over his shoulder as if he's just remembered something and then takes a step away from me. "I've got someone in the car, and—"

"Fuck off, Felix." Why should I care if he brought a woman up here? It's not like we're...anything. We had one stupid, tequila-fueled, admittedly mind-blowing night that meant nothing. Even if the result means everything to me. I need to tell him, obviously. But I'm not going to have that conversation at the moment.

What I *would* like to do is kill my sister for not warning me he was coming. She knows I came here to escape drama, not to have it delivered to my door in the form of a six-foot-five defensive end with commitment issues and the ability to make me forget my own name with just a kiss. Not that we're kissing ever again. That was a one-time thing. Felix Barlowe is a gorgeous, athletic, surprisingly tender mistake who's brought another woman to the cabin where I'm trying to figure out my life.

I suppose he has as much right to be here as I do. His brother did marry my sister, after all. We're family. Sort of. In the most technical, non-blood-related, we-accidentally-made-a-baby-together way.

"At least do me the courtesy of keeping her quiet." I aim for casual indifference and land somewhere around bitter resignation. Because I might have to hear him with another woman while my hormones are doing whatever the hell they're doing, which is trying to fangirl all over him.

"Wear earplugs," he says, that smirk widening into a full-blown grin as he disappears out the front door. But not before I catch him muttering something that sounds suspiciously like "who needs sedation" and shaking his head.

I stand there for a full minute, Kindle still clutched to my chest, dignity hanging out on the floor with my shoe. The secret of my pregnancy sits like a stone in my stomach as I wonder how my peaceful mountain escape just turned into...whatever this is.

The universe has a twisted sense of humor. And right now, the joke's on me.

PREORDER SOMEONE TO Stay now to get all the Piper & Felix goodness.

ABOUT THE AUTHOR

USA Today and Top 5 Amazon Bestselling author Michelle Major writes swoon-worthy stories full of heart, heat, and guaranteed happily-ever-afters. When she's not dreaming up romance, you'll find her hiking the trails (or avoiding housework) in her home state of Colorado.

Connect with Michelle
website: michellemajor.com
Instagram: @michellemajorauthor
Facebook: michellemajorbooks

www.ingramcontent.com/pod-product-compliance
Lightning Source LLC
Chambersburg PA
CBHW010735130726
47899CB00015B/3268